D Wolf

CHAPTER ONE

The late afternoon sun was a short period away from turning the Arizona sky into a crimson hue. The long, criss-crossing shadows of the desert cactus were painting eerie pictures along the basin floor as the beast broke from his run and fell into a fast-paced trot.

As he trotted he let his lower jaw hang slack and gulped in the cool afternoon air. In as much as the fresh air invigorated his lungs, the clotted mass of blood from a recent kill was matting the thatch of hair under his chin and it was beginning to cause him some irritation.

A professional magazine photographer, by the name of Greg Morris, was exploring the desert canyon floor a short distance south of the oncoming beast. He had spent two days camped at the location and he had collected a variety of plant life snapshots. The afternoon sun had extinguished any chances for more photography of flowers for the day, so he was casually making his way back to his campsite.

Greg was forty-five years old and slightly overweight. He had thinning brown hair, but his hairline hadn't started receding yet. He was not a tall man as he stood at five-foot, four inches. He was dressed in jeans with a long-sleeved blue cotton shirt and hiking boots. He wore no belt, so the shirt was not tucked into the waist of his jeans. His camera was hanging from a leather strap draped over his neck and he had a canvas shoulder bag full of assorted lens that he was carrying in his right hand. He wore a ball cap with a frayed bill that was once colored red, but it had faded to show spots of russet and rose.

He was simply poking his way along when he stopped by a small tuft of grass and dropped to one knee. He sat his shoulder bag aside and he wiped the brow of his head with the sleeve of his shirt, then readjusted his ball cap afterwards. As he was searching the terrain for possible photos that he could take the next day, he absent-mindedly picked up a handful of pebbles.

The only thing that caught his attention was a discarded fruit drink can that lay under a tuft of brown grass. He dropped a pebble into his right hand and smiled as he tossed it at the tin can.

The stone pinged against the side of the can and twisted it sideways. A small chuckle escaped his mouth as he knew that he wasn't particularly good at throwing stones with any degree of accuracy.

The beast planted his forefeet to abruptly stop. He spun his head towards the south and sniffed the air. He turned his sensitive and pointed ears towards the direction of the noise and listened for any further disturbance. He had stopped breathing in order to make sure that he could detect any sounds other than himself.

After a moment of intense concentration, he was convinced that there was something lurking nearby. He began to cautiously creep southward.

Greg had continued his slow and careless walk and he had placed the bag strap over his left shoulder. He had four pebbles in his left hand and one in his right hand as he sauntered slowly along. He was simply looking for another discarded can or bottle to use as a target as he was making his way up a small hill.

When he made it to the top of the hill, he stopped next to a giant saguaro cactus and turned his head towards the west. The sun was sinking low so that only half of the orb was visible on the horizon. The open desert before him had numerous saguaro cacti, which cast long shadows over the sand. The clouds surrounding the setting sun had turned a deep red they billowed softly due to a slight breeze.

He took a deep breath and whispered out loud, "Ain't nothing prettier, man! Nothing at all!" He dropped the pebbles and placed his canvas bag on the ground next to the wide cactus. He took his ball cap and sat it on the bag as he took a kneeling position and used both of his hands to place the camera in front of his face. He spoke aloud again, "One more picture of one more sunset won't hurt anything."

He was focusing his camera lens when he felt hot breath strike the back of his neck. His nose captured the scent of a slightly foul odor and his hands began to shake.

The next breath coursed down the back of his cotton shirt and his chin began to tremble. Greg's eyes closed tightly as a small tear fell from the corner of his right eye. He kept his eyes closed as his mind tried to figure out what had caught him off guard. He screamed in his mind, "Dog! Gotta be a dog!"

Keeping his eyes shut, he dared not to move his hands, but he decided to slowly turn his head and see what was standing so close behind him.

The beast watched Greg's head turn towards him so he leaned back on his haunches and tensed his leg muscles.

With all of the inner strength that he could muster, Greg fluttered his eyelids and opened both of them very slightly. His pupils immediately focused on an entity that he couldn't have possibly prepared for. He watched the huge and grotesque animal unhinge his lower jaw and then lunge for his face.

Greg didn't utter a sound. He died the instant the beast's jaws snapped closed and one large canine tooth penetrated his skull's frontal bone.

The beast stood over Greg's body with his front legs spread across the man's chest. He still held Greg's face in his mouth as he tightened his jaw muscles until he heard the familiar bone crunching sound. When he heard the noise, he shifted his weight to his hind legs again and slowly stood up. He kept raising his body with Greg lodged firmly between his upper and lower teeth, and when he reached his full height, Greg's feet dangled a few inches off of the desert floor.

The beast dipped his head slightly and loosened the muscles of his mouth. He snapped his head to the left and sent Greg falling to the ground. Greg landed with a sickening thud with his arms and legs splayed outwards. The camera strap remained attached to his neck as the camera landed lens first onto the dusty ground at his shoulders.

The beast slowly lowered his body so that he stood on all fours and then he sniffed the air once more. He inched his way to the lifeless body of Greg Morris and paused when he stood close to the man's chest. He placed his nose close to the man's face and inhaled deeply. He then produced a very low growl that sounded more like a grunt than it did a warning.

He walked to the canvas bag lying next to the saguaro cactus and used his sense of smell once again. There was no scent from the man or his equipment that put the beast on alert, so he simply turned his head and took one final look at the prone body. He grunted again, then trotted away in the same direction from whence he came.

He habitually killed for reasons outside of hunger. It was his own unique nature.

CHAPTER TWO

Meacon, Arizona is a small, sleepy, town, located near the Papago Indian Reservation. The reservation itself is situated in the lower, central, southern part of the state. The Santa Rosa River, which is nothing more than a branch of the Gila River, makes its final stop a few miles east of Meacon.

At the end of the river's flow, it dumps into a shallow reservoir at the foot of the Comobabi Mountains. The reservoir is referred to as a lake by the residents of Meacon because it's the only fishing spot available for a hundred miles.

Geographically speaking, the region around Meacon is described as rugged desert terrain. The lands south and west of Meacon are covered with the giant saguaro cactus and the plants called Brush Dalea. Whenever the brush and the cactus are in bloom, the landscape becomes picturesque with yellow and blue flowers. A small evergreen tree called the Red Justicia makes its presence known in several places south of Meacon, but for the most part, the land is brown sand, rolling hills, deep crevices, and flat-topped hills.

In spite of an average rainfall of only two and one-half inches per year, Meacon has some successful ranches and farms. Irrigation pumps pulling water from the Santa Rosa River enable the growth of alfalfa and Bermuda grass hay, which feeds local livestock, but no one in Meacon grows the hay for commercial purposes.

The local industry is the military munitions factory located five miles north of town. Most of the munitions assembled at the factory are the belted thirty and fifty caliber models, but periodically, the Marine Corps Bases in California order supplies of forty-five caliber pistol shells. It's not a large factory by any standards, but it employs more than three-hundred locals and operates both a day and a night shift. The name of the factory is the *Eisenhower Munitions Factory*. It was so named after Dwight D. Eisenhower, but not in honor of his presidency.

When Eisenhower was a first Lieutenant in 1915, he was given an assignment to locate a place for a small arms munition factory and he chose the isolated township of Meacon for this honor. Primarily due to the fact that a railroad existed close by and it joined California to Arizona and it was impractical (if not illegal) to have a munitions factory built close to any sizeable city or township.

When the plant opened in late 1916, it began producing rounds for the Browning M1917 machine gun and was such a successful operation that the Army, Navy, and Marine Corps grew to rely upon their steady production capabilities.

Meacon is the central township located in Pinal County. Pinal County is an area covering five-thousand and three hundred-seventy square miles and is bordered by Maricopa, Gila, Graham, and Pima Counties. Located within the boundaries of Pinal County are the Gila River Indian Reservation, the Maricopa Indian Reservation, the Tohano O'odham Indian Reservation, and the Papago Indian Reservation. The Papago Indian Reservation is located south of Meacon. The population of Meacon fluctuates between twenty-three hundred and twenty-five hundred annually.

The grade school, middle school, and high school are at three different locations in three different buildings. The High School, also named after Dwight D. Eisenhower, is located two miles north of town, while the grade school and middle school buildings are located at the southern edge of the township. Student population in Meacon is three-hundred and twenty and that includes all three facilities.

The other municipalities in Pinal County are seven settlements and three more townships. The settlements consist of nothing more than a few houses with a gasoline station, while the townships have less than a thousand residents each. Meacon is the County Seat.

One block off of Main Street in Meacon is the County Court House. The building is of the old Spanish adobe style, which means that it's a brown stucco, one-story structure that houses the Sheriff's Office, County Clerk's Office, and the District Judge's Chambers.

A very young man named Wallace Sand is the Sheriff of Meacon. He's thirty-four years old and he's a quarter-blooded Navajo Indian originally from Mesa. He's six-foot-two inches tall with broad shoulders and narrow hips. He has a very dry sense of humor and he's a very quiet man by nature. However, when dressed in his uniform, he commands a lot of respect by having an overbearing presence.

He had never liked his given name of *Wallace*, so he adopted the nick-name of Wally very early in life. Very few people knew that his real name was actually Wallace so he was simply called Wally by some, and Sheriff Sand by most others. His wife had various nick-names for him and she rarely used one twice in a row.

His last name of *Sand* was his tribal name. His mother gave him only a first and last name without once considering a middle appellation. She was a very beautiful half-breed Navajo woman who bore Wally out of wedlock and raised him alone. She supported herself and Wally by working as a waitress at a diner and she did part-time work for a landscaper on the weekends.

When Wally was old enough to work (age thirteen) he took a job with the same landscaper who pursued his mother romantically. He worked for the man until he reached the age of seventeen and graduated high school. His mother and the landscaper never married.

When Wally was seventeen, he met and fell in love with a very thin and small breasted girl named Jo Ann. Jo Ann had the opposite personality than that of Wally. Where he was sometimes irritatingly introverted, she was outgoing, friendly, and extremely funny at times. When they graduated high school they decided to elope.

Eloping wasn't a common practice in the year 1967. It was the time when young adults practiced free love and all of the pitfalls that go with it. So, the two of them actually sitting down at a table and discussing how and when they were going to elope was quite unusual. But, not quite as unusual as the fact that they included Wally's mother in the conversation.

As a single mother of a teenaged son, she recognized the seriousness of his intentions and decided to give the two of them her blessings. Along with some personal recommendations. She had a brother that lived in Meacon, who was recently widowed and she knew that he would be lonely, so she advised them to go to the small town in southern Arizona and begin their lives together there.

She went so far as to take Jo Ann and Wally to the Mesa Court House and sign the legal documentation to allow her son to wed at age seventeen. She even talked Jo Ann's mother into doing likewise, but both of them insisted that the kids take their marriage vows in Meacon. Their reasoning behind that decision was to not burden their children with undue scrutiny that would surely come from their classmates. It was a logical request as far as they were concerned.

The night of their high school graduation came and then the morning afterwards, the two of them hitch-hiked to Meacon to meet a man neither one of them had ever met so they could become a new part of his family. Wally's mother had made the arrangements with her brother sometime before the two teenagers left Mesa.

Wally's uncle turned out to be a man fifteen years older than his mother. His age wasn't discussed by Wally's mother, so he was slightly surprised at the difference between the two of them.

Never-the-less, Wally's uncle was delighted to have someone living under his roof besides himself, so the first thing that he did upon their arrival was to take them to the Meacon

Court House and get them properly married. Once that was completed, he called his sister and let her know that her son and new daughter-in-law had arrived and they were getting settled in.

Wally's uncle was a Pharmacist and he owned the only drug store in the town of Meacon. Wally and Jo Ann were immediately put to work in the Pharmacy. Her as a clerk and him as a stock boy. Their wages were simple. They earned ten percent of his gross profits and they lived under his roof rent free.

Although Jo Ann was not a beautiful woman by most people's standards and definition of the word, she was a handsome young lady just the same. Her inner beauty was what made Jo Ann the most precious. She had a charming personality and she communicated easily with people of all ages. She laughed easily and she had a sharp wit that she used to her advantage in almost every situation. She had light brown hair, which she never let grow long enough to touch her shoulders, and she had high cheek bones. Her eyes were blue and her lips were slightly pouty. Her breast size was a thirty-four, and her legs were shapely in spite of being slender.

Shortly after she became the Pharmacy Clerk, people would drop in just to say hello or listen to her recite the daily activities of the townsfolk. And, then, of course, no one wanted to be thought of as a bad customer, so everyone bought something when they visited. The store profits grew significantly under her stewardship.

In 1967 the Army was still utilizing the draft system for obtaining new recruits. Wally received his draft notice in March of 1968. He and Jo Ann had been married for seven months.

This was the time in America where young men shirked their responsibilities and moved to Canada in order to avoid military service. The war was not a popular war, but with Wally, he harbored no feelings *for* or *against* it. He simply felt like he was a young man and he was being called upon to do something for his country, so he didn't ponder the issue for any length of time. The only misgiving that he had was that he was being forced into the Army. That misgiving was only because his mother told him that his father was a soldier and that he had abandoned the two of them shortly after Wally was born.

The morning after he received his draft notice, he bought a bus ticket to Phoenix and joined the Marine Corps. He then took his customary one-week prep-time to get his personal affairs in order before reporting to boot camp.

Going off to war has a sobering effect on anyone facing that reality. He and Jo Ann shared intimate moments together whenever they could before he had to leave home. They were always very close, but during that seven-day period before reporting to boot camp, they both realized how deeply committed they were to each other. They had professed their love towards each other many times, but the separation forced upon them brought their relationship to its highest level of devotion.

Wally completed his basic training in ten weeks, then he completed his infantry training in four weeks, and then he found himself sitting in an airplane headed for Da Nang. He had a window seat. The airplane taxied away from the airport in Los Angeles and he stared blankly out of the window. He was eighteen years old with a young wife at home and an uncertain future. He felt very alone.

The plane rocked slightly as it rolled down the runway and young Private Wallace Sand was lost in his own thoughts. The plane stopped at the far end of the runway and he could hear the Pilot throttling up the jet engines preparing for takeoff. With the increasing sound of the jet engine roar and before the plane made its lurch towards the takeoff moment, he remembered something his uncle had said. He hadn't given the statement any thought before, but at this moment, the words made absolute perfect sense.

Wally's uncle had survived World War Two and he only had this advice to give his nephew, "When it comes to war, Wally...if you think you're going to die...you will."

The plane lunged forward and it sped down the runway at an ever increasing speed. Just as the front wheels lifted off of the ground, Wally made himself a vow. "I will return home!"

Wally was assigned to the 9th Marine Regiment based out of Saigon. It was March of 1968 and the Tet Offensive was in its last phases, but that's when the fighting was the fiercest. His regiment was in the forefront of the push to remove the North Vietnamese, which meant that Wally was no sooner put into the regiment did he come under fire.

The North Vietnamese were constantly attacking the Soldiers and Marines around Saigon until March 28, but upon that very next day, they abandoned the effort and allowed themselves to be chased out of South Vietnam. Wally was part of the pursuit.

It was a frustrating to chase an enemy so well trained in the art of camouflage. Wally's regimental commander grew angrier and angrier at his lack of successful engagements with the fleeing enemy. He blamed his unsuccessful attempts on the jungle foliage, so he called for a bombardment of a region with a new chemical defoliant called Agent Orange.

Wally had a thirteen-month tour of duty in Vietnam. In 1968, there was no such thing as a six-month break for combat troops. That regulation came later the next year, so Wally spent thirteen months in the field except for a two-week aid station stay when he was wounded in the upper left arm by a piece of shrapnel.

Wally's tour in Vietnam ended in April of 1969, but he wasn't shipped back to the United States. He had been meritoriously promoted three times while he was in the 9th Marines and he had obtained the rank of Staff Sergeant. This meant that his combat experience was extremely valuable, so he was offered a job of combat instructor on the island of Okinawa. The Marines made him a deal. The commanding officer of the 1st Marine Division told a group of men like Wally that he would limit their terms of service to eighteen months instead of twenty-four months if they would train men in jungle warfare for four months. Wally jumped on the deal.

Wally returned home to Meacon, Arizona on October 3, 1969. He was fully discharged from the Marines and had no idea what he was going to do from that point forward. That's when Jo Ann took over their married life and organized their careers.

The two young people had as happy of a reunion as they could manage, but when October 13, 1969 arrived, she had Wally sitting in the lobby of the Court House filling out an application to become a deputy for the Sheriff's Department.

Her speech went like this: "We're both twenty years old and neither one of us have an education! You're going to go into law enforcement and I'm going to go to the Community College in Santa Rosa!"

Wally tried a weak protest. "Why do I have to go into law enforcement?"

She took him by the chin with her right hand and smiled as she explained, "You're young…you're handsome… you know how to handle firearms…you look good in a uniform."

He returned her smile and answered, "Well…since you put it that way."

She continued, "Then, when I graduate in two years, I'll put you through college."

He frowned and tried another weak protest. "I never thought about going to college before! What do I need college for, anyway?"

She kept smiling as she put a hand on each side of his face. She pulled him close to her own face and whispered, "Because you can't become the Sheriff without a college education!"

Wally worked as a deputy for Sheriff VanGlenn from November of 1969 until November of 1976. During that time, Jo Ann graduated from the Technical College in Santa Rosa with a two-year Associates degree in Healthcare and went to work at the Meacon Hospital as a Nurse's Aide. Wally graduated from

Tucson University with a degree in Criminal Justice, Safety, and Law Enforcement.

He was twenty-seven years old and Sheriff VanGlenn was seventy. The sheriff took Wally aside one day in July of that year and had a private conversation with the young man. It was a life-changing conversation.

Sheriff VanGlenn started the conversation by handing Wally a stack of papers. "Here...fill these out."

Wally took the thick stack of papers and asked, "What are these?"

"Registration forms and legal documents."

Wally looked at the man and asked the obvious question, "Legal documents for what?"

VanGlenn's expression never changed as he answered, "You have to file your intention to run for County Sheriff. Better get cracking on it, the deadline for submitting your application ends the day after tomorrow."

Wally was immediately flustered. He sputtered his reply, "But...but...how...how did you know that my wife was..." He never completed his statement. VanGlenn smiled and interrupted, "Me and Jo Ann have been working on this for years! I'm retiring in November, and you need to get your ass elected!"

Wally argued, "But...I don't know how to run a campaign! I don't know how to get elected!"

VanGlenn shook his head slightly, but he was smiling when he replied, "Jo Ann was right...sometimes you just have to be pushed in the right direction. Now...listen to me...me and Jo Ann have it all under control. The posters are made...your campaign speech schedule is booked...we've taken care of all of that. All you have to do is quit talking to me and go fill out these damn forms."

On November 22, 1976, Deputy Wallace Sand became Sheriff Wallace Sand. He was elected as a Sheriff of Pinal County by a margin of sixty-five percent. He was twenty-seven years old; a combat veteran; a recent college graduate, and he was entering into the early stages of AL Amyloidosis. A rare disease caused when an abnormal protein, *amyloid*, enters the tissues or organs. In his particular case, it was Agent Orange.

Jo Ann grew up in Mesa without a father. Her mother worked as a grocery clerk during the week and a Buster Brown shoe salesperson on Saturday. Jo Ann went to work as a cleaning person for the same grocery store where her mother worked when she turned fourteen. She worked afternoons on school days and all day long on Saturday, and kept the job all through high school.

She was in the same grade of school as Wally, but never in the same classes with him. They had known of each other's existence since they were pre-teens, but their social lives had never crossed each other. The primary reason for that was actually due to the fact that the both of them worked to help their single mothers.

One day during their Sophomore year of high school, Jo Ann witnessed a tall and tough Wally Sand break up a fight between a bully and a younger boy. She saw Wally pick the bully up by the collar of his shirt and punch the ruffian in the stomach. That short fight (such as it was) immediately earned the admiration of Jo Ann.

When the bully ran away, she strolled to Wally's side and introduced herself. "Hi there! I'm Jo Ann. Your new girl-friend."

Wally was speechless at first, but he managed to reply, "I'm not looking for a girlfriend."

She cocked her head and squinted her eyes as she stared at him. She retorted, "Are you sure? I'd be perfect for you."

He couldn't help but chuckle. Somehow the skinny girl made him feel relaxed and not nervous the way all other girls made him feel. He answered her, "How do you know you'd be perfect for me?"

She teased him instantly, "You're tall. You're handsome. I love your shoulders and arm muscles. I'm cute as a bug and you really do need me as your girlfriend."

He was close to laughter as he replied, "You haven't told me why you'd be my perfect girlfriend...I think your avoiding answering the question."

"Well for one thing...mister...I'd protect you from bully's like the one that just hurt your fist."

Wally couldn't hold back. He laughed loudly as he said to her, "Now...that would really make you the perfect girl-friend!" He offered her his hand and continued, "Your name is Jo Ann...My name is Wally...can I walk you to school, Jo Ann?"

She took him by his right elbow and started leading him towards the school house. She was smiling up at him as she replied, "My last name is Wilkerson. I think your last name is Sand...am I right?"

As they walked along, Wally had the best conversation with a female he'd ever experienced. He replied, "I'm Wally Sand."

"You're also part Indian, too, huh?"

He confirmed, "One-quarter Navajo."

"What about the rest of you?"

"Don't know. Mom never said."

She made it a point to have him notice her looking him over as they walked side-by-side. She shrugged her shoulders once she stopped looking at him and replied, "I'll have to go with Irish...maybe some English, but I'll go with Irish/Indian for now."

He teased her a little as he asked, "Which do you prefer? Irish or Indian?"

She answered quickly, "Indian."

"Really?"

"Yeah."

He scratched his head and asked another question. "Why the Indian part?"

She continued teasing him as she replied, "Easier to come up with Indian nicknames. I like giving people nick-names."

During the summertime between Jo Ann's and Wally's Junior and Senior years of High School, Jo Ann was injured in an automobile accident. She and her mother were hit by a drunken driver that ran a red light at fifty miles an hour. His car smashed into Jo Ann's vehicle at the right front quarter panel, which spun the women's auto around and slammed them into a telephone pole.

The car that Jo Ann's mother owned was ten years old. It had no seatbelts and there was no law making them mandatory. Jo Ann was flung from the vehicle and landed on a concrete barrier that just happened to be at a construction site. She was taken to the hospital by an ambulance. She was suffering from internal injuries and she was unconscious.

Jo Ann was hospitalized for nine days and Wally sat with her during the day every day. He couldn't spend the night in her hospital room because he wasn't related to her, but he did spend all of the visiting hours by her side. He left her only when her mother arrived to spend the rest of the evening and night. Jo Ann suffered no scars from the accident, but she did have to have an operation to repair some internal bleeding. The end result of that, of course, was that Jo Ann would never be able to have children.

The drama and tragedy of Jo Ann's accident somehow faded from her and Wally's memory, and by the time their Senior year of high school arrived, they were simply happy to be together.

Wally never had sex with Jo Ann until they were legally wed. She was perfectly willing, but he had told her that he considered premarital sex a dishonor to a woman. At first, she chided him about it. She said such things as, "Where did you get the idea that having sex is dishonorable?"

He didn't fall into her trap. He simply replied, "My mother tells me that my people have a strict code about young people coupling before being wed."

"Coupling? Your mother called it *coupling*? That's so...

old fashioned!"

He argued, "It's not old fashioned...it's a tribal tradition."

She folded her arms across her chest and raised her voice, "Tribal? You're only one-quarter Navajo, for Christ's sake! How can anything be a *tradition* to you?"

He took her hands and removed them from her chest and held them in his own. He had a very serious look on his face when he explained, "My mother said that she was dishonored by the man who was my father. She said that she brought shame to her family, but that because she had me...she could live with the shame. To her...I was not a *shame*...I was her only pride."

Jo Ann choked slightly when she replied, "Oh..." She turned herself to be at his side and took him by the arm and walked away. As they walked slowly down the side of the road by her house, she spoke to him softly but firmly. "Alright... I won't let you *shame* me...but...on our wedding night...I'm wearing you out!"

And she did.

CHAPTER THREE

The beast was sitting on his haunches while he was on top of a small plateau. He was panting slightly and he let his tongue hang out of the side of his mouth as a means of helping him cool himself down. He liked to travel fast because he had learned that game was scarce and in order to eat, he had to cover a broad territory.

The hour of the day was growing late. The shadows of the saguaro were long and running towards the east. Every breeze brought a puff of dust in the distance and each one caught his attention. He snapped his head left and right each time a pillow of dirt twirled into the air. After a bit, the dancing sand irritated him and he growled his displeasure.

He was hungry. The day before, he had not taken the time to hunt or kill because his instincts forced him into establishing a hunting territory first. He traveled a great distance and had marked a tract of land covering most of the southern part of Pinal County and several hundred acres of the Papago Indian Reservation. He had two ways of marking his territory. He urinated on some large rocky outcrops, then he chose several trees to scratch bizarre shaped cuts into with his front claws.

Finally, far into the distance and north of his plateau, he spotted something big. He could barely make out the shape, but he was certain that it was a bovine of some sort. He'd killed and eaten them before.

He closed his jaws and smacked his lips. He opened his mouth slightly and took a deep breath as he slowly stood up on all four of his feet. He leaned back slightly and stretched his front legs. Then, he used his rear legs to launch himself off of the flat hill top and break into an extraordinarily fast run. His agility was another sight to behold. He wove himself among the brushes and cacti and never lost a bit of his velocity.

The way his feet and legs were designed, he could launch himself into huge strides that sometimes reached as much as twelve yards in length. He could then pull himself forward with his front claws and then propel himself forward with his rear legs. Puffs of dust stirred up behind him as he dashed towards the unsuspecting bovine.

A five-strand barbed wire fence stretched out before him, but he never broke his stride. He leaped over the top wire and landed on the other side with seemingly no difficulty at all. His victim was two-hundred yards in front of him, so he opened his huge mouth and unhinged his jaws. He would clear the distance in a matter of seconds, so he prepared himself for a launch.

It was a black angus bull. It was alone in a pasture sparse with grass, but he was near a watering trough. The bull sensed the approaching beast and snorted in surprise. When the bull turned to see the approaching animal, he bellowed at the top of his lungs out of fear.

The beast leaped into the air and lofted over the watering trough. He landed upon the back of the angus bull and dug his razor-sharp claws into both sides. His mouth clamped over the neck of the bull and his oversized canines punctured the bull's throat. The bull's next bellow was stifled with blood shooting from his mouth and nostrils.

The beast's lunge was so powerful that it knocked the bull to his knees and that put the angus into full panic mode. He clamored to his feet and tried to run away even as the beast held him in his clutches. It was a death embrace. The bull staggered while the beast dug his claws deeper into the flesh. The beast released his first bite, then clamped his teeth over the bull's neck again, but this time closer to the base of its skull. The bull was still having a hard time trying to scream out his fear. His windpipe was blocked with free-flowing blood.

The bull staggered and spun as the beast snapped his

jaws together once more. This time, one of the oversized canines severed the spine and the bull fell limply to the ground. There were no kicks of retaliation or any further attempts to fight back. The bull's eyes were glassy as he lay on his side so he was moments away from death, but his chest was still rising and falling as he tried to breathe.

The beast had dismounted his victim and stood growling at the head of the angus. It wasn't a victory growl. It was a growl of contempt.

The beast walked slowly to the bovine's exposed stomach and used his right front paw to slash open the belly muscles. Intestines spilled upon the dry earth and bile poured out of the wound.

The beast then grabbed a mouthful of intestines and started pulling backwards. He extracted a long section of intertwined guts, then shook his head violently. Intestinal fluids and undigested grasses flew away from the beast's head. He then plunged his mouth into the open cavity and withdrew another mouthful of organs and intestines. Once again, he shook his head forcefully and sprayed fluid around himself for several feet.

He coughed and spat at the same time, then dipped his head back into the open wound. This time he pulled out portions of a lung and he had the heart clamped between his upper and lower jaw teeth. He kept pulling backwards and stretching muscles and sinew until they were shredded.

Finally, he stopped and looked at the extracted organs. He grabbed the exposed heart and chewed twice before swallowing. He then searched the bloodied ground for another organ and spotted the liver. He used his teeth and his front claws to separate pieces of intestines tangled around the organ, then chewed and swallowed it also.

He exhaled another grunt, then moved himself to the hindquarter of the bull's left rear leg. He began using his canines to slice his way through the upper Round section and then he chewed his way down the Shank until he reached the lower marrow bone. He planted his front feet and grabbed the large section of meat with his teeth and then began to tear and rip the muscles away from the bone. Within seconds he had a slab of dripping meat in his mouth that was gruesomely ripped from the body of the bull.

He lay the large chunk of meat and hide on top of some exposed intestines, then took a moment to sniff the air. He searched the land around him for any possible intruders and quickly ascertained that he was alone. Nothing would threaten to take his kill.

He walked calmly to the water trough and began lapping at the cool water noisily. He had made himself thirsty. As he lapped water, blood dripped off of his snout and into the trough where it dissipated and turned into a pink cloud.

The water trough didn't leak, but it did have an enormous amount of sweat forming along the outside of the metal container and dropping onto the ground near the shell. The sand was wet and saturated for about a foot around the outside circumference of the trough. The beast had his front paws standing in wet soil while he drank his fill.

When he moved away from the trough and returned to his severed meat, he left two perfect indentations of his front paws in the shallow mud. He picked up his evening meal and held it lightly in his mouth as he took a moment to consider where he would go and finish gorging himself. The sun was almost completely down and the afternoon air had begun its fall in temperature. He spotted another flat-topped hill in the distance, then decided that would be a good place to spend the night. He liked sleeping on hilltops. Especially when there were stars above and a bright moon to light up his night.

CHAPTER FOUR

The cool, crisp air of the early morning was in stark contrast to the searing heat that smothered the desert by mid-afternoon. Because of this, residents of Meacon performed their domestic chores early in the morning. If grass had to be mowed or a hedge needed trimming, the power tools were rattling the morning air along with the sounds of lawn mower engines.

It was summertime and the teenaged boys and girls hired themselves out to older couples or working couples as lawn care workers. Meacon had two grocery stores, but one of them was more of a convenience store than a full-service grocery store. There were two restaurants in town, but both of them had full-time waitresses, so the only work there was part-time waiting and providing a busboy service. Young people's summer jobs were somewhat limited. That's why lawn maintenance was so popular. It was one of the better choices.

A person had to be twenty-one in order to work at the munitions factory, so high school kids were left out of that particular trade. Industrious young boys and girls found houses or garages or even barns that needed painting and bargained for the rights to use paint rollers or brushes.

The ideal summer job for high school boys or girls around Meacon was landing work at the Jeff Watkins Ranch. It was a large spread located ten miles south of Meacon and the old man ran it like it was a factory. He had large fields of hay that needed tending to; he had goats and sheep; he operated a brooder house for chickens; he raised feed cattle and show cattle alike, and he bred horses. The horses that he raised and trained were for both ranch work and rodeo stock. A lot of his rodeo stock were horses bred with mustangs captured in the wild. His working stock horses were strictly the Quarter Horse breeds.

His cattle were strictly the Limousine breed. He favored the Limousine for both beef production and show animals. He used the local FFA charters to show his cattle and he utilized school kids of all ages to show his beef. He was a savvy business man in that aspect. His Limousines had won many top honors at many livestock shows and he used those trophy's as prime advertisement for his beef herds.

When Jeff Watkins sold livestock, Jeff Watkins received top dollar. He was a wealthy individual and he employed no less than twenty high school kids every summer. He had a full-time staff, but he liked to be around kids that were teenagers. He liked their lingo, as he was fond of saying. He taught boys and girls alike to build fences, tend to animals, repair barn doors, shingle a roof, set up corrals, earmark cattle, sheep, and goats, plow fields, bale hay, and hundreds of other labors associated with ranching. He was also picky about the boys and girls that he chose to work for him. If you were not a straight "A" student, you could apply elsewhere. He paid them all, boy and girl alike, ten dollars an hour. Considering that this was 1984 and the minimum wage was three dollars and thirty-five cents an hour, Meacon kids studied hard to keep their grades up and land an opportunity to work for Jeff Watkins.

Jeff was sixty-four years old and he was lean from hard work and a strict diet. His skin was tanned and his hair was speckled gray with few strands of dark brown. It wasn't thinning or receding as most men his age had to contend with. His legs were slightly bowed, but that was from spending most of his life riding horses.

Jeff shaved every morning and he wore nothing but jeans, boots, and long-sleeved work shirts. He favored the denim variety of work shirt. His wife had died two decades ago and he had never remarried. They had no children, so his summertime ranch hands were his substitute kids.

Allie Thompson was the Dispatcher at the Sheriff's Office. She was twenty-four years old and she had light blonde hair with a round face and almond shaped eyes. The eyes were blue-gray in color. Her nose was petit and her chin was small, so she was a very attractive woman in the face. She was five-feet-six-inches tall if she was wearing flats, and she hardly ever wore heels. Her favorite footwear was leather hiking shoes, which always went well with her faded jeans and white work shirts. The white work shirts were the two breast pocket models with a name tag identifying the person working at the Sheriff's Office. They were mandatory. The jeans and shoes were not.

Allie liked to run in order to keep herself in shape and she was in very good shape. She didn't have an ounce of fat on her body and her curves were the envy of many other women her age. Not to mention the lust of many men as well. She did her running during the early hours of the morning so that she could shower and change clothes and be at work by eight o'clock sharp. She was smart and she was dependable and Wally counted on her to keep his office affairs in order along with dispatching his deputies or taking emergency calls.

Barry Kramer was the District Judge. His office was connected to the courthouse, which was part of the overall building layout, but there was only one passageway between the Judge's office and the Sheriff's Department.

Judge Kramer was seventy years old and he had no intentions of retiring any time soon. He was slightly overweight for his six-foot frame and his hair had vanished from the top of his head when he was fifty years old. He was a jovial man for the most part, but he could portray the hardcore judge when called upon to do so.

For the most part, Judge Kramer was called upon to render decisions in divorce cases, petty theft sentences, drunken brawls resulting in property damage, and numerous other small town legal matters. This is not to say that he had no experience with serious matters of the court. Over the twenty-two years that he had been the District Judge, he had to provide sentencing for both kidnapping and murder cases as well.

It was nine thirty in the morning and Jeff Watkins was sitting on top of his favorite mount. It was a bay gelding with white stockings and it was pawing the ground with its left hoof and snorting. He was nervous.

Two young girls were astride two other horses and they were on each side of Jeff. Their horses were showing signs of nervousness also. All three of them were staring in disbelief at the mangled body of the angus bull.

The young girl named Karen spoke first. "We found him like this almost two hours ago. We were riding fence on the south side and we found an open spot. Wires were broken, but it didn't look like someone cut them."

Jeff nodded and asked, "You followed the tracks and found it here?"

Both girls answered at the same time, "Yes sir."

Jeff was mumbling his thoughts as the girls tried to hear what he had to say. He had one hand holding the horse's reins and he was rubbing his chin with his other hand. "South land is Kermit land. This damn thing came from his place."

The other girl's name was Becky and she thought she might be missing an order or some request from her boss, so she spoke up, "I'm sorry Mister Watkins. We can't hear you."

Jeff shifted himself in the saddle before he answered, "Sorry girls...I was thinking out loud...that's all." He pointed at the flayed bull and sounded sarcastic as he said, "That's why I don't raise angus. Damn things are stupid."

The girls didn't laugh, but they both smiled at his remark.

He continued, "Well...damn! Ordinarily I'd just call the game warden and be done with it, but seeing as how this bull belongs...*belonged*...to the Kermit's...I guess I'd better call Sheriff Sand. I'll need a police report in case the asshole wants to go to court about it."

That remark caused the girls to chuckle softly.

Jeff took a moment to look around before he continued speaking. He pointed into the distance and said, "Whatever did this is gone, and I'm going to have to ask you girls to stay here with the carcass until I get the Sheriff out here. I don't like it, but I don't want the coyotes to get at it either. Do either of you know how to use a rifle?"

Becky spoke up. "I do mister Watkins."

Karen added, "She's a good shot, too."

Jeff pulled his 30-30 rifle out of the holster attached to his saddle and handed the weapon to Becky. She took it from his hand and he then reached inside of his saddlebag and took out a box of shells. He handed the box to Becky as he remarked, "Rifle's not loaded. Load it. I'm going to go make a couple of phone calls and be back directly."

He offered no other advice. He simply turned his horse and started trotting towards his house. Becky and Karen walked their horses to a nearby brush and dismounted. They tied the reins to separate branches and then they took a seat on the ground.

Becky handed Karen the box of shells so she could give them to her one at a time. Becky began pushing shells into the loading slide and decided to ask her friend a question. "What do you think it was?"

Karen shrugged her shoulders and replied, "Mountain lion most likely."

Becky continued loading the rifle as she remarked, "Mountain lion, huh? I didn't think we had any of those around here."

Karen replied, "Looks like we do now."

Allie was standing next to Wally's desk holding a stack of papers with her left arm and she was handing some documents to Wally one at a time. She simply placed the documents on the desk in front of him and pointed at certain spots and instructed him, "Sign here...initial there...sign here..."

As she was getting forms signed, Judge Kramer entered Wally's office and took a seat in the chair next to where Allie was standing.

Allie didn't move her head away from Wally as she cheerfully said, "Good morning Judge."

He replied quickly, "Good morning Allie. Keeping the Sheriff straight?"

She chuckled politely as she answered, "There's no helping him. You know that."

Wally remained silent and simply kept signing documents. The judge and his office clerk were just making small talk that had no particular purpose other than showing signs of friendship.

Wally signed the last sheet of paper presented to him, then Allie scooped it off of his desk to put with the others. She announced as she left the room, "I'll take these to the post office. You two behave yourselves until I get back.

Neither man offered a reply. Wally sat back in his chair and spoke to the judge. "What can I do for you this morning, Judge?"

"Edna Ivers" he answered without any voice inflection.

Wally lowered his head and took a short breath before he answered, "Oh God...again?"

That remark brought a smile to the judge's face. "Yep... she missed her court date yesterday...again."

Wally sat up straighter as he replied, "Do you really want me to bring that crazy woman in again?"

The judge raised both of his hands and answered, "How about if I give you a reprieve?"

"Talk to me."

Judge Kramer took a deep breath and answered, "My wife wants to go visit her mother. I'd be gone...say...three days...how's four days from now sound?"

Wally smiled as he replied, "I'll take it!"

"Alright...four days it is...you'll have to work on Saturday, though."

"I'll still take it."

The judge was now smiling as he remarked, "Edna's a fighter, Wally. She beat your deputy, Herman up the last time you tried to bring her in."

Wally was close to laughter as he replied, "She didn't beat him up...she just gave him two black eyes...that's all."

"I don't know...sounds like an ass-whipping to me."

"Don't let Herman hear you say that."

Wally thought for a moment then he playfully suggested, "Hey...it's a simple battery charge...how about I take you to see Edna...you pronounce her guilty of assault...give her a fine to pay...I'll collect the money...you go home...everybody's happy."

Judge Kramer stood up from his chair and started to leave. He answered before he made for the open door, "If it were only that simple. I'll see you Saturday." He then walked out of the room.

Allie was right behind him as she stuck her head into the open doorway and said, "Hey. Pick up line two. Jeff Watkins wants to talk to you."

Wally was lifting the phone receiver when he remarked, "I thought you were going to the Post Office."

"I am...pick up line two."

She disappeared from Wally's sight as he spoke into the receiver, "Good morning Jeff."

The voice on the other end had a static noise to it due to a poor connection. "Wally! I need you to come out to my place this morning. I got a situation with one of my neighbor's bulls and you need to come check it out."

Wally leaned back in his chair as he spoke again into the mouthpiece, "What kind of situation?"

"Damnedest thing I ever saw. Something tore that bull up. There's blood and guts everywhere."

The static noise in the line faded Jeff's voice slightly, so Wally had to ask him if he understood correctly, "Something?

You mean the bull was killed by an animal?"

"Yeah. Something big got to the bull. Don't know what it was, but it had to be something big."

Wally leaned forward in his chair and tried to understand why Jeff was wanting him and not simply take care of the problem himself. He asked, "Jeff...if it's an animal attack... you want the game warden...not me. Besides...You got enough people out there to hunt it down if you have to."

Jeff raised his voice slightly and argued, "Nope! Better if you come out here! And that's a good idea about the game warden! Bring him along with you!"

Wally chuckled to himself as he answered, "You want a police report on that bull, don't you?"

Jeff quickly admitted that a report was exactly what he wanted. He said, "You and I both know that old-man Kermit will drag my butt into court over his prize bull! I'll need evidence of what happened before I call him and tell him about the damn thing."

Wally leaned back in the chair and smiled again. He decided that he wasn't going to get rid of Jeff, so he might as well agree to go to his place and see what all of the excitement was about. He sighed and said, "Alright, Jeff. I'll come out there. Give me a little while to find Bob Bernoit and we'll both come see you."

Allie was leaving the Post Office and walking towards her government vehicle. It was a car belonging to City Hall, but they kept it at the Court House for the Sheriff's Department to use. It was an older model and the City Manager had four other newer ones for his own employees to use, so he left the old one at the Court House.

She was climbing down the concrete steps out of the building and holding the car keys in her right hand. There were only five steps, so she didn't bother using the handrail. When she descended the stairs, she saw Bob Benoit pass by the parking lot in his Jeep.

She stopped walking and stood in place to watch him drive by, and then stayed there until he drove out of sight. She took a deep breath, then sighed and walked the rest of the few steps to get to her car. As she opened the door to the vehicle she thought to herself as she slid into the front seat, "I gotta think of something to get that guy's attention. So cute. So single." She turned the ignition key and started the car.

Allie was pulling into her assigned vehicle parking spot when she saw Wally coming out of the Court House. He saw her at the same time, so he waited for her to come to him.

As she approached him, he said, "I have to go out to the Watkins Ranch for a little while. I don't know how long I'll be, but I have to find Bob Benoit and take him with me."

Allie's face lit up as she replied, "I just saw him! He was headed down second street towards the coffee shop! I'll bet you can find him there!"

Wally turned to make his way to his own car and waved at her as he walked away, "Thanks. I'll look there first."

Bob Benoit was twenty-seven years old. He was six feet tall and had dark brown hair that he kept short on top, but allowed the back to grow out and touch his shirt collar. He was tanned from excessive exposure to the sun and he weighed a very athletic one-hundred and seventy pounds.

He had been a Pinal County Game Warden for two years and that's how long he'd been a resident of Meacon as well. He had transferred to Meacon from the Tucson Office and he felt very lucky to get the posting. It was a job that he desired very much. He wanted to be a game warden in an area where he worked alone and set his own hours. Meacon was a dream come true for him when he applied for the transfer.

Bob's uniform was the brown standard issue, short-sleeved shirt, with the brown trousers being optional. He chose jeans over the brown trousers and he wore slip-on hiking boots that were also brown in color.

Game wardens in Arizona wore the official campaign cover seen with so many other professional offices. Bob didn't like hats. The only time he wore his was when he had a visitor from the state office or some other important political figure.

His work vehicle was an off-road Jeep that had a canvas top and removable doors. During the summer, he preferred driving with the doors removed. The canvas top was good for keeping his head and face from getting sunburned, so he left that in place.

During his two years of living in Meacon, he had not found or even attempted to look for any female companionship. This was a fact known by every single female in Meacon and that included the high school girls. After two years of fending off female flirting advances, the rumors were starting to form concerning his sexual preference. He was not homosexual. He was shy.

He was in a coffee shop located at the north end of town on second street. He liked the small café because it was at the very edge of town and it was small establishment. Meaning that it was never crowded, even if it was full. He liked the two regular waitresses because they were older than he was and they tended to just serve him coffee without any conversation. The summer help was another matter, though. High school girls were chatty. Or so it was in his particular case.

He walked into the coffee shop intending to get a cup of coffee and a sandwich. He figured that it was close enough to eleven o'clock and it was a good enough time to grab an early lunch, so he was going to do just that.

As soon as he walked through the door, he winced. The two older waitresses were not on duty. Just the flirty little high school girl named Wanda. She was not his favorite person because she always wanted to chat him up. (That's what he called it.)

Wanda was standing behind the serving counter with her elbows propped on the edge. She was obviously reading a magazine of some sort when Bob entered the café. When she glanced up and saw who it was, she gave him a large grin and said, "Hi, Bob!"

Wanda was a fairly good looking teenager. She had blonde hair, blue eyes, nice figure, and she was five-feet-seven-inches tall. Her biggest drawback, for Bob anyway, was that she was seventeen years old.

Bob took a seat at the counter that was two stools down from where she was standing. He smiled back at her and then he hit her with a vicious tease, "Hi there, Wanda. You still dating that sheep herder from Mexico?"

She closed the magazine with a rough manner and frowned as she replied, "You're mean sometimes, Bob."

Bob thought to himself, "Good. That put her off." He then said to her, "I just want a ham sandwich and a cup of coffee, Wanda."

She grabbed an empty cup and used the spigot of the coffee pot to fill it as she grudgingly said, "Alright. You want mayo or mustard?"

"Mayo."

As she sat the coffee mug in front of him, they both turned to see Wally enter the café. He didn't speak to either of them as he made his way to Bob and took the stool next to him. As he sat down, he greeted the young man. "Morning, Bob. You got some free time today?"

Bob answered, "I guess so…what's up?"

"Jeff Watkins wants us to come look at a dead bull."

Bob stared at Wally for a second before he replied. "Really? A dead bull? And he wants the both of us?"

Wally answered as honestly as he could, "He wants me because he thinks the bull belongs to the Kermit's and he wants me to fill out a report for him in case he gets taken to court. He wants you because it was some kind of animal that killed the bull."

Bob took a drink out of his coffee cup and pretended to be very serious when he said, "Some kind of animal, huh? He was *that* specific?"

Wally snickered and spoke to Wanda, "I'll have a cup of coffee, too, Wanda."

She grabbed another empty cup and was filling it as she asked, "You want a ham sandwich, too?"

Wally turned to Bob, "You having an early lunch?"

"Yeah."

Wally then spoke to Wanda again, "Yeah...ham sandwich for me too."

She sat the cup in front of him and asked, "Mayo or mustard?"

He answered, "Dry."

She turned to Bob and said sarcastically, "He's a better customer than you." Then she walked away from the counter towards the kitchen.

Wally whispered to Bob, "You make her mad about something?"

"She wanted to flirt...I didn't...she thinks I'm an asshole now."

Wally raised his coffee cup to his lips as he offered, "Well...she's too old for you anyway."

Bob almost snorted coffee out of his nose.

Becky and Karen had been sitting under the shade of the tall bush for almost three hours. They were bored as they'd exhausted all of their talk about boyfriends and other generally interesting subjects. Becky stood up first and brushed the sand off of the backside of her jeans. She was a fairly muscular girl, which is to say that her shoulders were slightly broader than most females. She also had strong hands to go along with her strong arms. Her hair was black and she had a dark toned color to her skin. Her eyes were brown, but not very dark. People told her that she had soft brown eyes. It was a point of pride with her.

She looked down at Karen as she put the rifle over her shoulder and announced, "I'm hungry. I'm going to get my lunch out of the saddlebags.

Karen got to her feet and brushed the dirt off of her jeans and agreed with her friend, "Me too. I brought a roast beef sandwich. What'd you bring?"

"Meatloaf."

The girls stepped to their horses and opened up their saddlebags. They both had leather pouches with top zippers that they used for their lunches and that's what they took out.

Karen wasn't a petit girl, but she was smaller framed than Becky. Karen's hair was a very light shade of brown and long enough to braid into a ponytail so that's the way she wore it. Like her friend, she was dressed in jeans and a long-sleeved shirt with western style boots. Both of them wore the standard straw hat used by all ranch hands. After they retrieved their lunch pouches, they both removed the hats and hung them on their saddle horns.

The girls had wisely chosen a place to stand guard that was on the opposite side of the water trough where the mutilated bull was laying. They couldn't see the carcass and they weren't forced to look at the swarming flies either. The shade from the brush where they were sitting was getting smaller due to the sun rising higher in the sky. They had to sit closer to the brush in order to have any shade at all while they ate their sandwiches.

The girls had been riding the fence lines since four o'clock that morning. It was their job to inspect all of the ranches' fence lines and to make any necessary repairs that they may find. Their saddlebags contained fencing tools needed for such work and they both knew how to use them. Karen's horse had a thick canvas bag tied to the saddle horn that contained a fifty-foot roll of barbed wire. Sometimes fence wire had to be spliced and both girls knew how to do that very well.

Normally, when one considers the job of the line rider, they think of a young man. Jeff Watkins had other opinions regarding the job. His logic was that females were naturally more attentive than boys. Becky and Karen were his fence riders because they had proven themselves capable of doing the work and they didn't need supervision. That was all he needed for approval.

Becky had the rifle leaning against a low-hanging branch of the brush as she ate her sandwich. She was talking to Karen while chewing her food at the same time, "We're not gonna get much fence line inspected today."

"Nope" Karen agreed. "We'll have to go fix that hole as soon as Mister Watkins gets back. I guess we can start all over again tomorrow."

"Yep" Becky replied.

Suddenly the girls heard the distant noise of an automobile engine and they stopped eating. They listened for a moment, then Becky rationalized, "Here comes Mister Watkins..." They both took larger bites out of their sandwiches and chewed faster. As soon as their hands were empty, they untied their horses and put their hats on their heads. Becky grabbed the rifle with her left hand and they both moved closer to the water trough. Both horses snorted to demonstrate their displeasure.

Jeff and Wally were in Bob's Jeep. They decided that the off-road vehicle was the best choice due to the road to the water trough being nothing more than ruts through the sand. Wally and Bob were in the front seat while Jeff was in the back seat along with several boxes of gear.

Bob stopped the Jeep about forty yards away from the water trough and turned the ignition key off. They all sat in silence for a moment, then Bob remarked with a tone of amazement, "Holy, shit!"

Wally was wearing a pair of sun glasses and he slowly removed them from his face as he echoed the sentiment. "Holy shit is right."

Bob turned his head to look at Wally and asked, "How you wanna do this?"

Wally tucked his sun glasses into his shirt's left breast pocket and cleared his throat before speaking. "Let me get some pictures. Several of them. You hang back here until I'm done, then you and I'll inspect the carcass together."

Wally turned in his seat to face Jeff and asked politely, "That alright with you, Jeff?"

Jeff simply nodded and answered, "You two do what you gotta do. I just need to get my girls back to work if you don't mind."

Everyone exited the vehicle and Wally folded the passenger side front seat over so Jeff could make his way out. When Jeff was standing next to the front door opening, he reached back into the vehicle and pulled out two pistols along with their holsters. He spoke to Wally first, "I'm giving these to the girls. Never had any use for them before, but I'm playing it safe for now."

Wally shrugged his shoulders and replied, "Agreed." He then reached into the back seat and took out a plastic case. He sat the plastic case on the floorboard and opened it. He took out a 35mm camera and film pack, and then began loading the film into the base of the unit.

Jeff slung the pistol belts over his right shoulder and made his way to the girls. Bob followed the rancher and he didn't notice it when Becky grabbed Karen's arm and whispered, "Bob's coming over here!"

Karen was all smiles as she replied, "I'm the oldest...let me do the talking!"

"You wish! Besides...you're older by three days, only!"

As Jeff approached his workers he raised his voice and asked them both, "You girls ate anything yet?"

Becky answered, "Just now Mister Watkins."

Both girls then spoke at the same time, "Hello Bob!"

Bob smiled and replied, "Hello girls." He paused for a second and then added, "Karen and Becky, right?"

Both girls were having trouble trying not to giggle when Karen answered, "That's us."

Jeff interrupted and took the pistol belts off of his shoulder. He handed the firearms to the girls and said, "Ones a twenty-two, the other ones a thirty-eight. Who gets the big one?"

Karen reached for the thirty-eight and took it from Jeff's hand. Becky grunted and took the twenty-two. They both strapped the pistol belts over their hips as Jeff continued, "I don't want you two out here without a gun anymore, alright."

Both girls answered at the same time, "Yes sir."

Jeff nodded his head in agreement, then asked, "I suppose you didn't see anything while I was gone, did you?"

Becky answered, "No sir. We didn't see anything at all."

Bob was facing the water trough when he interjected, "How about noises? You hear anything unusual while you were guarding the carcass?"

Karen squinted her eyes and asked, "Like what?"

Bob replied, "I don't know…growling…howling…snarling…stuff like that."

Becky answered that remark, "No. Nothing at all. It was all quiet here."

Jeff then interrupted and spoke to the girls, "You two better get over to that busted section of fence. I'll need it stitched up before the day's over."

The girls didn't hesitate for a moment. They both moved to the left side of their horses and climbed onto their saddles. Becky was seated in the saddle when she asked Jeff, "You want the rifle back, Mister Watkins?"

Jeff waved her off and replied, "Yeah, but…just bring it in with you this afternoon. I'll get it from you back at the house." He then reconsidered his answer and changed his mind, "On second thought…no. Keep the rifle and the gun belts. You can use them again tomorrow."

"Yes sir" they answered and reined their horses towards the south. Bob called to them as they started to ride away. "Be careful! See you guys later!"

He didn't hear them softly giggling as they rode away from the watering trough. When they were almost a hundred yards from the dead bull, Karen teased her friend, "He was eyeing me more than he was you!"

Becky quickly retorted, "In your dreams! His eyes were all over me!"

Back at the watering trough, Bob was oblivious to the amorous banter. He was simply watching Wally move slowly around the bull and take picture after picture. Jeff stood at his side and remained silent.

The two of them watched Wally kneel down next to the water trough and aim his camera. They were close enough to hear the clicking of the shutter and the buzzing of the flies. Jeff remarked off-handedly, "This is gonna get smelly in a little bit."

Bob replied quickly, "No doubt."

Wally remained kneeling as he called to Bob, "Bob! Come take a look at this first!"

Bob replied, "You finished with the camera?"

"Yeah! Come look at this!"

Bob made his way to the water tub and stood beside Wally. Jeff was beside him when he stopped and looked down at the two foot impressions. Bob didn't speak for a very long time. Jeff grew impatient and asked, "Well?"

Wally stood up and moved aside. He said to Bob, "Kneel down and get a closer look."

Bob dropped to one knee and rested his elbow on the other one. He still remained silent as he stared at the two footprints.

Jeff snorted and remarked, "So...any ideas?"

Bob didn't answer.

Wally waited for a long moment, then he too became concerned. He spoke softly, "Bob?"

Bob remained kneeling as he answered, "I've seen this before...I'm trying to remember..."

Jeff snorted again and remarked, "Well, if you've seen it before, then you know what it is."

Bob shook his head and replied, "No...I've seen it before, but I don't know what it is."

Wally and Jeff stared at each other. Bob stood up and looked at them both before he spoke, "It was a drawing...I saw these prints in a drawing...I'm trying to remember what it was all about, but it's not coming to me."

Wally shrugged his shoulders and replied, "So...what do you want to do next?"

Bob was quick to respond, "I need to make a plaster casting. I have the kit in the Jeep, just let me grab it and I'll make a solid impression."

Wally replied, "Anything else?"

"Yeah! I'll need to measure the bite radius."

Jeff squinted his eyes and asked sarcastically, "What?"

"The bite radius. It's important. I can use these prints and the measurements of the teeth marks on the bull and then I can tell you how big this thing is."

Jeff was growing impatient as he replied, "You can't tell us *what* it is, but you can tell us how big it is?"

Bob walked away from the two men and made for his Jeep. Jeff turned to Wally and whispered, "He can tell us how big it is...don't you need to know *what* it is for your report?"

Wally shrugged his shoulders and answered, "More or less."

"More or less...how about he tells you how big it is and I tell you how angry it is? Can we take it from there?"

Wally chuckled as he answered, "Patience, Jeff. He'll figure it out."

Jeff couldn't help himself. He chuckled along with Wally and replied, "Oh, alright!" He then took Wally by the arm and said, "Well...let's get out of his way so he can do his work." They stepped away from the scene as Bob knelt down next to the foot impressions again.

It was ten minutes until noontime when Jo Ann came walking through the Sheriff's office front door. Allie was writing in the log journal and talking on the dispatch radio at the same time. She was calling for the deputy named Jesse. "Jesse, this is base, over."

A crackling voice replied, "This is Jesse."

"Jesse, what's your twenty?"

"Highway 76 at the Papago Fuel Stop."

She made a note in the book and then replied, "Roger. I'll check back with you later." She waved a hand at Jo Ann and said, "Hi!"

Jo Ann sat in the chair across from Allie's desk and smiled as she said, "I see my husband's out...we were going to have lunch together, but I guess it'll have to wait until dinner."

Allie explained, "He's out at the Watkins Ranch. Don't know how long he'll be, but I don't expect him back in time for lunch."

Jo Ann thought for a second, then asked, "How about you? You hungry?"

"I could do a salad."

"Me too. Let's go to the Palm Café and get a Caesar."

Allie stood up and picked a hand-held radio unit out of its cradle. She used the clip to attach it to her belt and then said, "Let me grab my purse."

The Palm Café was an old establishment. It specialized in southwest dishes that had a TexMex character, but it offered a decent barbeque menu as well. Allie and Jo Ann were having what they called a "light" lunch. Chicken Caesar Salad with vinegar dressing. They were both drinking water.

Somehow the conversation got around to Bob Benoit. Jo Ann accidentally moved it in that direction when she asked, "You dating anyone these days, hon?"

Allie sat her fork on her table napkin and answered, "You know who I'd like to date? Bob Benoit."

Jo Ann smiled slightly and replied, "That introvert? Why him?"

"You don't think he's cute?"

Jo Ann shrugged her shoulders and said, "Not particularly."

Allie put her elbows on the table and leaned forward, "Why not?"

Jo Ann took another bite of salad as she answered, "I'm married…my judgement of *cute* went away a long time ago."

Allie sat up straight again and started eating her salad. She replied, "Fair enough. You can take my word for it."

Jo Ann wrinkled her brow as she thought of another question. "How you gonna do it?"

"Do what?"

"Get him to ask you out."

Allie took a drink of water from her glass and thought for a second. "I don't know…like you said, he's so introverted that it hurts."

"I got an idea" Jo Ann offered.

"Tell me."

"Next time you see him, walk right straight up to him and say *I need a date tonight…and you're it.*"

Allie sat her fork down again and replied, "Oh…funny! Ha-ha!"

Jo Ann pretended to be hurt as she said, "What's wrong with that idea?"

"It's too bold!"

"No it isn't!"

"You want me to prance right up to him and give him an order to date me? I'd make a fool out of myself!"

"Not if you showed him some cleavage."

Allie snorted a loud laugh. "You're impossible!"

Jo Ann answered, "And you're endowed."

Allie cocked her head to one side and sounded peeved when she replied, "You're embarrassing me."

"You wanna date him or not?"

Allie sighed and said, "This is the best advice you can give me?"

Jo Ann put her fork alongside of her salad plate and put one elbow on the table. She leaned forward and said with a very serious tone, "You got any experience with introverts?"

"Uh…no."

"Well I do! So you need to listen to me!"

Allie smiled and replied, "Ok…go ahead…I'm all ears."

Jo Ann took her elbow off of the table and answered, "It's about time. So…here's what you need to do…oh, and forget about that cleavage thing…that can come later…for right now, you need to understand that the first move is yours. Not his."

"Alright."

"Don't go driving around town looking for him…that *would* be too bold. Just remember that the next time you see each other, you have to make the first move."

Allie interrupted, "You have something specific in mind that I should say?"

Jo Ann shook her head as she said, "Nah…it'll come to you. You just gotta get close enough to him to make him nervous. That way he won't turn you down."

"You make it sound easy."

"Oh…it's easy enough…trust me. You're looking at the expert introvert handler right here."

Allie took a deep breath and surrendered, "What have I got to lose? I'll do it."

Bob was letting the thin liquid plaster from his impression kit dry while he used a flexible measuring tape to get some sizes of the wounds on the bull's body. Wally and Jeff simply stood silently by and let him work. Bob was taking measurements, then writing a note in a small booklet concerning each one. He had a small plastic case lying on the ground next to him, and he appeared to be through taking measurements. He put the flexible tape into the plastic case, then removed a long metal tong that looked like a giant set of tweezers.

He used the tongs to lift away a section of muscle from the open wound at the bull's flank, and frowned as he stared at the recess. He looked up at Wally and asked, "You got enough film to take one more picture?"

Wally still had the camera in his hands so he just stepped forward and answered, "Whatcha need?"

Bob pulled the muscle back and pointed at the slice in

the meat. "You see that?"

Wally nodded his head as he said, "Jagged cut. More like a rip, actually."

"Can you get a good close-up of it?"

Wally pulled the camera to his face and replied, "Sure." He snapped a picture and asked, "Want another one?"

"Sure."

He took another one, but he held the camera closer that time. He let the camera drop from his face as he asked Bob, "Are you through?"

"Yeah."

"You know what it is?"

Wally saw Bob glance nervously up at Jeff, then he saw Bob shake his head slowly in the negative. "No."

Wally frowned and thought to himself, "Bob's lying...he knows something, but he won't say it in front of Jeff."

Wally decided that Bob was probably exercising extreme caution, so he simply remarked, "Well...then, can we pack up and go?"

Bob stood up slowly and replied, "Let me check the plaster. If it's dry, we can go."

Wally watched Bob go to his plaster casts and he spoke to Jeff. "Let's pack up, Jeff. Time to go."

"You got enough for a report?"

Wally snickered, "No. Gotta get the pictures developed first. Gotta get Bob's input, then I'll get you a report. Probably take a day or two."

Jeff sighed, "Oh, well...can I call old-man Kermit?"

Wally answered off-handedly, "Yeah, you should probably do that today. Let him know that Bob and I are looking into it."

Jeff seemed happier when he replied, "Good! Thank you."

Karen and Becky had their horses tied to a section of fence close to where they were working on the broken section.

They decided not to weave any new wire onto the old ones. They cut the broken strands off and rolled them up into a small ball, then stretched new strands between the wooden poles and stapled them into place.

They had the repair completed in less than half of an hour, so they decided to ride the south fence line for a couple of more miles before heading back to the ranch. They would have to allow themselves enough time to tend to their horses before quitting for the day, so they only had about two more hours of work time available.

They rode side-by-side, slowly walking their horses and simply looking at the fence and scanning the brushy hills for nothing in particular. They were told to be on the lookout for some sort of big animal, but they weren't too preoccupied with that particular search. Becky had the rifle butt resting on her saddle pommel with the barrel point towards the sky as she rocked slightly with the rhythm of her horse's walk.

Karen decided to make an offhanded remark, "How do you feel about wearing pistols?"

Becky joked as she replied, "Like a regular Annie Oakley."

Karen chuckled as she said, "Me too…sort of."

Becky had another thought, "You know what? I'll bet our boyfriends wouldn't argue with us about anything if they saw us armed like this."

Karen agreed, "Yeah…we look pretty formidable, don't we?"

Becky reined her horse to a stop. She was looking at a distant plateau as she said, "What's that?"

Karen tried to see what she was looking at, but had to ask, "What do you see?"

Becky nodded her head in the direction of the flat-topped hill and answered, "There. Top of that plateau. I think there's something sitting up there."

Karen stood up in her stirrups and strained her eyes to make out what Becky was alluding to. The heat waves were dancing off of some rocks and bare earth places, but she finally said, "I think I see it! It's black! Oops! It moved to the other side."

Becky cursed softly, "Damn! I wonder what it was."

The girls sighed to each other, then nudged their horses to start them walking again.

Bob and Wally dropped Jeff off at his ranch house and made arrangements with each other to meet and talk when they were away from the rancher. They drove their vehicles away from Jeff's place and stopped underneath some tall pines that were along the side of the road. They both exited their vehicles and stood facing each other.

Wally started, "You know something, but you won't say what it is."

Bob confirmed, "I *think* I know something, but it's insane, and I don't want to say it out loud."

Wally folded his arms across his chest and put a serious look on his face. "Try me."

Bob replied, "Let me explain something first...when I saw the foot prints, I was certain that I'd seen them before. I had to think long and hard, but I finally remembered..."

Wally dropped his arms to his sides as Bob continued. "There is a newsletter that circulates among colleges...it's called the *Rubicon Journals*...people in the scientific community publish articles and the journal gets circulated around to various campuses."

Wally was not following the narrative, so he said, "So?"

Bob continued, "A few years ago...I read an article about regressive genetics...quite interesting stuff, actually."

Wally frowned, "Get to the point."

Bob sighed and continued, "The animal that killed that bull...it's a mutation. It's a throwback. Those prints and those bite marks were made by an animal that doesn't exist today."

Wally was growing impatient with the game warden. He cocked his head and said, "What you're suggesting is not logical…to me, that is.”

Bob had to sigh again and agree with Wally. “You’re right. I can’t firmly state what that animal is, but I know what I have to do in order to find out.”

That statement calmed Wally slightly. He said, “Talk to me.”

“I gotta take your pictures and my casts to the College in Vera. There’s a professor there that teaches zoology. He’s a Mammologist, actually…and a damn good one.”

Wally brightened up somewhat. “Professor Wilcox. I know him. Had him for some biology classes. Tough SOB.”

Bob interjected, “Then you agree? I can take our stuff to Wilcox and get his opinion?”

“Yeah…that’s probably the best idea…but I have to say something first.”

“What?”

“We’re dealing with an animal. That’s your department, and not mine. I don’t have the resources to chase after animals. Only the human kind.”

Bob was smiling as he replied, “You’re putting the ball in my court, huh?”

Wally used his right index finger to point at Bob’s Jeep. “You have my camera and case in there. Go get the pictures developed and meet me back at the office. I want to look them over before I let you take them to Vera.”

“Fair enough. I’ll see you in a couple of hours, then?”

“Yeah…but first…”

Bob squinted his eyes and frowned. He knew what was coming next.

Wally finished his statement. “Tell me what you *think* killed that bull.”

Bob’s voice was barely above a whisper as he answered, “Dire wolf.”

CHAPTER FIVE

Bob Benoit entered the Sheriff's Office front door at 4:15 in the afternoon. He was carrying Wally's camera case and a large brown envelope and he was walking towards Allie's desk. When she saw him, she gulped and took a quick breath. She held her breath until he spoke to her.

"Hi. I've got the Sheriff's camera and he needs to see some photos that I just got developed." (The local discount store had a dark room where they developed customer pictures, and they had an arrangement with the Sheriff's Office to give them top priority on any and all film development.)

Allie used her thumb to indicate Wally's office, which was behind her desk and to her right. She said, "He's in his office. Go right in."

Bob walked around Ellie's desk and she lowered her head slightly. She tried to calm herself in her mind, "Now... don't get nervous! Don't get nervous! You can do this!"

Bob sat the camera case on the floor next to Wally's desk and handed him the envelope. He explained as Wally took the package, "We got almost three dozen pictures. Four of them didn't turn out. Too fuzzy."

Wally snickered softly and replied, "I'm getting better, then." He opened the brown envelope and pulled out three more smaller white envelopes. He spread the pictures out of one of them on top of his desk and looked at each one. He chose four individual photos out of the picture envelope and set them aside. He put the rest of them back into the original packet and picked up the second one.

He repeated the process without any comments and

chose three photos out of that one. When he inspected the last white packet, he frowned slightly and held one particular photo close to his face. He then spoke to Bob, "This one...that gash you had me shoot...does it look clear enough to you?"

Bob quickly answered, "Oh, yeah. Very much so."

Wally didn't choose any photos from the third packet. He simply put them back in place and reinserted the packets into the brown envelope. He handed it to Bob and asked, "What's next?"

"I called Professor Wilcox. I told him what I had and he's agreed to see me. He gave me address and he's wants me there between six-thirty and seven."

Wally glanced at his wristwatch and replied, "Plenty of time. Vera's a little more than an hour away."

Bob replied, "I'm leaving now. Maybe he can see me earlier." He tucked the envelope under his left arm and walked out of Wally's office.

Allie had moved away from her desk and she was standing between Bob and the exit door. As he was walking towards her, she glanced at her top shirt button and quickly said to herself, "No!"

He was beside her desk and she started taking bold strides towards him. She held up her hand and said, "Hold on, Bob."

Bob smiled and stopped as he replied, "Allie..."

She had a few more steps to take before she would be directly in front of him and she kept talking, "I have a bone to pick with you!"

"What?"

"You heard me!" She was directly in front of him when she stopped and folded her arms across her chest. "You heard me. I need you to take me out for pizza tonight."

Bob stammered, "Uh...uh...Pizza?"

She took a step closer and Bob tried to inch his way backwards. The back of his legs touched Allie's desk and blocked him.

She kept her arms folded and continued, "I'm tired of you not chasing after me, so tonight you're taking me out for pizza."

Bob stammered again, "I…I…I'm sorry, I have to go to Vera…right now."

She inched herself closer to him and had her face directly in front of his. "Vera, huh? Don't they have a pizza place in Vera?"

He tried to lean backwards, but she had crowded him to the point where he couldn't think straight. He tried to explain, "I…have an appointment…I have to leave right now…"

Allie unfolded her arms and put her hands on her hips. She leaned to the left side of Bob and called to Wally, "Sheriff Sand!"

Wally's voice was muffled as he replied, "Yeah?"

"I'm leaving work early!"

There was no pause before he answered. "Alright…how come?"

"I have a date!"

There was a slight pause, then he answered her, "By all means, then!"

She stood up straight and kept her face directly in front of his as she said, "You ready?"

Bob swallowed audibly as he replied, "Uh huh."

She stepped aside and took him by the elbow with her left arm and started walking towards the front door. She was smiling as she remarked, "Now, see…that wasn't so hard, was it?"

He walked dutifully beside her and pushed the front door open for the both of them before he replied, "No…you made that pretty easy."

The sidewalk sloped slightly towards the parking lot and made a slow right hand curve. Bob's Chevrolet pickup was parked next to the Handicap stall and he had the windows slightly rolled down so the heat wouldn't build up inside. He walked Allie to the passenger side and opened the door.

She looked inside and saw a cardboard box sitting on the passenger seat, so she grabbed it and put it in the floorboard before stepping inside. She turned to him and took the brown envelope from under his arm and then climbed into the vehicle. She sat the envelope on top of the cardboard box and slid herself close to the steering wheel as Bob made his way to the driver's side.

Bob was still nervous and speechless as he slowly stepped into the cab. He settled into his seat apprehensively, and then started the engine. He let the engine run for a moment, then he turned the air-conditioning on at its highest setting.

It was an automatic transmission, so he dropped the shift lever into reverse and started to back up. He let the vehicle roll for a few inches, then put his foot on the brake. He turned to her and said, "I had no idea you were like this."

She smiled and replied, "Are you saying that I'm bossy and forward?"

He shook his head very slowly and answered, "No...I meant...sexy."

She couldn't help herself. She put her face onto his and gave him a quick kiss on the lips. She slipped her left arm around his shoulder and replied, "Let's go...and...I want you to drive real slow through town, OK?"

He backed up cautiously and then put the vehicle into drive. He steered towards the parking lot exit and asked, "Slow? Why?"

"I want everybody...and I mean *everybody* to see us together. Just like this!"

He smiled and shrugged his shoulders, then pulled out of the parking lot. While his head was turned, she unfastened the top button of her work shirt.

Fourteen miles southwest of Meacon, and in the open desert, there is a parcel of land that has three very large and very deep gullies. They are situated at the bottom of a sloping valley and they run in the same general direction. The largest gulley is the one situated at the very bottom of the valley and it runs due north and south. The cliff walls are over forty feet high in some places and the width of the cut varies between ten and sixty-five yards.

A small and shallow creek trickled along the bottom of the cut, which allowed the growth of some salt brush and tiny pines. Due to the mineral content of the soil, the creek's edges had deposits of brown moss and slime clinging to rocks along the rim of the water.

There are five natural caves located on the high cliffs and each one of them had a wide ledge leading up the side of the rock face to allow access. During the early part of the century, camping was a popular adventure and people from around the state of Arizona hiked to the gulley and made their camps among the caves. By the time the forties had passed, the main gulley and its sisters had lost their public appeal. They became places of solitude and a haven for quail, and there are no roads leading to the ravines.

That was how the gulley received its name. The cubbies of quail flourished there, so people referred to it as the Quail Cut. The other two gorges didn't have any name or designation other than the east cut and the west cut. The Quail Cut was also dead-ended at the southern end. The creek sprang out of the southern end and flowed out the northern end where it eventually became a trickle and finally made its way to empty into the Gila River.

Halfway through the gorge's expanse, and on the western side, the largest of the five caves was seventeen feet high off of the fissure floor. A twenty-foot rock overhang kept it from being seen from above, while a wild growing Chiricahua Mountain Dock hid the opening from the opposite side of the gorge.

The hole itself was an opening that a person would have to stoop in order to enter, but it expanded outwards and upwards to form a large round room almost twenty-feet in diameter. The floor was covered with a shallow layer of dirt, which made a comfortable place for an animal to lay. The beast was stretched out on his right side and he was sound asleep.

Highway 89 runs north out of Meacon for twenty-five miles, then it joins with Interstate Highway 19 at Green Valley. Twenty miles north of Green Valley, State Highway 12 branches off towards the west and Vera, Arizona is five miles from there.

Vera is a college town that caters to the southern Arizona natives. It offers a four-year degree in business, accounting, and law, but it's considered an AG college, so agriculture and economics are its primary purpose. Both Wally and Jo Ann are graduates of Vera State University.

The speed limit for State Highways and Interstate Highways is fifty-five miles an hour. This makes the fifty-mile drive between Meacon and Vera take somewhere around an hour, or a little longer. Bob was driving the absolute speed limit while he and Allie talked to each other.

As soon as they had left the town limits of Meacon, she started grilling him for details about his life. Her first question was, "I hear you come from northern California, is that true?"

He confirmed, "Close to Oregon. Small town. About the same size as Meacon."

"You like living in small towns?"

"Oh yeah. I had to work in Tucson for almost a year and that almost choked me to death."

She chuckled as she continued, "I don't much care for big cities either. How do you like being a game warden?"

"Best job in the world."

"Yeah? Does it keep you busy a lot?"

He glanced at her and saw that she was smiling broadly. He answered, "Some. I do game counts for the state which keeps me fairly busy. I work with ranchers and farmers mostly. Sometimes I have to work with the fish hatcheries, but mostly I keep track of wildlife numbers."

She sounded like she was teasing when she asked, "So… you run around counting critters, huh?"

He caught the gist of her humor and joined in the jest,

"Yeah...birds are the hardest...I have to count them while they fly overhead."

He returned his gaze to the highway, then asked her a personal question. "How did you come to work for the Sheriff's department?"

She moved herself slightly closer to his side and answered, "Oh that's easy. I kicked this guy in the nuts and Sheriff Sand hired me on the spot."

He turned his head and stared at her disbelievingly. She put a hand on his knee and explained, "See...I had this girlfriend in high school, and this fat guy named Joe Johnson was trying to take my friend's shirt off. Right there in broad daylight, too. Joe was a dumbass and a mean dumbass at that. My friend, Beth... she was screaming and trying to fight him off. The Sheriff and one of his deputies...I'm pretty sure it was Jesse...were driving by and saw what was going on. Well, before they could get out of the police car, I ran up behind Joe and kicked him in the nuts."

Bob started smiling more and more as the story progressed. He interjected, "So...you blind-sided his cods, huh?"

"Yeah...put the bastard in the hospital for two days too."

Bob was close to hysterics. He pressed her for more details. "So...Sheriff Sand saw you and went up to you and said, "Hey...nice nut kicking...wanna go to work for me?"

Allie was close to laughter as she answered, "Not exactly. I was still in high school, so he waited until I graduated. Then he came to my graduation and offered me a job that very night."

Bob teased her. "Wow...almost like a fairy tale."

"It's my favorite story." She looked down at the cardboard box and pointed at it. "What's in there?"

"Paw casts."

She thought for a second, then asked, "Like those bigfoot plaster casts you see on TV?"

He answered her quickly, then changed the subject. "Yeah...just like those. Are you going to college?"

"My last semester is this fall."

"What's your major?"

"You'll think I'm lying when I tell you."

He glanced at her then returned his eyes to the road. "Why?"

"I'm studying veterinary medicine. I don't want to be a Veterinarian just yet. I want to work as an assistant with Doctor Madlow in Meacon for a few years, then maybe start my own clinic."

He looked surprised as he asked, "Why did you think that answer would make me think you were lying?"

She rested her head against his shoulder as she said, "Well...you're the game warden, and I like working with animals...so I thought...maybe...you'd find that a little strange."

He quickly responded, "No! Hell, no! I think that's...I think that..."

She nudged him in his ribs. "Spit it out!"

"I think that's fantastic. No wonder I've always wanted to ask you out!"

She sat up straight and roughly squeezed his leg with her hand. She leaned closer to his face and raised her voice, "You wanted to ask me out? I've had the hots for you for over a year and you wanted to ask me out? I should kick you in the nuts! Making me wait all this time!"

They passed a road sign that said, GREEN VALLEY / 5 MILES. She kept her grip on his leg and then she started smiling as she relaxed her grasp and said, "You apologize to me...right now."

He was wincing from her clench as he said. "I'm sorry."

She patted his leg and put her head back on his shoulder. "You owe me lots of dates, Bob. Lots of them..."

It was five thirty in the afternoon when Becky and Karen brought their horses into the barnyard and unsaddled them. The stable hand was an older gentleman that worked for Jeff full time. His name was Todd Endoran and he was a deaf mute. When he approached the girls so he could take their saddles into the saddle house, Karen greeted him with sign language. "Hi Todd. We have pistol belts and a rifle for you to store."

Todd nodded and signed back, "Let me do saddles first." He saw that Becky's saddle was unbuckled, so he pulled it off and carried it into the barn. There was a large room with wooden stands used for holding saddles. It was referred to as the saddle house.

As he walked away, Becky commented to Karen, "I wish I knew sign language. I'd like to say hi to Todd sometimes, too."

Karen agreed, "Yeah. He's a nice man. I can teach you some simple stuff if you'd like."

Becky agreed, "Sounds good. Maybe you can show me some stuff starting tomorrow."

Karen left her unbuckled saddle on her horse as she and Becky made their way to the saddle house. There was a gun rack inside, so they were simply going to put their weapons on it for the evening. They had removed their lunch pouches and left the fencing tools in the saddle bags. Todd would replace the barbed wire roll in the canvas bag so that the girls would have a fresh one for in the morning.

As they walked side-by-side, Karen asked her friend, "You think we should tell Mister Watkins that we saw something today?"

Jeff's voice came from behind them, "Yes…you should tell Mister Watkins what you saw!"

The girls jumped, then they both giggled. "Nice one, Mister Watkins" Becky said.

Jeff put himself between the two girls and the three of them made for the barn. Becky tried to explain, "Well, Mister Watkins…we don't exactly know what it was. It was a long way off and it was sitting on top of a plateau."

Karen offered, "It was black. We saw that much."

Jeff frowned, "Black huh?"

Karen continued, "Yes sir. Sorry, but with the heat

waves from the sand and all…all I could see was a big black shape."

Becky offered, "When I first saw it, I thought it looked like a dog when it sits on its back legs. Sort of a shape like that."

The three of them entered the barn and made for the saddle house. Todd passed them on his way out. Jeff mumbled out loud, "Well…I guess that's something…big dog or wolf, maybe."

Becky took Karen's pistol belt and she hung the two of them on a peg of the rifle rack, then she gently lay the rifle across one of the cradles. Jeff automatically asked, "Those are unloaded, right?"

Karen answered him, "Yes sir. Absolutely."

He nodded his head and then asked, "Where are you two working tomorrow?"

Becky answered that particular question. "Your north range is next, Mister Watkins. We want to start with the fence line beginning at the Elkins gate." (Pasture gates were named after the ranches they opened up to.)

Jeff agreed. "Good. That's good. That's rocky country for a long stretch, so check your horse's shoes before you head out in the morning."

Both girls answered him at the same time. "Yes sir."

The beast rolled onto his stomach and yawned. He got to his feet and then shook himself violently so he could jog away the dirt from his black fur. He grunted softly, then made his way out of the cave's entrance.

He stopped just outside of the cave and sniffed the air. Nothing caught his attention, so he sat on his haunches and scratched his right shoulder with his right rear leg. When he had satisfied the itch on his shoulder he stood on all fours and looked over the ledge. The trickling water below made him realize that he was thirsty, so he trotted down the wide ledge leading away from his cave. The ledge was rock face and wide enough for a person to easily pass over. The wind currents in the gorge kept the dirt from accumulating on the strip so he left no footprints.

The bottom of the gorge was completely covered with a dark shadow. The sun was well down so daylight didn't penetrate the entirety of the ravine. His fur was black in color. Very black. It could easily be referred to as jet black or raven black. He was a sleek animal, which meant that his fur did not grow thicker over the shoulders or thinner over his haunches. His muscles rippled underneath an even coating of short-hair fur. He had odd shaped ears in as much as they were broad at the base of his skull and formed extremely sharp tips at the ends.

His front paws resembled a normal four toed wolf paw with an exceptionally broad back pad, but his hind paws were only three-toed. His front paws measured nine inches in length, and his hind paws measured ten. It was the configuration of his hind feet that gave him his great speed and agility.

His snout was long and his eyes were a pale yellow in color. They were good for seeing well in either daylight or darkness. His jaw muscles were oddly shaped because nature had given him a malformation at the base of his jawbones. There was a cartilage connection between his zygomatic arch and his condyloid process that allowed his mouth to open far wider than his snout would indicate possible. His jaws didn't *unhinge* as much as they stretched to unbelievable lengths. However, when he readied himself for an attack, and he opened his jaws to reveal his teeth, it certainly would appear that the jaw bones had dislodged themselves.

His canines were another birth defect. They were seven inches long and curved. The backside of the teeth was jagged and sharp and they hung outside of his mouth. He couldn't be called *saber-toothed* because the base of his canines was too small. His front teeth were dagger-like and he used them well when he killed his prey, but they were not the extremely oversized canines depicted by a true saber-toothed creature.

His tail was long and heavy with a natural curl at the end. Just like a wolf's tail. He was a wolf. A wolf with structural and functional birth defects, but a wolf, none-the-less. He weighed two-hundred pounds.

Wally had both of his hands pressed against the shower wall and he was letting the water hit the back of his neck and cascade over his shoulders. He had the water temperature at the warm setting and was about to adjust it so that it was cooler.

His eyes were closed as he heard the shower door open and he smiled at the sudden interruption. Jo Ann stepped behind him and put both of her arms around his waist and pulled herself to him.

He stood up straight and let her caress his chest, then he moved to allow her to stand under the water herself. She used her hands to steady herself by clutching his hips and slipped under the shower head. Wally took the wet washcloth off of the soap den and lathered it with a white bar of soap. He started at her neck and gently rubbed her throat and face, then moved the cloth to her chest and breasts. She spread her legs slightly and let him clean her stomach, vulva, and thighs.

Once he had washed her past her knees, she turned to face the spraying water and let him scrub her backside. He put the washcloth back onto the plastic bar above the soap dish and then picked up the shampoo bottle.

Jo Ann stepped fully under the water spray and let the soap rinse away from her body. Once her hair was saturated with water, she lowered her head and let him start shampooing her scalp. Wally scrubbed the shampoo vigorously into her hair and it formed a thick foam that dripped over her face. When he had thoroughly scrubbed her scalp, he grabbed strands of her hair and squeezed the excess lather off of her locks. He then guided her head back under the falling water and massaged it gently to allow the lather buildup to wash away.

She pulled herself close to his body and rested her hands over his buttocks while he worked the strands of her hair.

She felt the last of the lather drain off of her shoulders, then used her hands to guide him under the spray. She picked up the washcloth and the bar of soap and repeated the perform-ance on his body.

Once she saw that his scalp was free of shampoo, she reached behind him and turned the water faucets to the off pos-ition. She pushed the shower door open with one hand and used her other one to hold onto his arm so she could step out of the shower without slipping. As he stepped out of the shallow tub she pulled him out of the bathroom and said as she led him away, "We don't need a towel. I'm gonna do you wet."

Their bed was only a few steps away from the bath-room, so she pulled him to the side of the mattress and released her hold. She grabbed the top covers and jerked them off of the bed and let them fall to the floor. She pushed his shoulders and made him fall backwards onto the mattress.

He pulled himself across the mattress and she scram-bled to lay on top of him. She wrapped her arms around his shoulders and started kissing his lips passionately and roughly at the same time. He groaned softly as she gyrated her hips and pressed herself against his manhood.

The sheet on the mattress was wet and felt cool to his skin. His hands were interlocked together around her waist as he pulled her even tighter against his body.

She continued kissing him as she moved her right arm from around his shoulder and raised her hips slightly. She grabbed his member with her hand and held it softly as she slid herself onto it. She began rolling her hips slowly and then thrusting herself up and down. Wally groaned with pleasure and moved his hands to the back of her shoulders.

After a long and sensuous session, she felt him stiffen slightly so she wrapped her legs around his and made herself thrust faster. His release filled her with a warmth that immedi-ately triggered an orgasm. She squealed softly and went limp.

They were both breathing deeply as they lay perfectly still. Her wet hair had fallen over his chest and part of his face, but he made no effort to brush it away. After a long moment, she lifted herself off of him and sat on his legs. She smiled down at him as he was smiling at her as she said, "Now, I'll get us a towel."

Bob slowed his pickup down to the posted speed limit of thirty-five miles per hour and said to Allie, "Hey…how well do you know your way around Vera?"

She responded, "Where are we going?"

"Corner of Fourteenth Street and Elm Avenue."

Her left hand was still resting on his right leg as she used her other hand to point to the next intersection. "Turn left at the light" she said.

He had to stop and wait for the turn signal arrow to indicate that he could move, and as soon as he had completed the turn, Allie instructed him again, "Thirteen blocks to make it to Fourteenth Street, then turn right. There won't be a light, so I'll let you know when we get close."

He snickered softly, "Wow. I'm really glad you came along, now."

She shrugged her shoulders and remarked offhandedly, "I go to school here, so I sort of know my way around."

They passed through the intersections and only had to stop for one traffic light. When they were half of a block from Fourteenth Street, she said, "Next intersection. Turn right."

He turned right onto the narrow street and she then instructed him, "Elm is four blocks from here. Do you know which corner house?"

"He said it was the stucco one with the beige roof."

She suddenly realized where they were going. She remarked partially excited, "Are we going to Professor Wilcox's house?"

He glanced at her as he made his way slowly down the street, "You know the Professor?"

She answered, "He's my biology teacher. Did you know that he's also famous? He writes books about extinct creatures."

Bob saw the stucco house that he was making for and he saw that the driveway was empty. He pulled next to the driveway and parked close to the curb. He answered Allie when he put his vehicle into park. "He's a mammologist. That's why I'm taking this stuff to him. I want him to look at it."

She asked quickly before she slid towards the passenger side door, "Is it important stuff? Can I get course credits for this?"

He laughed softly as he opened his door and stepped out onto the curb. He replied, "Maybe. I think it's important stuff. You want me to ask him for you?"

She opened her door and stepped out onto the pavement as she replied, "Nah. I'll hit him up about it next semester."

He met her at the passenger side door and she had his picture envelope in her right hand. She said, "I'll carry the envelope, you get the box."

He reached past her and took the box into both of his hands. He stepped back and she shut the door. He had his keys in his trousers pocket so he didn't bother trying to lock the vehicle.

As soon as Allie shut the pickup door, they both heard the front door of the house open. The door opened into the interior of the house, then they saw a man push open a screen door and hold it open.

Professor Wilcox was a pudgy man with a balding head. His face was oval and he had large eyebrows above his dark brown eyes. His nose was slightly bulbous from years of overindulging with alcohol, but during these last few years he had gotten control over his drinking.

He was dressed in a white tee shirt with knee-length denim shorts and his shoes were a pair of brown slip-ons. He called to Bob when he saw the couple walking up his driveway. "You could've parked in the driveway! I use the garage."

Bob called back, "Sorry. We didn't know. The truck'll be alright there for a little while, I'm sure."

"Well, come on in, then" he continued as he held the screen door open for Bob and Allie. He stared at Allie quizzically as she walked by and then he closed the doors behind them. He spoke to Allie as they made their way to the living room, "Aren't you Miss Thompson...the veterinary student?"

She turned her head to look at him as she smiled and affirmed, "That's me. I'm in your biology class."

Professor Wilcox grunted as he replied, "I thought so...I never forget a "B" student."

Allie complained, "Hey! I work and go to school!"

He didn't answer her. He simply instructed Bob, "Let's go to the dining room. I have a big dining table and I'm dying to look at those casts that you brought to me."

Everyone sat at the table. Allie and Bob sat on one side while Professor Wilcox sat on the other. Bob pushed the box across the table towards him and said, "I made these at the Watkins Ranch in Meacon. These were the only decent impressions that I could get. There were a lot of claw marks around the kill that were its hind feet, but none of them would have made a decent cast."

Allie sat the picture envelope on the table in front of her and remained silent. She kept her focus on Professor Wilcox's face as the man opened the lid on the cardboard box. She saw his eyes narrow and his jovial expression fade as he looked down into the box.

His hands were holding the sides of the cardboard lid as he silently stared at the contents. He didn't move a muscle for a very long time, and neither Allie nor Bob had the inclination to interrupt him. They just let him stare in silence.

After what seemed like a very long period of time, Allie and Bob heard the man whisper, "No...this...is impossible."

Bob took the envelope off of the table and opened it. He withdrew three white packets and pushed them across the table to the Professor. He explained, "Sheriff Sand took these for me."

Professor Wilcox reluctantly pushed the cardboard box aside and opened a packet of pictures. He looked at each one very closely before setting them down and opening another packet. He repeated his inspection of that set of pictures, then opened the third packet. Allie saw his eyes widen as he pulled one photograph close to his face. She heard him remark, "Oh...oh my goodness."

Allie turned her head to look at Bob but said nothing. She elected to sit quietly and let her professor initiate a conversation. It didn't take long after he had studied the one particular photograph. He let his hand fall to the tabletop and looked directly at Bob. "Mister Benoit...what...what was your first impression when you discovered this...animal?"

Bob's cheeks visibly blushed and Allie caught it. Bob answered, "I'm a little embarrassed to say."

The professor took a plaster cast out of the box and held it with both hands as he replied, "Then let me guess what your brain said...it said *Dire Wolf* didn't it?"

Bob sheepishly replied, "Uh-huh."

Allie's brow winkled as she whispered to Bob, "Dire Wolf?"

Professor Wilcox jumped at the opportunity to explain it to Allie, "The Dire Wolf is scientifically named Canis Dirus, which means *fearsome dog*. You see...it's not really a wolf, but a hybrid...more closely related to the Red Wolf. It died out ten-thousand years ago."

Allie couldn't help herself. She asked the obvious question, "So this is a ten-thousand-year-old dog?"

Bob snorted and Professor Wilcox smiled. The professor continued speaking, but he directed his words to Bob instead of Allie. "Mister Benoit, the front feet of this animal are almost exact duplicates of casts made by archeologists and zoologists. Almost...but not quite."

Bob interjected, "I sort of thought that also, but my second thought was that the animal was mutated."

"That's my belief. It's a wolf with a birth defect more than likely. It's very rare for an animal to have both structural and functional deformities, but it does happen."

Bob offered another bit of information, "I measured the bite radius and to tell the truth, it's shocking. I looked at the depth of its footprints and I estimated the animal to be around one-hundred and eighty pounds, but the size of the bite marks indicates an animal twice that large."

Professor Wilcox offered, "Go with the footprints to guess its weight. If it has deformed feet, it could also have a deformed head."

Bob nodded in agreement as he replied, "That's what I thought when I saw the way its canines ripped apart flesh and meat. If it has oversized canines, then it has to have some way to compensate his mouth in order to use them."

"Very flexible jaw muscles" commented the professor.

Allie interrupted the conversation again, "Can either of you tell me what this deformed wolf looks like?"

Professor Wilcox answered, "If it looks like a Dire Wolf, then it's taller at the shoulders than it is at its hind legs. It would be either black or brown. Nobody knows for certain which, but it was most likely brown."

"Why?" asked Allie.

Bob answered for the professor, "Northern Mexico was a rugged mountain range ten-thousand years ago. The Dire Wolf fed on large game, such as elk or bison or even mammoth. Brown was the color scheme of virtually all of those animals."

Wilcox smiled and added, "Brown is as good of a guess that there is. But...like you said, it hunted and killed large animals, and by the looks of these pictures, your animal didn't have any problem taking down a full grown bull."

Bob agreed with the man. "It mangled the bovine. Almost like it was tearing at it in a rage."

Professor Wilcox then stated, "Well...if you came to me for verification that you have a dangerous creature on your hands, then let me confirm your suspicions. I'll only offer this advice...it's a carnivore. It kills its prey and eats, and there is little to no doubt that it can do to a human being what it did to this cow."

Bob lowered his head and whispered his answer, "I've come to that conclusion, but I was hoping that there would be another solution other than to hunt it down and kill it."

Wilcox agreed, "Nature is harsh, Mister Benoit. It's not a struggle between right and wrong to protect lives and property. I strongly suggest that you don't try and capture this animal." He had picked up a plaster cast and held it up for the couple to see. He was pointing at the size of the claws on the end of the cast.

Bob instinctively knew that his visit with the professor was nearing its end. He started to stand up, but asked one more question before he did so, "I'll start looking for it tomorrow. Do you know anything about the Dire Wolf habits that may be helpful when I start trying to track it down?"

"Oh…good point…let me see…yes! If it's a product of wolf parents, then it may have a tendency to hunt either late in the day or after dark. It will mark its territory and jealously guard over it…be especially vigilant during the afternoon and evening hours." He paused and rubbed his chin before he spoke again, "Then…if it's a wolf…and neither of us know for certain that it is…it would like to hole up in a den."

Bob chuckled at that last remark. He replied, "Well… there's about a thousand good dens out there in the desert, so that should narrow my search down some."

Professor Wilcox stood up from his table and asked Bob, "What do you plan on doing with the plaster casts and the pictures?"

Bob and Allie both stood up as Bob replied, "I'll need them for a few more days, I guess. You want them when I'm done?"

Wilcox smiled as he replied, "That would be very kind of you. I have a place for them at the university."

Bob took Allie by her arm and started to lead her away as he answered, "It would be my pleasure to pass them to you. Just as soon as I'm done with them."

Bob let Allie walk ahead of him as they made their way out of the front door. She had the picture envelope and he had the cardboard box. The professor followed and told them goodnight as they walked down the sloped driveway. They heard him close the screen door and then latch his front door behind them.

Bob followed Allie to the passenger side door and she opened it for them. She took the box from Bob and placed it on the floorboard and then lay the envelope on top of it before she entered the vehicle. Bob closed the door after she had moved her feet over the box.

When he opened the driver's side door, she was sitting close to the steering wheel again and turned slightly to watch him get inside. He closed his door and she put an arm around his shoulder as she said, "That was interesting."

Bob agreed. "It was helpful in some ways. He's very sharp when it comes to animals." He started the engine and started to put the shift selector into drive but looked at her instead. "You hungry?"

"You owe me pizza."

He dropped the selector into drive and remarked as he pulled away from the curb. "And beer?"

"Hey...you can't have pizza without beer. I tried it once...didn't work out."

Greg Morris' body had lay in the desert sand all night Monday night and all day Tuesday. His head wound had left a dark circle in the sand around his head and shoulders. The buzzards found him early Tuesday morning and they had feasted upon his carcass throughout the day. They had to claw their way through his denim shirt, but once it was opened, they had pecked his rib cage down to the bone.

Flies buzzed around the open cavity and lay their eggs within. Maggots burrowed their way deeper inside of his chest cavity and feasted upon the rotting flesh. Greg's eyes were missing and his shredded lips made an open socket into his face.

The buzzards had gone to roost for the night, but the flies continued their feasting and breeding. By Wednesday morning, his limbs would be swelled to the point of bursting and they would split open by the time the sun came up.

Greg's body lay within the boundaries of the Papago Indian Reservation and their tribal police had jurisdiction over the entirety of the reservation. When Greg failed to contact his wife Monday, she waited until the end of the day Tuesday to make a missing person's report.

She had the phone number of the tribal police station that was located in the northern territories, because her husband had utilized that region many times in the past. It was a tribal regulation for anyone camping within their boundaries to register themselves with the police before setting up a campsite. A short form had to be filled out stating the start date and ending date of your venture, but it wasn't strictly enforced. Usually the forms piled up on a policeman's desk until the end of the month, and then they were discarded.

Each remote police station was manned by four deputies. Two worked the day shift and two worked the night shift. The Papago Chief of Police had his main office located further south near the geothermal wells and a small township called Tohono. The northern territory police station was given the designation of *Ohdam Station*.

When her phone call came into the Ohdam Station, it was the exact time for shift change, so a deputy named Geoff took the information and he gave it to one of his relief deputies. The relief deputy was named Lorenzo.

Both men were young. They were twenty-five years old and had very little formal training as a police officer. They were young and strong and could break up fights, so that was their chief qualification. The standard uniform for a Papago Deputy was a dark brown shirt with the reservation seal on a shoulder patch, a gun belt that held a flashlight and a baton, black trousers with black boots, and a brown hat with a visor.

The Ohdam Station had one official patrol car and it was seven years' old with one-hundred and forty thousand miles on the odometer. Lorenzo was sitting behind the wheel of the patrol car when Geoff handed him the message. He said to his fellow officer as he passed the note through the open window, "Missus Morris wants to know if we can look in on her husband. He didn't get in touch with her yesterday or today."

Lorenzo took the note and glanced at it. He then commented, "Says he's probably near the saguaro valley. I can check it out in about an hour." The car was idling so Lorenzo dropped the shift lever into drive and drove away.

The station house was manned by one deputy whose job it was to monitor the police band radios (which included the one in Meacon) and the man on the night shift with Lorenzo is named Palton. He was a much older and much heavier individual than Lorenzo, so he was better suited for office work than he was field work.

Lorenzo drove the police car down the dirt road leading away from the Ohdam Station and to the saguaro fields known as the Cactus Valley. It would take him an hour to make it to the valley because the top speed across the rocky desert terrain was thirty miles an hour.

Bob and Allie were sitting in the back corner of the pizza parlor called the *College Station*. They had chosen a booth instead of a table and Allie insisted that they sit next to each other instead of on opposite sides of the table. Their pizza hadn't been delivered as of yet, so they were each drinking a glass of beer while waiting on their order. They were in the middle of a conversation that was strictly meant for them to get better acquainted. Allie was speaking, "So...my mom passed away when I was in grade school. She had cancer and it must have been really bad because she got sick and didn't live long after the diagnosis. I lived with my Dad, of course, until I graduated High School and then I moved out on my own." She took a small sip of beer and then continued, "Of course, working for the Sheriff's Department helped me afford that. Sheriff Sand pays his people really well. My place is small, but the rent's cheap and I like it."

Bob interjected, "And your college classes? Do you pay

as you go, or are you on a grant?"

She swallowed another sip of beer and replied, "Believe it or not, I'm on a partial scholarship. As long as I maintain a two-point-eight GPA, I get half of my courses paid for."

"That's nice. Where'd you get the scholarship?"

"FFA. I showed registered Limousines for Mister Watkins while I was in High School." She sat up straighter and put her hand on his knee as she said with pride, "You know what I did for him two summers? I was one of his Line Riders."

He looked somewhat impressed as he replied, "Line Rider? You mean you inspected and repaired fences?"

She flexed her arm and made a muscle as she answered, "Yep! See…Line Rider Girl's gotta be tough."

He laughed softly as he replied, "I can't imagine someone as pretty as you stretching barbed wire and nailing it onto fence posts."

She was smiling as she replied, "Well…I did. And I was good at it."

He had a sudden thought. "That means you know how to ride horses."

She shrugged her shoulders as she admitted, "Well…I can't bust broncs, but I can ride fairly well."

The waitress appeared at their table and sat a metal pan in front of them. She then placed two ceramic plates next to the pan with two napkins rolled around a knife and a fork. Allie took her hand off of his knee and separated the two plates. She used her hands to tear apart two slices and put them on the plates. She let him take the first bite of food, then she followed after him. It was just one of those acts that most people consider good manners and it didn't escape Bob's attention.

The conversation lagged while they ate their first slice of pizza, then when Allie put another slice on their plates, she began again. "Another thing I like to do, besides riding horses is swim."

He was chewing a hot piece of cheese as he answered her, "Uhm…me too."

"Really? You like to swim? You're not just saying that?"

He smiled and pointed to her right bicep. "I make it a habit not to lie to tough girls."

She laughed and covered her mouth with one hand. The only thoughts going through her head was, "He's so comfortable to be with…God, he's so handsome!"

Bob's mind was speaking to him likewise, "I never knew that a woman could be so easy to talk to…"

There were small rolling hills leading to the saguaro valley and because the sun had gone down, Lorenzo had to slow down to twenty miles per hour as he used his headlights to follow the dirt road leading to the flat areas where people liked to park. There was an outcrop of tall pine trees near one flat area and Lorenzo had made his mind up that he would check that area first.

He rolled slowly down the last hill and came to a stop next to four tall pine trees. The dust trail from his tires floated past his windows and he kept them rolled up until the dirt had drifted away. He then put his vehicle into park and turned the ignition switch to the off position. He wasn't wearing a seat belt and the truth of the matter was that the receiver part of the belt had been buried under the driver's seat for four months. None of the deputies had a particular desire to wear a seat belt.

He opened his car door and took his flashlight out of his utility belt. He shined it towards the trees and immediately saw the outline of a Jeep SUV. He made his way towards the other vehicle.

The vehicle looked as if it had been abandoned. It doesn't take long for a layer of dirt to build up on cars or any other stationary object in the desert. The dust had formed a film over the windshield as well as the back window. The Jeep's side glass was tinted, so when Lorenzo shined his flashlight against the glass, he wasn't able to see much of the interior.

He took more than a minute to look at the vehicle before he decided that nobody had been around for several hours.

He took a deep breath and then made his way to the back of the SUV. He had a notepad in his shirt pocket along with a pencil, so he jotted down the license plate number, and then walked slowly towards his police car.

He opened the driver's side door and reached inside to turn the ignition key to the start position. The car's engine purred to life and then he grabbed the radio microphone off of the dash holder. He put the microphone to his mouth and pressed the side button, "Hey, Palton...pick up."

The crackling voice from the other end replied, "Whatcha got?"

"Hey...check that permission slip on the Morris guy. See what his license plate number says."

A short moment passed and then Palton replied, "AZR (dash) 140."

Lorenzo frowned as he replied, "Yeah...this is his car alright."

"Where's it at?"

"Top of the canyon before you get to the saguaro fields. He's nowhere around and it looks like he hasn't been here for days."

The radio sounded distant with an echo in the background as Palton asked, "You gonna go look for him?"

"Yeah...for a little bit. I'll walk around some and call his name. He could be anywhere, so if I don't have any luck, we'll have to do it tomorrow during the daylight."

Lorenzo answered, "Alright...just be careful out there. Don't step on something that bites."

"Ha...ha! I'll call you back in a bit." He replaced the microphone on the dash clip then turned the car's ignition switch off. He then turned back towards Greg Morris' car and switched his flashlight on.

Bob and Allie had returned to Meacon and they drove straight to the Sheriff's Office. Allie's personal vehicle was still in the parking lot, so their first date was ending outside of the

Courthouse. When they pulled into the parking space next to her car, she turned to him and said, "I had a real nice time, Bob. Thanks for letting me tag along."

He was smiling and searching his brain for something to say that wouldn't sound stupid. All he came up with was, "I don't think I've ever enjoyed being around someone so much as you."

She snickered and said, "That was corny, Bob."

He quickly apologized. "Sorry."

She put her left hand behind his neck and said, "I'm gonna kiss you now, Bob. It's gonna be a fantastic kiss, so get ready."

She put her other hand behind his neck and pulled him to her face. She pressed her lips against his and let her tongue flicker inside of his mouth. She moved his head slightly back and forth as she pressed her lips tightly against his, and she groaned softly."

He didn't hear himself, but he groaned with pleasure as well.

When she released him from the kiss, she still held her hands behind his head. She smiled and said, "See...I told you."

He coughed slightly, then asked, "Can I see you again tomorrow?"

She was all grin as she replied, "Pick me up after work. We'll figure out something to do. I don't care what we do as long as I do it with you."

His only reply was, "Wow."

She moved away from the driver's seat and opened the passenger door. When she was standing on the parking lot pavement, she held the door open as she said, "I get off at five. I'm assuming that you do to."

He answered quickly, "I...I set my own hours...I'll be here at five."

As she started to shut the door, she had a sudden thought. She stopped and said, "Hey...do you know where I live?"

"Uh…no."

"Okay…follow me home. I won't invite you in, but you need to know where I live. Tomorrow you can show me where you live."

"Yeah…that sounds good."

She closed his passenger side door and walked to her own car.

Lorenzo was following a foot path that sloped downhill and southward. The bushes and the grasses that appeared periodically made odd shaped shadows from the beam of his flashlight and every now and then, he'd call out, "Mister Morris! Can you hear me?"

It's as hard to judge distances in the dark as it is to keep track of time when you aren't wearing a watch. Lorenzo hadn't realized that he'd actually walked for almost a mile and he was still walking southward.

The trail veered to his left and he decided that it was time to give it up for the night. He had limited visibility and he was alone. His common sense told him that he needed to return to his vehicle and check in with Palton.

While he was standing still on the narrow path, he caught the faint smell of rotting meat. It was a smell that he was familiar with, so he stood perfectly still so he could judge the direction that the wind was blowing. He looked to his right and said to himself, "West." He pointed the flashlight in that direction and moved with the beam.

He didn't like it, but the smell was getting stronger and that meant that he was obligated to make sure that it was just a dead animal or something. His mind was certain that it was only a dead animal. Could be a dog, rabbit, cow, wild horse, or any number of things he kept telling himself.

He stepped off of a short drop on the ground and froze in place. The beam of his flashlight hit the dead body of Greg Morris and he immediately felt queasy. He spoke out loud and it was almost a yell, "Oh, no! Oh, God, no!"

He forced himself to move closer to the body, and when he was five feet from the dead man, his flashlight illuminated the grotesque figure that had been feasted upon by buzzards. He disturbed the nocturnal activities of the flies and a swarm buzzed out of Greg's chest.

Lorenzo coughed and spun around as flies bounced off of his face. He held onto his flashlight, but he only made it as far as the first bush. He fell to his knees and vomited. Not once, but three times.

Lorenzo made his way back to the narrow footpath, but his steps were faltering and unsteady. He couldn't keep the image of the dead man out of his mind and every time that he had an image of the face with the gaping hole, it made him heave.

He thought that he'd been walking forever when he finally made it back to the tall pine trees and he was breathing hard from the exertion and the excitement. When he arrived at the side of his police car, he stopped and put his hands on his knees. He let his head hand down as he preached to himself, "Get a hold, Lorenzo...get a good hold of yourself and don't sound like a baby!"

He opened the car door, started the ignition, took the radio microphone off of the dash clip, and took a deep breath. "Palton...pick up."

The answering voice still echoed. "Whatcha got Lorenzo?"

"Mister Morris is dead."

There was a pause before the echoing voice replied, "Well, shit! You know how it happened?"

"Too dark to see anything except the mess that the buzzards made."

Another pause and then an answer with a faint voice. "I'll have to call our main office. Chief Brigswall will need to know this right away."

Lorenzo took another deep breath and he tried not to sound disappointed or upset when he replied, "I'll have to stay here until the other units arrive. The body's...I don't know... maybe a mile or so from his car."

"Okay...you sit tight...it'll be a few hours before anyone joins you for sure."

"Yeah...alright."

At the Meacon Sheriff's Office, the night dispatcher named Horace Fannin was listening to the Ohdam Station radio transmissions. As he listened to the voices describing the discovery of a man's body, he made some quick notes on a piece of scrap paper. He jotted down the time and the date and a quick overview of what he had heard. After several minutes of radio silence, he ascertained that Palton was on the telephone informing his superiors about the discovery. He sighed and pulled the nightly log book closer to him and made the proper notations in the book.

CHAPTER SIX

It was five o'clock in the morning on August 22. Allie habitually ran three miles a day, and usually starting at four-thirty in the morning, but on this morning, she was fifteen minutes late. She had slightly overslept, but she managed to be fifteen minutes into her daily routine by five o'clock.

She didn't jog. She ran. She stretched and warmed up, then started jogging slowly, but she picked up her pace quickly and was moving at a very rapid clip within a hundred yards or so. She had several routes that she used each day and each one of them were meticulously measured so that she obtained her self-imposed three-mile workout.

She didn't run the entire mile and a half first leg of her routine. She ran approximately a half mile, then walked a few hundred yards to cool down and catch her breath, then she'd take off running again. She had stopped running for the third time this morning and she had her hands on her hips as she walked towards her half-way point.

She was dressed in blue running shoes with white socks and she had on blue jogging shorts with a pink exercise halter and a pink headband. She was breathing deeply when she stopped in front of the First Baptist Church of Meacon and she smiled when she read the small billboard beside the front side-walk of the building. The sign read, *Gospel Group Reassurance / 7:00 PM to 9:00 PM/* August 22. As soon as she read the sign, she muttered out loud, "Guess where you're taking me tonight, Bob."

Horace Fannin was short and portly. His hair had

turned grey when he was forty and he was now fifty-five years old. He was clean shaven, except for a small mustache. He had spent eight years in the Marine Corps as a younger man and would have stayed on active duty until retirement, but he had to accept a discharge when he was injured in an automobile accident. The accident shattered both of his knees and he couldn't maintain the physical requirements after he had recuperated. He had no trouble walking, but physically running or carrying heavy loads was no longer possible.

He had been the nighttime dispatcher for eleven years and he was quite satisfied with the job. He liked the work hours and the lack of hectic activity that went along with the night shift. His boss was a former Marine and that was important to him.

Allie worked from 8:00 AM to 5:00 PM, then Horace worked the front desk from 8:00 PM to 8:00 AM. The three hours between the two of those shifts was covered on a rotating basis by Wally's deputies.

Because Horace was portly and friendly, his nickname was Bubba. He liked it and nobody called him by his given name anymore. It was ten minutes until 8:00 AM and he was actively writing in the log book when Wally walked through the front door. Wally greeted the man with a friendly hello, but Horace didn't reply. He had the dispatch radio volume turned up loudly and he continued writing.

As Wally approached the front desk, he was able to hear part of the conversation, so he stopped to listen more closely. He heard a familiar voice say, "The Tribal Coroner is here now. Chief Brigswall will show him the body, so I'm coming in to give the vehicle to Geoff."

The radio voice of Palton answered, "He's here now waiting on you."

Horace stopped writing so Wally asked, "What's going on, Bubba?"

"Lorenzo found a body last night somewhere near the saguaro fields. It seems that the deceased is a photographer named Greg Morris. It's taken Chief Brigswall most of the night to get four deputies and now the coroner on site to start his investigation."

Wally nodded as he replied, "So…no details yet, huh?"

"Not really. I took notes and logged the activities, so I'll let Allie know what's going on and she can keep track of this when she gets here." He glanced behind Wally and saw Allie walking through the front door. "Speaking of which…"

Wally turned and waved at Allie as he said, "Good morning." She waved back and walked across the lobby. Wally turned to Horace and said, "Tell her to keep me informed" and then he made for his office.

The beast had the mangled body of a Pronghorn Antelope hanging limply from his mouth as he walked slowly up the ridge leading to his lair. The head was missing as was one front leg and one rear leg. The antelope had been disemboweled and its chest had been mostly shredded. Blood dripped off of the carcass and dotted the stone pathway.

The beast had hunted most of the night without any success and he had become both hungry and angry at the same time. When he spotted the lone antelope, he chased after it for almost half of an hour before he overtook it. When he finally dragged the antelope down by its haunches, his anger level was quite high so he ripped at the small critter savagely in a fit of rage.

Normally the beast feasted upon a kill on the spot, but this time he decided to take what was left of the body to his cave so that he might gnaw on the haunches later. It was daylight time and he was ready to retire for the day.

Becky and Karen had been riding fence since four-thirty this morning. They had to travel along a narrow trail that led northward away from the Watkins ranch house and they both knew that it would take them over two hours to get to the north fence line. The sun was fully up at six-thirty when the girls had stopped at a small windmill that had a water tank and a watering trough that was fed by the windmill pump.

They had dismounted their horses and were letting them drink the cool well water as they sat next to each other on the side of the trough. Becky had the 30-30 rifle in a scabbard tied to her saddle and the girls were wearing their pistol belts like they were instructed to do so by Jeff Watkins.

Karen spoke first. "What'd you do last night?"

"Slept mostly. My mom let my boyfriend come over and visit me for a while, but she ran him off at eight-thirty."

Karen snickered as she replied, "Yeah…me too. Momma let Johnny see me until eight-thirty, so we sat on the porch and drank tea. He told me that he was going to college in Vera next year. I'm probably gonna do the same."

Both horses raised their heads out of the water trough and snorted. It was a signal that they were finished drinking, so Becky and Karen led them away from the water and stepped back into their saddles. When they were both mounted, Becky took the lead and they followed the trail northwards once again.

Karen was behind Becky and she called to her friend as the horses plodded along, "Hey! Johnny gave me a nickname last night!"

Becky called back, "Let me guess! Pistol Packing Momma, right?"

Karen laughed as she replied, "Well it *was* after I told him I had to wear a pistol at work now. He called me *Pearl Hart* and said that I was his gunslinger girlfriend."

Becky shrugged her shoulders and called back to Karen, "My boyfriend started to do that to me, but I stopped him before he opened his mouth."

"What'd you do?"

"I told him that I'd blow his dick off if he had something smart to say about it."

Karen laughed loudly as she replied, "You didn't!"

"I did! I seriously did."

Karen thought for a second then said, "I don't think it was your momma that ran him off last night!"

The Game Warden's Office was a white two-room, wood framed structure that had a bathroom attached and a small kitchenette. The floor was wooden planks that were in dire need of a new coat of sealant. The windows were slightly dusty, but not so much as to appear neglected. The driveway was a two-car type where Bob parked his personal vehicle and the official government Jeep stayed during his off duty hours.

Bob's rent house was on the east side of Meacon, while his office was on the west side. Bob was the only employee to occupy the building, so there were no radio communication devices on the premises. He only had a government issued telephone with speed dial numbers of other Game Warden locations. Including his main office that was located in Tucson.

He had been on the phone with his main office since seven o'clock and it was now eight o'clock and he was growing weary of explaining his situation. It took him the full hour of describing his predicament and requesting assistance to be fully denied help of any kind. All his boss wanted was the standard report faxed to him along with some pictures to be put in the mail.

Bob didn't slam the desk phone receiver down onto its cradle, but he came close to doing so. After he hung up on his boss, he took a 30-30 rifle out of a locked gun cabinet and grabbed an ammo can with one hundred rounds. He muttered out loud as he stormed out of his office, "Fine! I'll borrow a radio from Sheriff Sand and I'll see if Jeff Watkins has somebody that he can loan me!"

Bob arrived at the Sheriff's Office at eight thirty. When he walked in the front door, he saw Allie wearing her white work shirt and his attitude immediately changed. He went from aggravated to admiring in less than a heartbeat.

Allie was wearing a headset and monitoring the transmissions that were pouring out of the Ohdam Station, but she noticed Bob and smiled at him as he approached her desk.

He saw that she was busy, so he leaned over and whispered to her, "I need to see the Sheriff."

She used her thumb to point over her shoulder towards Wally's Office and whispered back, "See me before you leave." Then she started writing something in the log book.

Bob knocked on Wally's open door and stood to one side as he saw that Wally was on the phone. He couldn't help but overhear part of the conversation. Wally was saying, "I have two Deputies at the Papago Fuel Stop, Chief Brigswall. They can meet you at the Ohdam Station if you need anything. High-res camera? Yeah...I got one here in the office...you need it? Okay..." Wally saw Bob and his face lit up. "Wait a minute, Chief!"

Wally put his left hand over the mouthpiece and called to Bob, "Come in! I need your help!"

Wally put the phone receiver back to his ear and mouth and continued, "Chief, our Game Warden just walked in...can he bring you the camera? Fine! Good! I'll send him straight-away!"

Bob had a very concerned look on his face as he watched Wally place the phone receiver back onto the cradle. Wally pulled a desk drawer open and took out two boxes of 35 mm film and put them on top of his desk. He then started explaining, "Bob...last night the Papago Police discovered a dead body that looks like it was a victim of an animal attack. I don't believe in coincidences, do you?"

Bob suddenly realized what was going on. He quickly replied, "No sir. I do not."

"You know where the Ohdam Station is located?"

"Sure. Been there many times."

"Chief Brigswall doesn't want to move the body until he gets some high resolution photos. He says that his office isn't equipped to properly handle the investigation and seeing as how it's Indian land, the FBI might have to get involved. I doubt it, but that's what he thinks."

"You want me to get your camera to him ASAP?"

Wally handed Bob the film and he put the camera case on top of his desk and opened it. He answered, "Yeah. Head for the Papago Fuel Stop and don't follow the speed limit. I've got two deputies there that can escort you to the Station." Wally took the film boxes from Bob's hands and put them in the camera case. He handed him the case and said, "Go. I'll let the deputies know you're on the way...no! Wait! See Allie and get a hand-held radio. I want you to keep in touch with her today."

Bob smiled and carried the camera case to Allie's desk. He smiled at her and said, "Good morning!"

She stood up and gave him a quick hug as she replied, "Good morning!"

"Sheriff said to give me a hand-held. Wants me to stay in touch with you today."

She nodded and replied, "I expected him to say that." She took a hand-held radio out of her desk drawer and turned the unit on, then put in on channel fourteen. She handed him the unit and said quickly, "Hey! I want you to take me to church tonight if you can."

Bob smiled, "Wednesday service?"

"Gospel choir tonight."

"Hey...I'd like that."

He took the radio from her hand and said as he walked away, "I'll try to hurry and see you later!"

She smiled and then sighed as he walked out of the front door.

Becky and Karen had arrived at the far northwest corner of the fence line they called the Elkins Line. It was a mile and a half of five-strand barbed wire fence separating the Watkins spread from the Elkins Range and it ran due north to south. They were at the northwest corner post where there was a small tool shed that had wire, tools, staples, and some metal posts bundled inside. Outside of the shed was a stack of wooden posts, but they wouldn't need any of those. This particular fence line used metal posts with heavy wire wraps to secure the barbed wire. They were putting two posts each on the back of their saddles and grabbing a canvas bag of heavy wire ties. They also needed the heavy-duty wire cutters, so Becky grabbed those as well.

It was Becky and Karen's job to make sure that the fence lines on the Watkins Spread were in perfect shape before Jeff Watkins moved a herd of cattle onto it. Jeff rotated his ranges, sometimes three times a year. Grass was sparse in the desert, so it required irrigating and some elaborate water management in order to maintain class A beef. Wind storms constantly assailed barbed wire fences with brush and debris, so Karen and Becky had to clear any buildup areas they found as well as mend broken fences. If they found a brush starting to sprout underneath a strand of wire, then it had to be cut away or dug up in order to keep the wires from getting entangled with brush limbs.

The land was not flat. The north to south fence line followed the contours of the hills and gulley's, and in some places, the posts were very hard to get at. They had four such places where they had to dismount their horses and inspect the wires while on foot. There were two access gates installed on the Elkins Line. One on the north end and one on the south end. They were both heavy metal gates that hung on four-inch steel posts that were cemented into the ground. They were wide enough to allow passage of large cattle trucks and/or trailers.

Becky and Karen decided that they would walk the first section of fence line from the northwest corner to the north Elkins Gate. It was only about a quarter of a mile and they wanted to simply take a break from being in the saddle. Besides, they reasoned, walking is good for one's figure.

They chatted as they walked along and led the horses. Becky was reciting the tale of her previous boyfriend. "He was cute…sort of…he had this dimple in the middle of his chin, and he had blue eyes."

"What do you mean *sort of*?" Karen asked.

"Well…it's hard to describe. He wasn't skinny, but he wasn't muscular, either?"

"Was he taller than you?"

"A little. Not much."

Karen offered, "I like boys that are taller than me. Is that weird?"

"No…at least I don't think so…all of my boyfriends have been taller than me…I think that's the way it's supposed to be."

"Yeah…I think it might be a rule."

Becky took an opportunity to tease her friend, "You wouldn't date a shorter guy?"

Karen shook her head, "Nah…that's what they make short girls for."

Becky started to laugh, but she cut herself off. She stopped walking and pointed at a section of fence in front of them. "Well, shit! We got us a break."

Karen joined her friend in a curse, "Damn! I thought we'd get lucky on this line. This fence is not all that old."

They moved closer to the opening in the fence and both of them cursed at the same time when they saw that all five wire strands had been cut. After both of them had shouted out a disgusted swear word, Karen spoke first, "Son of a bitch cut all five wires! The asshole!"

Becky pointed at the dirt between the two fence posts with the cut wires. She said angrily, "Look at the tire tracks! It's that damn Hershel Span and his stupid four-wheeler!"

Karen was tying her horse's reins to a fence post as she answered Becky, "God, I hate that little shit! Just because his daddy has more money than Santa Claus, he thinks he can do anything that he wants!"

Becky was chuckling softly as she started to tie her horse's reins to another fence post on the opposite side of the opening. She said humorously, "You want we should chase after him and blow his dick off with our pistols?"

Karen couldn't help but laugh. She replied, "Maybe later! I get first shot, OK?" She opened the flaps of her saddle bags and started removing fencing tools.

Bob had arrived at the site where Greg Morris' body was located. Tribal Police Chief Brigswall had the body covered with a heavy plastic blanket and he had set out stakes with yellow crime-scene tape tied around the tops.

Bob was standing next to his Jeep while the Coroner and two of his assistants were leaning against his vehicle as well. The Chief had ordered everyone to stay back until he had personally taken enough photographs to properly record the scene. The Papago Deputy named Geoff was still sitting in the passenger seat of Bob's Jeep and he was casually smoking a cigarette.

The two deputies working with the Police Chief were simply placing numbered markers next to places indicated by the Chief's pointing finger. After ten minutes of taking photographs of the area surrounding the body, Chief Brigswall announced softly, "Alright...pull back the blanket...expose the whole body and step back."

When the blanket was slowly removed from Greg Morris' head and down over his chest, a swarm of flies swirled out of the chest cavity. Bob was watching the two deputy helpers swat at the flying insects and he frowned as he remarked to the coroner, "He knows that they make a spray called *Green Shield* for controlling that, doesn't he?"

The coroner whispered in reply, "He knows...he can't afford it is all."

Bob was saddened by the remark. He simply replied, "Too bad." He kept his eyes on the Chief and watched him as he was kneeling next to the body. He wasn't close enough to the body to hear the clicking of the camera's shutter, so he simply waited for permission to inspect the deceased. He had a sudden thought as he asked the coroner a question, "Have you seen the body?"

"He let me kneel next to the head, but that's all."

"You think it was an animal attack?"

The coroner had a sour look on his face as he replied, "No doubt about it. Skull's crushed and there's the biggest damn set of teeth marks on both sides of his face that I've ever seen."

Bob stood up straighter and looked at the coroner closely as he asked, "Anything unusual about those teeth marks?"

The coroner was a perceptive man. He stared back at Bob and replied, "You know something that I don't, right?"

Bob quickly answered, "Fang marks! Are there any teeth marks that look like knife wounds?"

The coroner stood up straight and answered, "Holy, shit! You do know something!"

Bob turned and looked at the kneeling Police Chief and replied, "God...I hope not."

Hershel Span was six miles west of the broken fence line and he was three miles south of Quail Cut. He was a twelve-year-old boy with an all-terrain vehicle and absolutely no discipline what-so-ever. He drove recklessly over dirt mounds, trail cuts, and small ravines. He weaved his vehicle around brushes, pine trees, and cactus plants and left dirt clouds in his wake. His ATV was less than four months old and he had a friend of his help him remove the muffler. His excursion was reckless, loud, and dusty.

Three miles south of Quail Cut was a flat-topped plateau that was only twenty-five feet high, and the eastern side of the hill had a very gradual sloping plane. Hershel raced his vehicle to the top of the plateau and began cutting circles in the slightly rocky sand. He had no regard or concern about his vehicle's mechanical abuse or the excessive tire wear that he was producing.

The extremely loud engine noise echoed off of the top of the plateau and moved through the broad valley's below. By the time the engine noise reached Quail Cut, it was a rolling thunder clap that couldn't be heard by a human being. However, to the beast, it was a sudden violation of his sensitive ears.

He was asleep and he was lying on his side on top of the cool sand inside of the cave. When the engine noise reverberated into his cave opening, he sprang to his stomach and let out a harsh growl. His leg muscles automatically tensed and he growled for the second time.

He cautiously stood up and eased his way towards the cave opening and he kept his keen ears pricked towards the air outside. He could hear the noise and although it was faint and it seemed to be moving away from him, he found the new sound aggravating and irritating and therefore worthy of an inspection.

Bob, the coroner, and the coroner's two helpers noticed that Police Chief Brigswall was through taking pictures. He had instructed his two deputies to let the plastic blanket remain on the ground at Greg Morris' feet. He then turned his attention to Bob and motioned the waiting group to come to the body.

The coroner automatically handed his helpers and Bob a white face mask and said, "Put these on. It's gonna stink down there."

Bob didn't argue. Neither did the two helpers. The only person that didn't bother taking a mask was Deputy Geoff. Bob had never been part of a crime scene before, so he naively asked, "Will the mask help?"

The coroner shook his head and replied, "Not in the least."

Bob was in the process of wrapping the rubber bands of the mask around his ears when he stopped and asked, "Then why'd you give it to me?"

The coroner couldn't help but smile as he took a small spray can from a pouch around his waist. He pointed the spray nozzle at Bob's mask and gave it two quick squirts. "Here... this'll help. Won't last long, though. Let me know when you need another shot."

Bob took a breath through his nose and he smelled a faint odor of cinnamon. He watched the coroner spray his own mask and then hand the can to one of his helpers. He turned to Bob and said, "Me and you first. I'll call them when we need the body bag." And with that, he strolled towards the dead man.

Bob followed quietly.

The coroner was a Papago Indian by the name of Amos Green. He was fifty years old and a very lean and muscular man with hair that was turning gray on the sides and the top. He was dressed in scrubs that were colored a light blue and he was wearing brown canvas hiking boots. His tool pouch was nothing but a large, black, fanny-pack. Like Bob, he hated to wear a hat, so he was bare headed.

They spoke very briefly to the Police Chief as they passed each other. The coroner simply said, "Get your SUV ready for the body bag. We won't be long." He led Bob to the head of the corpse and they both kneeled down to get a closer look at the wounds. Bob was wincing underneath his face mask.

The coroner didn't bother looking at Bob as he remarked, "If you gotta barf, don't do it on the corpse."

Bob grunted, then took a deep breath and held it. The coroner pointed to the crushed skull and held a finger next to the large hole above Greg Morris' ear. "Have you seen one of these before?"

Bob grunted a response, "Uh-huh."

"Know what it is?'

"No."

The coroner turned his head and looked at Bob as he said, "You're kidding."

"I've seen it before, but I don't know what it is."

Amos stood up and Bob followed suit. Amos commented first, "Well, do you have any idea what I can put in the autopsy report? Death by *I don't know* is hard to accept by family members."

Bob tried to answer the man, but he had a sudden urge to cough. Amos took him by the arm and led him away from the body and spoke softly to him as they moved away. "Look... whatever bit this man had a huge mouth. The teeth marks are on both sides of his head...which means that whatever it was had the man's whole head in his mouth when he crushed the skull."

Bob regained his senses and began explaining himself, "Yesterday, me and Sheriff Sand investigated a mutilated bull on the Watkins Ranch. I'm reasonably certain that whatever killed that bull killed this man as well."

Amos led Bob towards their vehicles and he called to his assistants as they approached them, "Go ahead and bag him, men. The Chief's SUV will take him to the hospital for me."

Amos released his hold on Bob's arm as he approached the Jeep. He stopped walking and faced the Game Warden as he said, "Tell me what you and the Sheriff saw."

Bob removed his mask and so did the coroner. Bob started explaining, "We found an Angus Bull with extremely large bite marks on a mutilated body. I was able to get two plaster casts of the animal's front feet and I took them to Vera College last night and showed them to a Professor Wilcox."

Amos almost smiled as he replied, "Well...now...at least that's something. Did you and the good professor discuss what kind of animal this might be?"

"We believe that it's a deformed wolf."

There was a long pause before Amos answered with his question, "A deformed wolf?"

Bob looked slightly embarrassed as he said, "Yeah."

Amos turned his head and watched his assistants pulling the deceased man's body into the black bag. He watched them struggle for a moment, then spoke quietly, "Well...tell you what...when you find out for sure what did this...you call me...*immediately*!"

Hershel Span wasn't wearing a helmet. His shirt sleeves had once been long, but he'd cut them away to expose his entire arm length. His jeans had once been full length, but they had been cut off just above his knees. He was wearing a black pair of hiking shoes with white socks that covered his exposed calves. His hair, face, neck, and exposed arms were covered with sweat stains and a layer of brown dirt. He had paused at the top of the plateau to rev his engine three times, then speed back down the eastern slope. When he made it to the bottom of the hill, he turned his ATV south and began his joy ride once again.

The beast exited his lair at a full run. He sped his way down the wide ledge and onto the gorge floor and then made his way to the north end entrance. The south end was blocked by a sheer cliff, so he had no choice but to use the one and only entrance into his hide-a-way.

As soon as he burst out of the gorge, he made a wide turn towards the south and made his way towards the offending noise. Like the ATV, the beast was plowing his way along the top of the loose sand and making a dust trail of his own.

When Hershel Span had cut the five strands of barbed wire on the Elkins Fence Line, he had done so at the middle two fence posts. This meant that there was an equal length of wire on each post at the five different levels. Karen and Becky had two types of repairs that they could choose from. They could tie a loop on each end of each exposed wire and splice them together with some heavy-duty repair wire, or they could cut the short pieces off at each fence post and replace them with new strands. They chose option number two.

Becky had the strongest arms, so she used the cutters to snip the strands while Karen gathered them up and twisted them together. Both girls wore very thick leather gloves that had a canvass gauntlet extending to their mid-forearms. Once the wires were cut away from the posts, Becky retrieved a small chain come-a-long from her saddle bag while Karen tied one end of a length of barbed wire to a post. Karen used a loop type attachment to the post that was woven back onto the barbed wire itself. It was fashioned so that the harder it was pulled upon, the tighter the loop became.

They started at the bottom strand and worked their way to the top one. Becky used the come-a-long to pull the strand tight between the two posts, while Karen secured the barbed wire to the post with her heavy-duty flex-clips.

They were putting their tools away and getting ready to

continue inspecting the fence line, when Becky suddenly said, "Hey! Do you hear something?"

Karen stood next to her horse and listened for a moment. She replied, "Sounds like an engine...without a muffler...it's a long way off...maybe way southwest of here."

Becky stepped into her saddle and replied, "I'll bet its Hershel. If that little dick-wad comes back over here...I'm gonna give him a hot lead vasectomy."

Karen snorted as she climbed onto her saddle. She remarked jokingly as she nudged her horse and began riding along the fence line once more, "How long have you two been in love?"

"Ha, ha! Very funny!"

Hershel was now four miles south of Quail Cut and he had paused his foray into the desert at a small gulley. He was sitting on his ATV looking at the opening in the ground and he started smiling broadly at the sight before him. The gulley was wide enough to allow his ATV to pass through and each end was sloped steeply. His immediate thought was that he could race his vehicle down one end and up the other and be able to lift all four tires off of the ground as he exited the cut.

He gunned his engine and spun the back tires as he made his way to one end of the cut. He steered the vehicle into the pass and leaned forward as he twisted his handlebar throttle. The ATV's tires slung dirt and small rocks as he guided his vehicle into the shallow gulley.

Hershel never let off of the throttle as his vehicle leaped off of the incline and soared into the air when he exited the other end. He stood up on the foot rests as the vehicle rose above the ground and leaned slightly sideways. He landed on his left tires at first, then the right two crashed to the ground and bounced once.

He squeezed his hand brake levers and came to a sudden halt as he screamed loudly, "Hell, yeah! Oh, hell, yeah!"

He sat down on the cushioned seat and used his left hand to shift the transmission lever into reverse. He backed up and turned the wheels sharply so he could face the other end of the gulley, then he gunned the engine twice and shifted into drive. He leaned forward and sped back into the open pit with dust clouds covering his tracks.

The beast was two miles away and the engine noise was getting louder and more irritating by the moment. He was running at his full capabilities and his tongue was hanging limply out the side of his mouth as he gasped for air. He made a soft grunting noise about every third time that his feet struck the ground and propelled him forward.

Hershel flew out of the other end of his gulley with almost the same results as the first time that he went airborne. He was screaming *YES* as he made the vehicle leave the ground. This time his rear wheels struck the ground first and his front wheels bounced twice before the vehicle frame settled down and he was able to brake to a stop.

He chuckled loudly and decided that twice was just not enough. He reversed course, aimed the front wheels towards the opening and leaned forward one more time. He revved the engine for two seconds, then sped forward once again.

The beast hadn't broken his stride once. He was headed straight for the irritating sounds and he was getting angrier with virtually every leap. He didn't concentrate his hearing on the noise anymore. He had identified its location and he was using his full speed in order to get there.

Hershel flew out of the end of the gulley for the third time. He didn't realize it, but his maltreatment of the sand with his vehicle tires was only diminishing the natural ramps at each end of the cut. His third leap out of the gully was significantly less intense than the first two. His wheels barely left the surface of the ground and instead of bouncing to a stop, he more-or-less rocked to a halt.

He voiced his disappointment immediately, "Shit! Son-of-a-fucking bitch! Mother-fucker!" Hershel didn't take it well when he was let down.

He grabbed his shift lever and slammed the stick into

its reverse position. He didn't even turn his head as he gunned the engine and turned his front wheels to the left. He backed up roughly and then slammed his shift lever into forward. That's when he let his mouth drop open in shock and surprise.

The huge black beast was mere yards away with his mouth fully open and he had launched himself at the young boy's face.

Hershel never uttered a sound. The beast crashed into the lad as his mouth clamped over the boy's face. The force of the lunge pushed Hershel backwards off of the ATV's cushioned seat and the beast's jaws snapped closed while they were both still propelling through the air.

Hershel's skull shattered under the force of the beast's jaws and the boy's body went limp in the beast's clutch. As soon as the beast's feet touched the ground, he began a violent shaking of his head with a vociferous growling coming out of his throat. Hershel's neck muscles stretched and tore and began to separate. The beast stood up on his hind legs and continued shaking the lifeless body until the neck muscles failed and the head separated from the torso.

As soon as Hershel's body flopped away from the beast, the crushed head was flung aside and the beast fell upon the exposed chest of the lad. His jaws opened wide enough to cover the ribcage from collar bone to sternum, and when he forced them closed, he shattered the entire length of ribs. Both lungs were sliced by the long canines. The razor sharp claws automatically began eviscerating the stomach and allowed the intestines to spew away from the body.

In a fit of rage, the beast held Hershel by his crushed ribcage and shook his head violently once again. He clawed as he shook and he mangled muscles, bone, sinew, and organs. He tossed the boy to the ground, where it rolled onto one side, and then he leaped upon the torso once again and bit through the upper arm. He severed the upper arm in half with one bite and flung it to one side also.

He had been ravaging the boy for less than fifteen seconds and he was beginning to feel the release of his rage. He was growling menacingly at the mangled body as he slowly backed away.

The ATV's engine had been idling the entire time of the attack. The missing muffler allowed the escaping exhaust gasses to pop loudly and irritate the beast all over again. But, suddenly, the engine sputtered and died and the beast woofed at it threateningly.

The hot engine crackled and popped as it started to lose its operating temperature. It wouldn't take more than fifteen minutes for it to cool completely down and stand mutely next to the slain body of its once self-indulged and spoiled owner.

It was three o'clock in the afternoon. Becky and Karen had started their journey back to the Watkins Ranch House while Bob had returned to the Meacon Court House and was in a meeting with Wally and a deputy named Jesse Blount.

Jesse and Bob were sitting in the guest chairs opposite of Wally, and Bob was doing the talking. "It was definitely our wolf. I have no doubts about it what-so-ever."

Wally immediately asked, "Get any footprints?"

"Ground was too old. Might have been done the day before, so the wind took care of any and all of them."

Wally asked his next question, "Have you informed your superiors in Tucson?"

"First thing this morning."

Jesse interrupted, "What did they say?"

Bob almost sneered as he explained, "He wanted a report and he wanted some photos sent through the mail?"

Jesse pressed the matter, "Help? Did he offer any help?"

Wally smiled slightly as he explained to his deputy, "Bob's boss is Shane Owens. Shane's sixty-four years old. His idea of help is to stay out of the way."

Jesse took the information to heart. He replied, "So... the matter's up to us, then?"

Wally leaned forward and put his elbows on his desk

and folded his arms across each other. He took a short breath and agreed, "Yeah. More-or-less." He looked at Bob as he spoke again, "Your animal has killed a human. That sort of makes it my business as well as yours."

Jesse interrupted again, "The man was killed on reservation land. Are you going to ask Chief Brigswall to help us?"

Wally answered his deputy with a soft voice, "Slow down, Jesse. We need a plan before I call Chief Brigswall." Wally pulled one of his desk drawers open and he removed a topographical map. It was rolled together and held with a rubber band. He removed the rubber band and handed the map to Bob. He removed another map from the same drawer and took the rubber band off of it also. He handed that map to Jesse and then said to both men, "Let's go to the meeting room."

The meeting room was two doors down from Wally's office. As the three of them left the Sheriff's Office, Bob stole a glance at Allie. She had her back turned to him and she was still wearing the radio headset and monitoring transmissions from the reservation. He smiled unto himself and felt a longing to be with her again as the three of them entered the Court House Meeting Room.

They lay the maps upon the tabletop and Jesse unrolled both of them. Wally fixed the maps side-by-side so that the topography lines matched up. He then took a grease marker and put an "x" on the spot where the Angus Bull was found. He handed the marker to Bob and said, "Show me where this Greg Morris was found."

Bob put an "x" on the second map, indicating a spot approximately fifteen miles within the Papago Reservation. Wally studied the two marks and then remarked, "That's about thirty miles apart." He looked at Bob and asked, "How far is a wolf's territorial range?"

Bob answered sadly, "A hundred square miles...most often."

Jesse leaned against the meeting table and asked, "For a single wolf? I thought that would be for a pack."

Bob answered truthfully, "Makes no difference. Lone wolf or pack, they range about the same."

Wally nodded his head slowly and offered, "Well…if you had to start looking for tracks somewhere, Bob…where would you begin?"

Bob tried to sound confident as he replied, "I'd start at the bull. I'd head for the plateaus to begin with. That's where I'd start finding small caves and dens."

Wally drew a line from the angus bull "x" to a portion of topography lines indicating several plateaus. He then re-marked, "If Chief Brigswall starts here (he pointed at the "x" indicating Greg Morris) and works his way here." (He drew an-other line on the map towards the plateaus.) "We could use two teams to work towards each other."

Bob nodded his head and so did Jesse. Jesse replied, "It's a start." He looked at Wally and asked, "How many men?"

Wally kept his eyes on the map and pondered the question for a moment. He answered slowly, "Eight for sure…I'd be happier with ten."

Bob asked quickly, "Does that include the Papago?"

"Oh no…no…they'll form their own teams. Us? I want eight or ten…spread out and looking for tracks." He glanced at Jesse as he said, "That don't include me and you. I want us to help Chief Brigswall if he'll let us."

Jesse was almost caught up in a fit of excitement as he asked, "What about helicopters?"

Wally rolled his eyes as he answered, "They're two-hun-dred and fifty dollars an hour, with an eight-hour minimum. Pinal county can't afford helicopter assistance."

Jesse didn't reply. He just continued looking at the map.

Wally turned his attention to Bob and said, "Me and Jesse will work on teaming up with the Papago. Go see Jeff Wat-kins and explain the situation to him. He's the only rancher with enough hands and horses to assist us, and he's got a stake in helping us find the animal anyway."

Bob asked quickly, "Stake?"

Wally half-smiled. "It'll make him look good in front of a judge when the time comes."

Bob snickered, "Oh...yeah." Bob thought for a second, then asked, "What time you want to start?"

Wally replied, "Early. Let Jeff Watkins choose the best time for him and we will follow suit."

Bob simply stood up straight and said, "I'll head out there now. I'll swing back by and let you know what he said." And with that, he walked out of the room.

He paused by Allie's desk and whispered to her, "Still want to go to that gospel singing?"

She quickly answered, "Oh, yeah! You can make it?"

"I got a quick run out to the Watkins Ranch. I'll try to be back about a half an hour before you get off of work."

She smiled and said, "Okay. See you in a little while."

Wally was talking to Jesse, "Run over to the Ohdam Station and see if you can get Brigswall to sign off on our plan." Jesse left the meeting room without comment.

Jesse Blount was thirty-two years old and a semi-professional weight lifter. He only competed on the state level, but he had ambitions of taking his passion to new heights. He went to the gym in Meacon four days a week and worked out with the heavy weights so that he could keep his physique as sharp as he could.

His diet was one of a man bent on turning protein into muscle, so that meant that he ate large portions of red meat. He ingested fruits as well, but he preferred to mix them in a blender and drink his fruit. He didn't do that too often with his vegetables, but he was thinking that he might begin such a regimen someday soon.

He stood six-foot-two-inches tall and he weighed two-hundred and twenty-two pounds. He had dark black hair that he kept cut in the crewcut style. He had experimented with shaving his head bald for a while a few years back, but he gave that up due to a suggestion. His girlfriend sort of persuaded him to grow some hair on his head. The crewcut was a compromise.

His afternoon trip to the Ohdam Station would have him discussing the proposition from Wally with Chief Brigswall, his two deputies, his friends Geoff and Marc, and possibly Lorenzo. He was hoping that Lorenzo would be part of the hunt, because he knew the young man was one hell of a tracker. He often told Lorenzo personally that he wasn't much of a police officer, but he was a fantastic outdoorsman. Lorenzo knew how to hunt and fish and he did so often. Which meant that the active outdoor lifestyle kept him fit and trim.

It was close to four o'clock when he left the Meacon Court House and his trip to the Ohdam Station would take him forty-five minutes or so. Depending upon the traffic, of course.

Bob was at the Watkins Ranch by four-twenty that afternoon. His meeting with Jeff Watkins was short. Bob caught Jeff supervising the off-loading of a cattle trailer. He was taking delivery of twenty yearlings and he was putting them in a corral near his main barn. They would receive health inspections and vaccinations over the next few days before they were released into pasture land.

Bob was leaning against a wooden rail fence next to Jeff as Jeff was commenting on the plan to hunt down the wolf. Jeff didn't refer to the animal as a *deformed wolf*. He simply called it a wolf during his conversation with Bob. The calves were bellowing their displeasure at being prodded off of the cattle car so the men had to raise their voices in order to hear each other.

Jeff tilted his cowboy hat over the back of his head as he spoke. "I can't spare any of my regulars. I can put ten temps in the saddle first thing in the morning, but my regulars are committed to transporting cattle."

Bob replied, "I'm not sure I'd be comfortable putting high school kids on something like this, Mister Watkins."

Jeff snorted as he answered, "Well, all of my grownups have CDLs. (Commercial Driver's License) None of my temps do, so we'll use the kids."

Bob started to argue his point, but Jeff cut him short. "Bob...are you a parent?"

"Uh...no."

"Well, let me tell you something...these high school kids are just as much an adult as most of the town folks in Meacon. They might be sixteen and seventeen years old, but... by God...they're reliable and that makes them adults in my eyes."

"I can see your point Mister Watkins, but what does that have to do with me being a parent?"

"I only bring it up because one day you will be. Might want to think about how you treat teenagers before you have one. I firmly believe that if you treat a teenager like an adult, then he or she will act like one."

Bob smiled and politely agreed with the man, "I see your point. You make perfect sense."

Jeff turned to face Bob, but kept one elbow on the wooden fence rail as he continued, "We need to get an early start. Daylight comes at six, so we should be saddled and ready to go by that time."

Bob suggested, "I thought some of us might start out at the place where the angus bull was attacked. By the way... what's been done about the carcass?"

Jeff answered quickly, "Burned it. I called Old Man Kermit and told him about the critter's demise by the wolf and all he could do was yell and scream about taking me to court. I figure it was stinking up my watering hole, so I had some boys burn it and bury the ashes."

Bob thought the answer was humorous. Extremely honest, but humorous none-the-less. He tried to offer another suggestion, "I was hoping we could work in teams of two. You have a lot of land to cover and there's other ranches that we'll be needing to cross as well."

Jeff looked serious for a moment then asked an important question, "That's true. I got forty-thousand acres myself. That's a little over sixty-two square miles and eight grazing ranges for us to cover. If we cross over onto someone else's land…say Old Man Kermit's for example…how are we going to show legal right. Lots of NO TRESSPASSING signs out there."

Bob answered quickly, "Sheriff Sand's working on it. He's drawn up a legal writ giving us permission to travel wherever necessary. Allie will make copies for me to distribute in the morning."

Jeff nodded as he replied, "Now that's a forward thinking man. That Sheriff of ours might be young, but he's not dumb by any means. I'll bet his parents treated him like an adult when he was a kid."

Bob snickered. "I've already bought off on your philosophy Mister Watkins. You don't need to keep proving it to me."

Jeff chuckled as he replied, "I'll remind you every now and then so as you don't forget how right I am." Jeff had another thought and asked, "That legal writ? Will it cover the Papago Reservation?"

Bob shook his head in the negative. "Sorry. That writ has to come from the Chief of Papago Police. Wally's working on it, but don't expect one by tomorrow morning."

Jeff agreed. "Yeah…that's pretty much how I figured it." He scratched his chin and then said, "We'll work in teams of two. Me and you'll make up one team and I'll assign the rest. You be here before daylight and I'll see you get outfitted with a horse and tack." He had another thought, "Guns! Hell, I got enough to outfit six people, but I need a little help in that category. What you got at the Warden's Office?"

"I can handle outfitting the other four. Including myself."

Jeff turned his attention back to the cattle car and then said to Bob, "Well…that ought to cover it for now. I'll see you in the morning."

Bob glanced at his wrist watch and saw that it was getting close to five o'clock. He thought quickly as he spoke to Jeff, "Mister Watkins. I need to call the Sheriff's Office before five. Can I borrow your house phone?"

Jeff used his thumb to indicate his house and said, "It's in the living room. Help yourself."

Bob trotted to the house and saw the black desk phone sitting on an end table. He picked up the receiver and dialed the number to the Sheriff's Office. Allie picked up the other end on the second ring. "Sheriff's Office, how may I help you?"

Bob couldn't help himself. He felt immediately elated to hear her voice. "Allie..." he said. "Allie I'm just now leaving the Watkins place. Does the gospel sing start at seven?"

"Hi, Bob! Yeah...seven o'clock."

"That gives me time to rush home, clean up and pick you up before seven. That okay?"

"Sure! I'll see you at my place. Hey...don't dress fancy... no tie or anything like that."

"What are you going to wear?"

"I got a new blouse I'm dying to wear, so just a blouse and some slacks."

"Okay...I'll see you before seven."

It was five-thirty that afternoon when Karen and Becky came into the corral next to the barn. Todd Endoran met them at the barn entrance and he signed to Karen, "I'll take care of horses. Boss wants to see you in house?"

Karen signed back, "What's up?"

He answered with one hand, "Meeting" and took both horse's reins in his other.

Karen turned to Becky and said, "We got a meeting at the house."

Becky nodded and said, "We need to put these guns away first." They made their way to the saddle house and stowed their weapons, then moved together to Jeff's Ranch House. Becky commented as they walked together, "Bet it's about that asshole Hershel."

Karen chuckled as she replied, "Would you forget about that ass? He's just a punk."

Becky couldn't help but remark, "If the little shit wasn't

twelve years old, I'd smack him around for a while."

They stopped talking as they moved through the front door of Jeff's home. Jeff had a meeting room set up at the back of the house and the girls made their way to it. They heard muttering from inside as they walked through the open door. Becky was the first one through and she spoke to the three boys sitting at the back of the room, "Bill, Sam, Elliot…what's up?"

The boy named Elliot teased Becky, "Been waiting on you two…that's all."

Becky smiled and replied, "Yeah? You'll grow old waiting on me Elliot Johnson."

Jeff saw the girls enter so he called to them, "Take a seat, girls. We can get started now."

Becky took an open chair next to Elliot and elbowed him in the ribs as she sat down. He made a small huffing sound and rubbed his side.

Jeff was standing as he started his explanation, "I'm suspending all ranch for work for you tomorrow." He paused for a second and then added, "I really don't know for how long, but we're all going on an assignment to help the Sheriff and the Game Warden."

His first remark caused a lot of anxious faces as most of the kids thought he was suspending work for the summer. But his second remark caused them all to relax somewhat. He continued, "I got word this afternoon that we have a lone wolf hunting in the region and we're going to help track it down."

There was an excited murmur immediately heard from the boys. Becky and Karen remained silent. They had seen this so-called wolf's work up close and they were choosing to wait for further information before offering any comment or expressing any concern.

Jeff continued, "We need to work in teams of two and we need to start at daybreak in the morning. I'll assign the teams and I'll assign the areas where all of you will hunt. Bob Benoit will be here in the morning to show you what kind of tracks you're looking for." He paused once again and then added, "I know you all have heard about the Kermit Bull, but you need to know that this animal has killed a man. Over in the Papago Lands. Happened a couple of days ago, I guess...but...because it has killed a person, this is now a matter for the police and we've been asked to help."

A boy named Joe Wills interrupted, "Mister Watkins... what do we do if we see it?"

Jeff snickered, "Shoot it, Joe."

The crowd let out a soft laugh at the boy's expense. Jeff simply continued talking, "If any of you have a rifle that you want to bring from home tomorrow, then please do so. Otherwise, me and the game warden will be supplying ammunition and firearms." He took a breath and then ended the meeting. "That's all. Be here early in the morning and ready to ride by daylight."

The boys and girls simply got up from their seats and filed out of the room. They talked among themselves as they made their way out of the house.

It was six-thirty that evening and both Wally and Jo Ann were sitting at their dining table eating the evening meal. Jo Ann was talking, "Hey...I gotta go to Vera tomorrow. I need a new vacuum cleaner belt and Smith's Hardware is the only place I can get one. We need some groceries, so I'll stop the market."

Wally put a bite of food in his mouth and grunted a response.

Jo Ann immediately knew that he was preoccupied, so she smiled and let him have one of her verbal jabs, "Hey, Cochise! I'm talking to you."

Wally stopped moving with his fork in his mouth, then finished taking a bite and replied, "Sorry...I was thinking about tomorrow."

"Hey, that's okay...just talk to me while you think about tomorrow."

He smiled and had a sudden thought, "You're the prettiest woman in the world, Jo Ann…" He took a breath and shared his thoughts with his wife, "There's some bad business over at the Ohdam Station and I'll have to be there first thing in the morning. I'm taking Jesse with me."

Jo Ann took a small bite of food and asked, "What sort of bad business?"

"Man got killed by an animal. I'm organizing a hunt."

Jo Ann rolled her eyes and put her fork down. She verbally jabbed him again, "Look…Tonto…stop trying to gloss over your job. Tell me what's going on."

Wally was smiling broadly as he replied, "It's a nasty business, hon. Normally, a dangerous animal is the responsibility of the game department, but this one's a man killer. Sort of makes it my business now, so I'm going to try and help the Papago look for it. Bob's going to work with Jeff Watkins and do some tracking in Jefferson County for me."

Jo Ann retrieved her fork and took another bite. She thought for a second, then replied, "Hell…Jeff Watkin's land is most of Pinal County. How many helpers you think Bob will get?"

Wally grunted, "Ten, I hope. That's what I asked for, anyway."

She nodded and replied, "Good. I like big safe numbers when there's danger about." Her plate was almost empty and she saw that he still had several bites left. She pointed at his plate and said, "Hey…finish eating and help me do the dishes. Let's just watch some television tonight and relax. I'll rub your shoulders if you think that'll ease your tension."

He was still smiling at her as he replied, "That sounds so good…you don't know…"

Sunset came at seven-forty-five that night. The beast came trotting out of his lair and made his way down the ledge and onto the gorge floor. He lapped at the shallow water for a moment, then made his way out of the north end of the cut. It was time to hunt.

Bob was sitting next to Allie in the middle row of pews on the east side of the Church. They were near the isle and had a good spot to hear the gospel group singing. At eight forty-five, the group sang their last selected number, which turned out to be a favorite of both Bob and Allie alike. The song that they sang was *in the Sweet, By and By*. Neither he nor Allie realized it, but sometime during the concert, they had moved closer together and held each other's hands.

CHAPTER SEVEN

When Jo Ann had quipped that Jeff Watkins owned most of Pinal County she was exaggerating. He didn't own most of it, but he owned a sizeable chunk of it. He was certainly one of the most prosperous citizens, if not *the* most prosperous. Jo Ann liked Jeff and once you became a friend to Jo Ann, you became a friend for life.

Sometime around one-thirty in the morning on August 23, a lone motorcycle rider stopped at a small bar on the outskirts of Vera. He was wearing worn leather pants with calf-high riding boots. The heels of the boots were rounded on their outer edges, which indicated that the man walked with his toes pointed outwards.

He wore no shirt, but he had a vest with four zipper pockets on the breast. The pockets were unzipped and one of them was bulging from being stuffed with two pill bottles. He had dirty blonde hair with an unkempt beard and he was not wearing a helmet. There was a chrome plated forty-five caliber pistol tucked into the backside of his leather pants.

He coasted to a stop in the dusty parking lot and cut his engine off. He sat straddle-legged of his machine as he looked cautiously about. He saw two cars in the parking lot, which meant that there were at least one customer and the bartender located inside.

His eyes were wide with nervous anticipation, but most of that was due to the effects of the pills that he kept in his vest pocket. He glanced at the highway behind him and he saw no traffic. He listened for a few seconds and decided that there were no other vehicles close by.

He lowered his kickstand and lifted his right leg over the motorcycle seat, then walked slowly towards the open door of the bar. He heard soft music coming from a jukebox or a radio, but he heard no conversations taking place as he walked through the front door.

He saw a heavyset bald man behind the bar and a very thin older gentleman sitting on the stool in front of the obvious bartender. He walked straight to the bartender and leaned against the counter. The thin man looked nervous as the motorcycle rider was standing very close to him.

The biker spoke with a voice that sounded rough and gravely. "Beer. Draft."

The bartender took a mug off of a rack and filled it out of a spigot located near the cash register. As he handed the mug to the biker, the dirty blonde biker passed a ten-dollar bill to the bartender.

The bartender stepped to his left and opened the cash register. At that precise moment, the biker drew the forty-five pistol out of his pants and shot the bartender in his right temple. The thin customer jumped at the sudden blast of the pistol, but before he could react, the biker swung his arm into the man's face and pulled the trigger again. Blood and brain matter splattered over the top of the bar counter.

The biker tucked the pistol back into his leather pants, took a slow drink out of the beer mug sitting before him, and then made his way around the counter to the cash register. There were three twenty-dollar bills, one ten-dollar bill (his), and six one-dollar bills. He shrugged his shoulders and then scooped up the money and left the bar.

He casually left the building and he took note of the soft music still playing and he thought to himself, "I didn't notice if it was a radio or a jukebox. Humph. I need to pay more attention." He swung his right leg over his motorcycle seat, used his right foot to push on the start lever, and throttled the engine to life.

He used the toe of his right boot to shift the motorcycle into first gear and slowly made his way out of the parking lot. Once he was on the highway, he turned south towards downtown Vera and eased his way along Main Street. There were no other vehicles on the road. When he left the outskirts of Vera, he increased his speed and headed straight for Meacon.

At four-thirty in the morning of August 23, the phone in Wally and Jo Ann's bedroom startled them out of a fitful sleep. Wally sat up straight on the first ring while Jo Ann groaned audibly. Wally had the receiver in his hand and next to his ear before the phone rang the third time. He sounded very hoarse as he said, "Sheriff Sand…"

Horace Fannin was on the other end of the line. He sounded gravely concerned as he said, "Sheriff, I hate to tell you this, but you need to come in. Two deputy marshals in Vera have discovered a double-homicide, and Marshal Tate said that he needs your help."

Wally coughed and replied, "Double…homicide?"

"Two people shot in a bar north of town. I've got more details for you once you get here."

Wally muttered, "Shit…" He then coughed and said, "I'll be right there."

He lowered the phone receiver back into its cradle and started to get out of bed. Jo Ann was rubbing her eyes as he switched the lamp next to their bed to the on position. She groaned again as she asked, "What is it, hon?"

Wally sat on the side of the mattress as he answered, "Some people have been killed in Vera. I have to go to work."

Jo Ann leaped out of bed and said loudly, "Shit!" She scrambled to their closet and began taking out one of Wally's uniforms. She knew that he was a dead-head when he first wakes up from a deep sleep, so she had learned over the years to help roust him and get him ready. She was calling to him as she was taking hangers out of the closet, "Get in the bathroom, honey! Wash your face and shave right quick! I'll get your clothes laid out and make you some coffee!"

Wally dutifully stumbled towards their bathroom.

Bob Benoit was parking his Jeep in front of Jeff Watkins house at four-forty-five this morning. When he exited his vehicle with no doors, he was carrying a 30-30 rifle and a cardboard box.

He was met by Jeff Watkins at the front porch of the house. Jeff called to him with a pleasant tone of voice, "Ah... punctual! I admire that in a man!"

Bob didn't reply at first. He made his way closer to the rancher and said, "You got any coffee?"

Jeff answered him with a question, "You got a thermos?"

Bob sounded disappointed as he replied, "No."

Jeff handed Bob a small silver thermos bottle and said, "I didn't think so. Here." Bob sat his box on top of the porch and leaned his rifle against the side of the wooden flooring. He quipped, "Bless you" as he unscrewed the bottle's cap and took a long drink.

Jeff picked the box up off of the porch and said, "Take another drink. The way my cook makes it, you need two swigs to get your heart started."

Bob obeyed without a remark.

When Bob started putting the thermos lid back onto the bottle, Jeff said, "Grab your rifle. The posse is at the corral getting ready to go."

Bob asked as he picked up his rifle, "Posse?"

He fell beside Jeff as they walked towards the corral. Jeff explained, "That's the kid's idea. They didn't care much for the designation of *search party*. They wanted to be called a *posse*."

Bob couldn't help but smile at the thought. He was still smiling as he and Jeff walked through an open corral gate and he saw ten teenagers putting saddles and other gear on horses. There were flood lights mounted on top of tall poles allowing good vision all around the corral.

Jeff used his free hand to point to two horses tied to a rail. "Those are ours. Mine's the big black. Yours is the bay. You'll need to adjust the stirrups before we leave."

Jeff called out to all of the teenagers, "Everybody gather around us as soon as your done setting your tack. The Game Warden has something to show us!"

Jeff then turned to Bob and whispered, "That's why you brought the box, right?"

Bob nodded in the affirmative and asked, "I don't have a scabbard for my rifle. Can I go tie it to the bay's saddle along with this stupid radio?"

"Yeah. Go ahead. How many rifles did you bring this morning?"

"Four. No scabbards."

"Ammo?"

"In the Jeep."

Jeff then teased him, "Well, outside of not bringing a thermos...I'd say you're pretty much prepared."

Bob simply shook off the jab and took his rifle to his assigned horse. Once he had tied the stock to one of the back skirt straps and had the barrel pointing downwards, he tied his handheld radio to one of the front straps, and went to stand next to Jeff again. Most of the teenagers were gathered around the rancher and waiting on him.

The last three teens to join Bob and Jeff was Becky, Elliot and Joe. Bob watched them approach the rest of the group and then he saw Elliot mouthing something to Becky. He then saw Becky's hand slap the back of the boy's head, and he snickered softly.

When everyone had gathered around him and Jeff, Jeff gave the box to Bob and said, "Okay...show them what we're looking for."

Bob opened the box and took out a white plaster cast of one of the beast's front paws. He only brought one of the casts with him and he had chosen the one that he felt was the best. It showed the claws and foot pads very clearly and demonstrated the size of the paw extremely well. He handed the cast to the first person standing next to him, which happened to be Karen, and as she took in into her hands, he spoke to the crowd. "If any of you have ever studied animal foot prints, which I'm pretty sure all of you have, you'll see a close resemblance to the track of a wolf's front paw. This one is much bigger, of course, which indicates that it's probably an oversized deformation."

A young boy named Bill Ivers had the cast in his hands as he asked a question, "Deformed? Like crippled?"

Bob quickly dispelled that theory. "Oh, no! Not deformed like crippled! Think of it as *deformed* like in *dangerous*."

The cast was making around the group as it was passed from hand to hand. Another young boy named Joe Wills held the cast and asked his question, "This thing is heavy! Do you have any idea how big this deformed wolf is?"

Bob answered the lad honestly, "Some...I'm estimating around one-hundred and eighty pounds."

Jeff Watkins quickly added, "That's about thirty pounds more than you weigh, Joe!"

Joe quickly passed the cast to the boy next to him and kept his mouth closed. After a full two minutes of inspections, the cast made its way back to Bob's hands and he placed it into the cardboard box. He held the box in his hands as Jeff then spoke to the group, "I've told all of you which pastures you're working this morning, so we have about twenty minutes or so before we leave. I want everyone to carry a loaded weapon with them, but don't do anything stupid like ride around with a bullet in the chamber. Keep the rifles on safety and those of you with pistols, keep them holstered." Jeff turned to Bob and said, "Karen, James, Charles, and Simon need rifles. Can they go to your jeep and get yours?"

Bob readily agreed, "Of course." He stepped towards Karen and handed her the box. "Put this on the front passenger seat for me, please. I'll adjust my stirrups while you guys go get the rifles. The shells are on the floorboard."

The four of them walked away from Jeff and Bob while the rest of the boys and Becky made their way back to their own mounts.

At four-twenty this morning, the biker was within eye-sight of the street lights of Meacon. He decided that the wisest thing for him to do was to find the first road off of the main highway and skirt his way around the town. He saw one the very moment that he slowed down to start his search.

He steered his bike to the right and slowed significantly as he guided it onto a dirt road with loose sand. He kept his speed very slow and his engine noise as low as he could as he didn't want to wake anyone in their homes or draw attention to himself by creating a dust cloud. He putted along for almost three miles and was traveling a relatively southward direction. He passed several houses that were alongside of the road, but they were all dark and showed no signs of life.

The sun hadn't yet broken over the horizon, but the daylight hour had begun to shine in the east. A faint glow started to grow slowly. As he eased his way along the dirt road, he spotted a small sign a few hundred yards ahead. It looked like a road sign to him, so he made for it.

As he approached the sign, the light was getting a little brighter so by the time that he reached it, he was able to read, *Papago Indian Reservation / 32 Miles.*

As he read the words, he suddenly had a thought. His drug soaked mind spoke to him, "Reservation? Sheriff's don't have jurisdiction inside of a reservation! No townships inside of a reservation…that's where I need to be!" He then forgot his stealth logic and sped away from the sign.

He was wrong about one thing when he reasoned out his direction of travel. Sheriff's do have jurisdiction within Reservation Boundaries. They regularly assist Reservation Police in all matters. They never do so without communicating with the Reservation Police, but they do have jurisdiction.

At seven o'clock this morning, the Meacon Sheriff's Office was filled with activity. Horace Fannin was actively engaged in radio chats with two Vera deputy marshal squad cars; Wally was in his office on the phone with the Vera City Marshal, and his two nighttime deputies were in his office along with Jesse Blount. The three of them were seated in front of Wally's desk awaiting orders and directions.

Horace was talking on the radio when he saw Andrew Span and his wife Melissa walk through the front door. Melissa was obviously distressed and clinging to her husband's arm.

Horace completed his radio transmission with the deputy marshal as he said, "Copy, Frank. Big motorcycle...possibly a Harley seen leaving Vera at around one-thirty...possibly two o'clock...no other traffic noted."

Horace put the radio microphone on the desk and spoke as the man and woman approached him, "Mister Span...Missus Span...what can I do for you?

Andrew spoke first. "My boy...Hershel...he didn't come home yesterday or last night. We've been driving around looking for him most of the night."

Horace stood up quickly and indicated two chairs in front of the desk, "Please have a seat...I'll get the Sheriff."

Andrew and Melissa sat down in the chairs slowly and she kept her hands firmly on her husband's forearm as she lowered herself. Horace moved quickly to Wally's office.

He saw Wally hanging his telephone receiver back onto its cradle and spoke urgently, "Sheriff...I think you better come out to the dispatcher's desk."

Wally wrinkled his brow and asked, "What's up, Bubba?"

"Missing kid" Horace answered.

Wally stood up and replied, "Shit!" He left his deputies sitting in their chairs as he moved out of his office and made his way towards the Span's."

The Posse was mounted on their horses and they were all facing Jeff Watkins. Bob was mounted as well and he was at Jeff's right side. Jeff was giving his last minute instructions, "We will all be in separate pastures today, so that means we won't be within sight of each other. In case of an emergency, we all need to agree on a means of giving a signal."

Becky raised her hand and said loudly, "Mister Watkins! Can I give those instructions?"

Jeff smiled as he knew what she was going to say. "Go ahead, Becky."

Becky spoke so all could hear. "One shot means that you're shooting at something. Two shots mean that you missed your first one. Three shots mean your ass is in a sling! We all go running towards the three-shot signal!"

The boys all groaned in unison.

Jeff continued, "You all have your Sheriff's Passes, so if you find tracks and you need to follow them off of my land, then keep them handy. If you don't have any questions, then head out."

The boys and girls broke up into their teams and slowly walked their horses away in different directions. Bob and Jeff turned their mounts towards the direction of the water trough where the angus bull was killed and as they plodded along, Bob asked Jeff a question, "Don't you think it would have been better if you told them to come find us if they located any tracks?"

Jeff didn't bother looking at Bob as he answered, "No... not at all. You see...just because they find tracks don't mean that they'll lead anywhere. This is the desert. Wind and flying dust and rolling weeds usually wipe out tracks fairly quickly."

Bob nodded slowly in agreement, then offered, "How about me and you do something different?"

That made Jeff look at his companion. "Like what?" he asked.

"Let's make our way to the water trough, then work our way towards the nearest plateau."

"What do you have in mind?"

Bob answered honestly, "Something Professor Wilcox said. He said, *if* the animal has wolf instincts, then it'll look for a den. Lone wolves do that as well as wolf packs."

Jeff returned his attention to the trail in front of his horse and then thought for a moment. He then stated, "Dens... lots of recesses and small caves around plateaus. Kinda makes sense."

Bob added, "Mind you...I'd be a lot happier following footprints. If you follow prints, you know what's up ahead. Scouting holes in the ground has a nerve wracking aspect to it."

Jeff chuckled and had another thought. "Bob...where did this stuff about a deformed wolf come from?"

Bob explained to the rancher. "There's a paper called the Rubicon Chronicles. It's a scientific paper circulated around college campuses that deals with a variety of subjects. There's lots of articles about studying the natural habitats and habits of wild animals. I found the ones about extinct mammals the most interesting."

Jeff interrupted, "Extinct?"

Bob continued, "Believe it or not, one of the most popular subjects in the chronicles is the Dire Wolf."

"Dire Wolf?"

"Big animal that was closely kin to the dog and the wolf. Sort of a hybrid we think."

"We think?'

Bob shifted himself in the saddle and continued, "It lived in the age of the Mastodon. We know quite a bit about it due to fossilized bone studies and there's been plenty of plaster casts made of footprints left behind in dried sediment beds." He paused and took a deep breath before continuing. "When I first saw the paw prints in the mud by that water trough, I was shocked at the similarities."

Jeff reined his horse around a large rock protruding in the middle of the dusty trail and then offered a comment, "You thought you'd stumbled upon a Dire Wolf, huh?"

Bob couldn't help himself as he chuckled softly and replied, "Well...yeah...I'll have to admit that I was fairly excited at first."

Jeff turned in his saddle and asked, "What changed your mind?"

"Common sense. I've studied enough congenital structural defects in mammals to know better than to jump to conclusions, but..." he paused.

Jeff was still facing him as he pressed, "But what?"

Bob grinned sheepishly, "That foot print sure was close to a Dire Wolf's!"

Jeff turned back into his saddle and picked up the rhythm of his horse's gait with his hips. He thought for a moment, then questioned another aspect of the conversation, "Bob...this *Rubicon Paper* thing...why is it called the *Rubicon*."

Bob answered almost immediately, "Stands for *DECISION*. Not the word, but the concept. Comes from the story about Julius Caesar crossing the River Rubicon into Rome with his army. Caesar made a calculated decision concerning his political career when he did that. People that submit articles to the Rubicon Chronicle make calculated decisions about their studies and opinions."

Jeff was frowning and staring at the ground as he replied, "I don't quite get it."

"Well..." Bob explained, "Well, if a graduate student... and most of the articles are submitted by graduate students, get their articles and opinions published in the paper and it receives favorable reviews from campuses around the nation...it's like a stamp of approval."

Jeff replied, "Humph...I guess I have a different take on the Rubicon story."

Bob spurred his horse into a trot and moved himself beside Jeff. He remained at Jeff's side as he asked, "What sort of take do you have, Mister Watkins?"

Jeff was grinning as he spoke, "Julius Caesar crossed that river knowing full well that he was strong enough politically and militarily to force his way into the number one leadership role of Rome. He knew that no one could stop him, so he forced his way into the position." Jeff took a breath and then added, "And he was wrong. His people killed him because they feared him." Jeff turned to Bob and asked, "And you know why they feared him?" He didn't wait for an answer. "They feared him because of his strength."

Bob had a confused look on his face for a long moment. He finally spoke to Jeff, "You think we're bent on killing this beast because we fear it, don't you."

Jeff answered, "Don't we?"

Bob reluctantly agreed, "Yes...I suppose there's a great degree of honesty in that assumption. It's a killer and it's dangerous...but..."

Jeff pressed the game warden, "But what, Bob."

Bob became extremely uncomfortable as he slowly admitted, "Jeff...there's some things about the animal that bother me. For one thing, I keep asking myself *where did it come from.* Another thing I keep asking myself is *how did it get its deformity.* Not knowing those two things makes me uncomfortable with the decision to kill it."

Jeff reined his horse to a stop and turned his head towards Bob. He looked directly into Bob's face as he asked, "You think you could catch it and study it?"

Bob lowered his head and muttered, "No."

Jeff pursed his lips and nudged his horse's ribs. His horse began a slow plodding walk again as Jeff replied, "Then we kill it and study its carcass." A moment later he added, "As far as where it came from, I'm assuming it was Mexico."

Bob agreed, "Yeah...me too. He was probably born there and simply made his way here following game."

The biker had to slow his motorcycle to almost a crawl. The sun was coming up over the eastern horizon and it was blinding his eyesight. He was agitated from the intensity of the glare and he cursed loudly. After a full minute of trying to squint his eyes and block the irritating sunlight, he gunned his engine and aimed for a small tree on the side of the dirt road.

He killed the engine, dropped his kickstand, and muttered loudly, "Fuck it! I gotta piss anyway!" He swung his right leg over the motorcycle seat and then walked towards the scrawny pine. He was unzipping his leather trousers with his left hand while he reached behind his back with his right hand. He grasped his pistol before he opened his trousers' fly and held it to one side.

He fumbled himself out of his open fly and sighed softly as the urine stream fell upon the dry ground. He didn't hear the beast walking softly towards his backside, but he stopped his urination in midstream the instant that he heard the vicious growl.

It sounded very ferocious and very close and he swallowed noisily from the sudden fright. His pistol was gripped tightly in his right hand as he thought rapidly as to what his next move was going to be.

The beast growled again.

He forced himself to take a breath, then he cursed himself for his foolishness. He spoke in his mind, "Well, fuck! Here you stand with your dick in your hand and some dumb-assed dog almost scaring the shit out of you! Shoot the mother-fucker and finish pissing."

He started to turn his head to his left to get a look at the intruder when the beast clamped his jaws onto the biker's neck. His canines plunged into the biker's shoulders while his lower teeth tore a path up the man's spine.

The man screamed and involuntarily pulled the trigger of his pistol. The forty-five blasted a lead projectile into the sand at his feet and sent a puff of dust into the air.

The explosion of the gun startled the beast and he released his grip from the man's back. The biker screamed again and fell to the ground and rolled to his side. His right arm was pinned underneath his hip as his eyes focused on the unholy monster standing in front of him. He whimpered and tried to pull his right arm out from underneath his body, but his injured spine was preventing his hands from doing his bidding. He watched helplessly as the beast let his lower jaw go slack and allowed blood to drip from his lower lips.

Another loud growl erupted from the beast as he launched himself upon the man's chest and clamped his mouth over the biker's left arm. The mouth slammed shut and the arm was severed at the shoulder. His right hand lost its grip on the pistol as the beast flung the severed left arm away his body, but he had the strength to produce another painful scream.

Before the biker could take another breath, the beast crushed his skull and then slowly stood up on his hind legs. As before, when he was fully erect, he snapped his head to the left and sent the biker's body rolling across the dirt. The man landed on his back with his legs splayed outwards. His heart had stopped beating so the blood only drained from the open wounds and saturated the sand.

The beast approached the dead body and sniffed softly. He woofed quietly, then took his right front paw and used his razor sharp claws to open the biker's stomach. When the intestines were exposed, he used both of his front feet to rake them out of the cavity and expose the liver. He grasped the man's liver with his teeth and pulled it out onto the dirt, where he dropped it. He then used his front claws to dig underneath the ribcage and remove the heart. He closed his mouth over the heart and separated it in one bite. He chewed twice, then swallowed the heart and turned his attention back to the liver.

He gnawed at the liver for a few seconds, and then swallowed it. He used his tongue to remove some of the body fluids from his upper lips, and then he turned his attention to the carcass once again. He grunted softly and approached the biker's right leg so that he could inspect it. It was covered with a strange smelling material that irritated his nose.

The beast snorted his displeasure, then used his right front paw to slice away the leather trousers leg covering the man's thigh. Once the thigh was exposed, he chewed and sliced away a large portion of meat, then stood astride the biker with the majority of the upper leg muscles hanging from his mouth.

The sun was almost up and the beast decided that it was time to return to his den. He was a long way from his lair, so he carried the dripping mass of muscle with him as he quickly trotted away.

Wally had pulled Mister Span and his wife into the meeting room and had them both sitting in front of his desk. Jesse was seated next to Wally and he was taking notes on a yellow legal pad as everyone talked. It had already been established that Andrew Span had waited until the sun was almost down the day before when he decided that his son, Hershel was later getting home than he was supposed to be and that there was probably something wrong. He was out riding his four-wheeler and he had either broken down or had injured himself. Or so everyone had surmised.

The Span's had explained to Wally that several family members and several friends had spent most of the night driving around looking for the boy. They had concentrated their searches over public lands only because the boy had been warned about trespassing.

As soon as Andrew Span had mentioned the "public" lands aspect of his story, Jesse and Wally turned towards each other at the same time. Their thoughts were the same in regards to the Hershel boy. He was known to them as a disobedient and spoiled child and they both had previous run-ins with the lad regarding trespassing issues. Wally stared at Jesse and said, "You thinking what I'm thinking?"

Jesse answered immediately, "He's off-roading. Only question is…where?"

Andrew Span looked confused as he asked, "Excuse me?"

Wally stood up from his chair and replied, "Mister Span, if you can wait here with your wife for a moment, I'll be right back." He left the room without waiting for a response.

Wally made his way quickly to Allie's desk. She was occupied with a radio conversation with Marshal Tate of Vera. Wally waited for her to complete the conversation before he interrupted. As soon as she placed the microphone handset on her desktop, he spoke to her.

"Allie, does Bob have a handset this morning?"

She was jotting a note on a pad as she answered, "Uh-huh."

"Did you give him a call sign?"

She stopped writing and looked at Wally incredulously. She blinked and replied, "Of course."

He picked up the radio microphone and asked her before he keyed it, "What's his number?"

"He's unit six."

Wally keyed the handset and spoke clearly, "Unit six, this is base."

The handset that Bob carried was tied to his saddle and he had the speaker volume turned to the "low" position. He and Jeff were still riding side by side as Jeff pointed to the small unit and asked, "Are your number six?"

Bob acted slightly embarrassed as he replied, "Oh...shit! Yeah, that's me!"

Jeff snickered softly as Bob untied the saddle strap holding the radio. He fumbled for a second, then held the unit to his face and keyed the mic. "This is unit six!"

Wally answered immediately, "Bob, are you with Jeff Watkins?"

"He's right here."

"Let me speak with him."

Bob looped his bridle reins over his saddle horn and turned the volume knob to a louder position and handed the radio to Jeff. He was smiling as he said, "It's for you."

Jeff reined his horse to a stop and took the radio. He frowned as he spoke into the mouthpiece, "This is Jeff."

Bob instructed him, "Push the lever on the side to talk."

Jeff muttered, "Oh...okay." He pushed the side button

on the unit and replied, "This is Jeff."

Wally spoke plainly and quickly, "Jeff...did any of your people happen to see young Hershel Span on your property yesterday?"

The question made Jeff pause, but he realized that his two line riders had told him about a cut fence and some tire tracks that they believed belonged to Hershel. He keyed the unit again and replied, "My two line riders mended a fence that had been cut and they said that there were ATV tracks all around the opening. Both of them thought that it could have been the Span kid."

Wally re-keyed his mic and asked, "You think he might still be on your property?"

Jeff sputtered as he replied, "No way! My girls closed up the hole in the fence and they told me that the tracks led off into the Elkins' pastures."

Wally lowered the microphone for a moment so that he could think. He then put it back to his mouth and asked, "Which Elkins gate? North or South?"

Jeff answered, "Girls said the break was near the North gate."

Wally keyed the microphone one more time and said, "Thanks, Jeff."

Jeff waited for a few seconds more then handed the unit to Bob. "I guess we're done."

Wally moved quickly to the meeting room and announced as he walked through the door. "There's a good chance that he's somewhere on Elkins property."

Andrew Span jumped to his feet and asked, "What? How?"

Wally raised a hand and stopped him, "Mister Span, we can deal with that later. How many people do you have helping you look?"

Andrew sputtered, "Uh...uh...seven pickups...including mine."

Wally continued, "I'm going to have Allie call the Elkins Ranch and let them know that you need to search his property. I'll send a deputy along with you just to make sure that the Elkins know that this is not a request. But..."

Andrew whispered a response, "But?"

Wally had to steel himself as he explained, "Hershel hasn't been missing for twenty-four hours yet. My hands are legally tied until then. I'll make sure that you have legal permission to search the Elkins ranch lands, but I really can't offer personal assistance until tomorrow."

Andrew took a deep breath and then replied, "Well...it's a good lead for us. We'll take it. Thank you, Sheriff."

Andrew Span and his wife, along with Jesse Blount, had no sooner walked out of the Sheriff's Office when Wally started talking to Allie. "Get me Marshall Tate and Chief Brigswall on the phone. Can you set me up with a conference?"

Allie nodded, "Of course. Your conference line is line three. I'll let you know when they're both on the phone."

Joe Wills and Elliot Johnson were two of Jeff Watkins' boys assigned to the far southwest pasture. It had taken them two and a half hours to make it to the southwest pasture entrance gate, so it was a little after eight-thirty when they led their horses through the opening. The southeast gate was the designated opening into that particular section of land. It wasn't a swing-gate. It was nothing more than a barbed wire gate stretched across two rigid posts. A wire loop had to be removed in order to open the gate.

Joe Wills was pushing the top of a wooden post so that he could loop it back into position as he spoke. "Well, now that we're here...do we get to say it?"

Elliot rolled his eyes, "Say what, Joe?"

Joe was stepping into his saddle as he replied, "I've always wanted to announce, *Let the hunt begin!*"

Elliot was seventeen years old, whereas Joe was sixteen.

Elliot thought that the boy was a little immature, but he was also a muscular lad with broad shoulders. Elliot decided to choose his words carefully, and he spoke in a lighthearted manner. "Joe...there's a thin line between *crazy* and *asshole*. I do believe that you've converged the two."

Joe was smiling as he replied, "I'm a crazy asshole, huh?"

Elliot nudged his horse into a slow walk and then answered, "If it makes you feel complete...Joe...you can announce the hunt."

Joe moved his horse so that it was walking behind Elliot's and then he answered, "Nah...you rubbed the fun off of it. No sense in doing it now."

There was a large valley spread out before the two boys, so Joe called to Elliot as they made their way down the first slope, "Where do we start?"

Elliot pointed to a windmill in the distance. "Over there."

"The windmill?"

"There's a cattle water tank and some feeding troughs. I think that the windmill would be a good starting place, don't you?"

Joe happily agreed, "Yeah...good idea. Wolf's gotta get water somewhere, huh?"

Elliot sighed, "Good thinking, Joe."

Wally's desk phone was on *speaker* mode as he talked to the two lawmen. He was apologizing to Chief Brigswall, "I'm sorry about this morning, Chief. I'm having a rough morning today. My deputy, Jesse Blount, will be at the Ohdam Station a little later. He's on another assignment right now...sort of an emergency here locally."

Chief Brigswall answered with his usual slow drawl, "I've heard it over the radio...that's some bad business in Vera."

Marshal Tate was on the other line so he answered for Wally, "It's a mess over here, alright. Coroner's still on site and I've closed the bar up for the time being. We've got some deputies trying to find out who did this, but I don't have enough people in the field right now."

Wally interrupted, "I've got some help coming in from Casa Grande, but they won't be here until this afternoon. I've called for four deputies."

Chief Brigswall was slightly taken aback, so he asked, "Four? You got some other trouble besides the Vera murders?"

Wally answered somberly, "Missing child. Jesse's helping the family for the moment, so that's why he's running late."

Chief Brigswall replied equally concerned, "Damn...I always hate those."

Wally remarked, "Yeah...me too."

Elliot and Joe were sitting in their saddles looking at the muddy ground on the eastern side of the water pond. The windmill was turning slowly and squeaking loudly as Joe spoke first, "Well, I'll be damned! Look at that!"

They were staring at one full print of a front paw and a partial print of a rear one. Elliot seemed slightly excited as he replied, "Sum bitch! I didn't think we'd see anything, but there it is!"

Joe reasoned, "Yeah. It stopped here for a drink for sure. Wonder which way it went after it got a drink."

Elliot thought for a second and then said, "Only one way to find out. Let's walk around the pond and see if there's any more of them."

Both of the boys turned their horses to the right and headed north in order to circle the pond and look for tracks. Joe mused as they looked for more tracks, "Good thing Mister Watkin's herds are in other pastures, huh?"

Elliot had to agree. "Yeah. No telling how many would have been killed by this thing if any of them had been at the pond."

Both of them reined to a halt and stared at the ground. The footprints had obviously turned northwest and moved away from the water hole. Their eyes followed the trail of paw prints and they saw that as soon as the wolf left the soft and moist dirt around the pond, they disappeared.

After a long moment, Elliot had a thought. "Well…it's headed northwest. I say we head that way and see if we can find any more prints."

Joe tilted his cowboy hat to the back of his head and had an idea of his own. He offered a suggestion to his friend, "Hey… you and I both know that these sands shift all day long. The best we're gonna do is find a print here and there…maybe."

Elliot was with him in thoughts as he said, "You're right. We'd better mark any trail or prints that we see. In case we have to look for more than one day, we would know where we left off the day before."

Joe unbuckled one of his saddle bags and drug out a thin rag. It was his saddle oiling rag and he held it up for Elliot to see. "Elliot…we both have one of these saddle rags…how about we tear off a strip when we find a print or two and tie it to the nearest bush. Or maybe cactus. More than likely it'd be a cactus."

Elliot smiled at his friend as he gave him a compliment. "Good thinking." They both pursed their lips and nudged their horses towards the northwest.

Jo Ann was driving her car towards Vera and she had made it to the halfway point. Several homes could be found on the side of the highway, but they were far apart and mostly older houses. She passed a Vera City Marshall police car that was parked on the left side of the road and it had its lights flashing. The vehicle was parked in front of a white wood-framed house and she could see a deputy talking to a man while they were on the front porch.

She didn't normally see a unit visiting a home with the lights flashing, so she thought that it was a strange matter, but she didn't ponder on it for long. She drove another ten miles and saw another Vera police car on her right hand side next to a house with its lights flashing and the deputy talking to a woman in the front yard.

This time, she thought to herself, "Gotta have something to do with that homicide they called Wally about." Again, she let the matter pass and continued on her way to Vera. She had some shopping to do and she was anxious to get to it.

Marshal Tate had dispatched all four of his deputies to interview people who lived along the highway between Vera and Meacon. It was his hope to find someone who might have noticed a motorcycle rider sometime during the wee hours of the morning. The crime was listed as occurring sometime between 1:30 AM and 2:00 AM on August 24. He cursed that part of the murder. Vera was a college town and if the crime had been committed on a Friday or Saturday night, the streets would have had many more people out and about. Wednesday and Thursday, however...Vera was like a monastery. Or so he told himself.

Marshal Tate was keeping himself in his office as was Wally keeping himself situated in the Courthouse in Meacon. The two of them were coordinating their efforts and communicating each aspect of the investigation. Wally had called for four more deputies to drive in from Casa Grande and be able to take over the investigative processes if they should require ongoing efforts after normal working hours. Two of them would assist Marshal Tate, and two of them would assist Wally.

Jesse Blount was still on assignment to work with Police Chief Brigswall, but his original timeline of joining the men at the Ohdam Station had been changed from eight o'clock in the morning to "whenever he could get there." He was at the Elkins Ranch House at ten o'clock this morning ensuring that the owner of the large section of land, Gary Elkins, was reluctant to let several strangers (and their vehicles) move about his property.

Gary Elkins was married to Fanny Elkins; whose maiden name was Renshaw. Her family once owned the property where the Eisenhower Munitions Factory now resided. This meant that she was quite well off financially, and consequently, it meant the same thing for her husband.

When Jesse first approached Gary Elkins (in the man's front yard) about letting the Span family search for their missing son on his property, he was not amenable to the idea. He wanted to argue that he had several ranch hands that worked his property on a daily basis and they had not reported any trespassing incidents in months.

Jesse was not a man to take the word "no" for an answer when he was performing official duties, so he readied himself for an argument with Gary when Fanny walked out of the house. She was a petit woman with long gray hair. She was wearing a light blue sun dress with dark blue house shoes and she was using a cane to steady herself as she walked out onto the front porch. She called to Jesse when she stopped at the edge of the wooden porch, "Good morning, Deputy Blount. How's your girlfriend?"

Jesse smiled and answered Fanny, "Good morning missus Elkins. Jennifer is fine and she's supposed to become my wife next month."

"Well now...that's wonderful. I'm happy for you." She then turned her attention to her husband and her voice tone became rather harsh. "Gary! Get your ass over here and help me down from the porch!"

Gary Elkins stepped away from Jesse and took his wife by the arm. Her voice returned to a pleasant overtone as she said, "Thank you, dear."

Once Fanny had both feet on the ground, she shook her husband's grip away from her forearm and walked stiffly towards Jesse. She looked up into the huge man's face and smiled as she said, "I overheard your conversation with my husband. I apologize for Gary...he can be a class-A dick sometimes."

Jesse snorted and Fanny continued. "You think this Span boy might be lost out on our property, Jesse?"

Jesse answered quickly, "There's a chance, missus Elkins. I don't know if it's a good chance, but there is a chance."

Fanny looked around Jesse and didn't see any other vehicles other than his squad car, so she asked, "You said there were family members…where are they?"

"Back at your property front entrance. I had them line up at the cattle guard and wait for me to tell them when it was alright to come inside."

Fanny frowned and then pointed her cane at Jesse's face. She said sternly, "Jesse Blount! You get your butt back to the front entrance and let those people get started looking! Shame on you for taking so long!"

Jesse was smiling as he apologized, "I'm sorry missus Elkins! I'll tell them right now."

As he was walking towards his police car, Fanny called after him, "I'll get my asshole husband to help!" She then turned to Gary and used her cane to steady herself as she changed her voice tone once again, "You heard me, Gary! Get your ass in the pickup and go help those nice people!" As her husband walked quickly towards their garage, she started muttering out loud, "Damn man! Sometimes I think he's got a mental problem! Wanting to refuse a family help to look for their boy! Damn bald-headed old fart!" She then made her way to the front porch and used her cane to pull herself up onto the board deck.

At ten minutes after ten o'clock, Jesse was inside of his squad car watching seven pickups drive slowly onto Elkins land and start to spread out in several different directions. Once the last vehicle moved over the cattle guard, he picked up his radio transmitter and spoke into the mic, "Ohdam Station, this is unit three. Come in Marc."

Wally was sitting behind his desk in his high-back chair. He was leaning back and he had his hands behind his head as he stared at the ceiling. He was so lost in thought that he was oblivious to the radio chatter coming from the lobby and Allie's desk. He was concentrating on the double homicide issue and he had a very blank look on his face as he was thinking. His mind was trying to turn the situation into a puzzle and then put it together one piece at a time.

His thoughts were a conversation within his mind. "Man walks into a bar...right at closing time...that was no accident." Wally rocked his chair slightly and continued his self-conversation, "He walks up to the bar...he orders a drink... a beer...hands the bartender some money...waits for the bartender to open the cash register...shoots the man in the head."

Wally removed his hands from behind his head and sat up straight. He had the vision of the crime in his mind. He pictured an assailant pointing a pistol at the bartender, then shooting him in the head and then immediately turning to the one and only other patron at the bar and killing him in the same manner. Wally muttered out loud, "Damn! That's some cold-bloodied shit!"

He then put his elbows on his desk and had a very reasonable thought. "A man can only be that cold-bloodied under two circumstances. Drugs or insanity. Either way, the man will have a criminal history." Wally suddenly felt like he was on to something. He smiled and had another thought, "He came from somewhere and that somewhere had to be close." He was still smiling as he picked up his telephone receiver and said out loud, "Tucson or Phoenix. Had to be one of the cities." He dialed the telephone number of the Tucson Police Department and sat back in his chair as the phone began to ring on the other end of the line.

Elliot and Joe had slowly worked their way northwest and in an effort to make sure they that didn't overlook any animal prints, they crisscrossed their paths constantly. It was noontime and the desert heat was at its maximum intensity. As the boys looked off into the distance, the heat waves danced off of the sand and caused bushes and cactus alike to become fuzzy to the eyesight.

The boys had grown weary, thirsty, and hungry. The next cattle watering hole was off to their left and at least twenty minutes away. They decided that the best thing for them to do is to mark their current spot; go to the cattle watering hole and have lunch. There was a windmill there, so there was shade and a place to eat their lunches.

They had discovered four footprints during the morning that indicated that the wolf was moving northwest. They had stayed on that trail for hours and as much as they were excited about finding foot prints at the beginning of the day, their luck hadn't been so good over the past hour.

Joe dismounted his horse; tore a thin strip off of his oily rag and tied it to a small brush. He leaped back into the saddle, then he and Elliot loped their horses towards the windmill.

The boys knew better than to overheat their mounts, so they didn't run them very far. They trotted for a while, then walked the horses to the windmill to make sure they weren't breathing hard when they got there. They tied their horses at the water trough so that they could drink, then took their lunch pouches to the windmill.

The best shade around the windmill was directly underneath the large structure. The windmill blades were spinning slowly and the pump rod was moving up and down, so there was some squealing and bumping noises filling the air.

Still, it was cool underneath the windmill, so Joe and Elliot removed their hats and sat on the ground. They chatted as they ate their sandwiches.

Joe spoke first, "You know, it'll take us the rest of the day to check this pasture."

Elliot nodded and answered as he was chewing a bite of his sandwich, "Yeah. We wasted a lot of time riding the horses over here this morning. We should have loaded them up in a trailer and brought them over here."

Joe agreed, but argued, "I know, but Mister Watkins has all of the stock trailers tied up right now. I heard he's got another hundred head of steers to bring down from Tucson, so there's not much chance of any of us getting to haul the horses over here."

Elliot nodded his head as he took his sandwich wrapper and balled it into his fist. He put the paper roll back into his lunch pouch and then removed the lid from his canteen. He took a long drink of water, then leaned against a windmill upright beam as he answered Joe, "I don't know how we'll keep from having to use horse trailers. There's only ten of us out looking around and we can't cover a whole lot of land in the time frame that Mister Watkins gives us. He has enough land that it would take all of us a week to search the way we're doing it right now."

Joe was leaning against another windmill upright as he shared his thoughts with Elliot. "Hey! You know what? You're right! Mister Watkins knows this, so I'll bet his plan is for us to look for tracks today and if any of us find some, then he'll truck some of us to that spot and make us start searching from there tomorrow."

Elliot cocked his head slightly and said, "Humph... you're probably right about that! Jesus...I'd have never thought..."

Joe asked, "Thought what?"

"That you'd have some intelligent logic and then make it come out of your mouth."

Joe picked up a handful of dirt and flung it at his friend. "Fuck you!"

Wally heard a voice answer his phone call, so he immediately leaned back and listened to the greeting. "Tucson Police Department, Sergeant Hankins speaking, how may I help you?"

Wally replied immediately, "Hello Sergeant Hankins. This is Sheriff Sand down in Meacon."

Hankin's voice immediately grew friendlier. "Hello Sheriff Sand. What's up today?"

Wally jumped right into the narration, "Me and Marshal Tate have a double homicide in Vera. Happened around one-thirty or so this morning and we think the murderer was riding a motorcycle. Not much to go on right now, but the way I figure it, he was a pretty bad hombre and someone that bad has a reputation. You got anybody up there that might fit the profile?"

There was silence on the other end of the line.

Wally waited for a long moment, then said softly, "Sergeant Hankins?"

There was a cough and a reply, "Uh…Sheriff Sand…I'm going to transfer you to Lieutenant Borden. I think you two should talk." There were no further words from the desk sergeant. Wally heard a light clicking sound and then another voice answered the phone. "Lieutenant Borden."

Wally began his narrative again, "Hello Lieutenant. This is Sheriff Sand in Meacon. Sergeant Hankins thought we needed to talk to each other."

"Oh?"

"Me and Marshal Tate have a double homicide in Vera. We suspect a biker, but we don't have a lot of information right now. We've got deputies looking for witnesses, but outside of two murders in a bar around one-thirty this morning, I don't have too much to share."

Wally heard the Lieutenant's voice turn serious as it answered, "So…you thought someone with enough gall to kill two people would have a history, right?"

"Sort of…yeah."

"Sheriff…I've been looking for a blonde headed neo-Nazi scumbag since yesterday afternoon. I've got a dead Hispanic gang member up here and two of his friends tell me that he was shot by a man named Vince Amirah. Vince is also known as *Crank*, and I assure you that he didn't get the name from drag racing."

Wally sat up straighter as he asked, "Do you have an APB out on him?"

"Nah. The two witnesses are less than reliable, so I'm just trying to locate him and bring him in for questioning."

Wally spun in his office chair and rested his right elbow on the top of the desk as he held the phone to his ear. He asked the next obvious question, "I don't suppose you have a picture of the asshole, do you?"

"You want his latest mug shots?"

"Just as fast as you can get them to me."

"Give me about ten minutes and then check your fax machine."

Andrew Span was running entirely on adrenalin and caffeine. He had driven over dirt roads most of the night and now he was driving over dirt trails and dodging huge rocks, large cactus, scruffy trees and brush, and trying not to let his pickup fall into one of many ravines. He had six other vehicles helping him search for Hershel, not including Mister Elkins, and each pickup had two people in the cab. His wife was at his side and she had refused to stay at home while he continued searching this day.

The faint dirt trail that he drove across headed southeast and it was mostly rocks, brush, and small ravines crossing his path. It was a bumpy ride and he jostled himself and his wife so much that they removed their seatbelts. Every time that they hit a bump, the belt cut into their waist and his wife groaned. He simply felt that it was stupid to be strapped in while he was trying to scout unfamiliar landscape. He would make his way to a high piece of land; pause for a moment, then look around, and drive slowly downhill. It was a time consuming process, and the truth of the matter was that the Elkins range was fifteen thousand acres in size. That made it almost twenty-three and a half square miles. He and his wife were currently twelve miles south of their son's mangled body and they were slowly moving further away.

Joe and Elliot had untied their horses and they were both mounted in the saddle. Just as they nudged their horses towards the rag marker they had left behind, Elliot had another thought to share with Joe. He raised his voice because Joe was riding behind him. "Hey, Joe!"

"What?"

"You know how we decided that Mister Watkins was getting all of us to see if we could find footprints of the wolf and then go tell him where they are later this afternoon?"

"Yeah…we covered that subject already."

Elliot stopped his horse and motioned to Joe, "Get up here beside me. I'm tired of yelling."

Joe eased his mount beside Elliot, then they both rode side by side as they talked. Elliot continued, "I don't think we have the right notion, Joe."

"What do you mean?"

"Well…it's pretty obvious that he wants us to see if there is any evidence of the wolf so he can narrow the search. That much is plain. But…"

"But what?"

"I just realized that all of us are assigned pastures that are fairly close to the Ranch House. Did you notice that?"

"Not so close." Joe argued. "It took us two hours by horseback to get to this field."

Elliot continued, "Yeah…and this is one of Mister Watkin's best pastures. Not a lot of grass, mind you…but lots of watering holes and feed troughs."

Joe sighed, "Get to the point."

Elliot adjusted the brim of his hat as he continued, "So…I'm just thinking…I'll bet Mister Watkins wants to find out how close to his main property this wolf is hunting. I'll bet he wants to make sure his new herds are gonna be safe and that's the primary reason we're out here looking for footprints."

Joe's nose itched so he was scratching it as he replied, "You know what I think?"

"What?"

"I think you think too much."

At one-thirty in the afternoon, Allie received a radio call from a deputy marshal by the name of Tom Weavers. "Meacon base, this is Vera unit four."

Allie answered, "Go ahead unit four."

"I have three confirmed sightings. I say again, three. All sightings along highway nineteen."

Allie replied, "Roger unit four. Do you have mile marker locations and people's names?"

"Roger base. I'm twelve miles north of Meacon. Will deliver info now."

Allie answered the deputy, "Roger unit four. See you in fifteen." She made a quick note in the log book and removed her headset. She walked quickly to Wally's office and looked inside. He was staring at some papers on top of his desk so she quietly spoke to him, "Sheriff...deputy Weavers is on his way here. He has witness information about your biker."

Wally glanced up at his clerk and smiled, "What's his ETA?"

She replied, "Fifteen minutes. More or less."

"Thanks." He replied and returned his attention to his paperwork. Allie went to her desk and put the headphones on again.

Wally had received a fax from Lieutenant Borden almost two hours earlier and he was still trying to digest the enormity of the rap sheet. The man had been implicated in several armed robberies; he had served time in jail for both larceny and drug distribution, and he was suspected of smuggling illegal aliens. Wally's attention kept returning to the smuggling aspect of the rap sheet.

He'd study the mug shots for a while, and then read the long list of crimes associated with the man, and then shake his head before returning to the part that mentioned smuggling. It took Wally a long time to realize why that fact was important, but he finally figured it out. He tossed the stack of papers on top of his desk and leaned back in his chair. He muttered out loud, "Mexico. He has ties to Mexico. That's where he's headed."

He stood up from his chair and stretched his arms. He took a deep breath; picked up three sheets of paper off of his desk and made his way to Allie. She saw him standing next to her desk, so she removed the headphones and looked up at him. He simply said, "Can you fax these to the Border Patrol?"

Allie answered as she picked up the papers, "Sure. Got a

message to go with them?"

"Yeah. Wanted for questioning regarding a double murder in Pinal County."

Allie moved quickly to the fax machine; picked up a pre-printed cover sheet; scribbled a note on the sheet, and then placed the stack of papers into the fax machine feeder tray. She dialed a phone number and watched the first page load into the machine, and then moved back to her desk. Wally had already gone back to his office.

Jo Ann was at home. She was putting food in the pantry and the refrigerator when she heard the phone ring. She was always anxious when Wally was engaged in serious matters, so she left the refrigerator door wide open as she raced to answer the telephone located in their living room.

She snatched the receiver out of the cradle and spoke into it as fast as she had put it to her ear. "Hello."

She breathed a sigh of relief when she heard Wally's voice say, "Hi, hon."

"Wally! How's everything going?"

He sounded stressed as he replied, "Slow. Too slow. I was calling to see if you could bring me a bite of lunch."

She glanced at the clock on the wall and replied, "Wally! It's almost two o'clock! You haven't eaten lunch yet?"

He sounded apologetic as he answered, "Been busy here, hon."

"You want me to fix you something, or grab you a burger?"

"Burger."

She laughed softly as she said, "Figures. See you as quick as I can."

She put the phone receiver back into the cradle and returned to the kitchen. She shut the refrigerator door, grabbed her purse off of the kitchen table, and then left the house to get Wally some lunch.

Jeff and Bob had walked their horses across Jeff's land from his Ranch House to the far northwest corner of his property line. It was two-thirty in the afternoon and they had not discovered any signs of wolf tracks what-so-ever. When it had come time for them to eat a bite of lunch, they ate sandwiches (supplied by Jeff's cook) while still in the saddle.

They were tired and aggravated and not very inclined to make conversation. They had investigated two plateaus and although they found four recesses, they found no signs of any animals living in or around them. Jeff stopped his horse and patted it on the shoulder as he spoke to Bob. "We need to head home. If we hurry, we can make it before sundown."

Bob sounded disappointed as he replied, "Yeah. I guess we better do that."

Jeff simply turned his horse's head towards the main house and let his horse set his own pace to return home. Both horses quickly realized that they were through working for the day, so they moved at a very fast walk with visions of grain playing in their minds. Both men let their reins go slack so the horses could control the direction and speed.

Deputy Marshal Tom Weavers and Deputy Jesse Blount was sitting in Wally's office. They both had their notebooks open and they were comparing notes. Jesse had been called back to the office shortly before eleven o'clock that morning. Police Chief Brigswall had organized a foot search for the beast that had killed Greg Morris and Wally didn't want Jesse to be part of that type of hunt. Besides, Jesse wasn't dressed for such a venture. He could be the following morning if called upon to be so adorned, but for this day, his assistance to the Papago was nothing more than an offer.

Jesse had spent the rest of the morning and the afternoon trying to find anyone who may have seen a lone biker ride through town during the wee hours of the morning. He had not located a single soul that had any information in that regard.

Tom Weavers, on the other hand, had three individuals that gave verbal testimony about seeing a man riding a motorcycle headed for Meacon.

Wally was listening to Tom recite his notes, "First sighting was ten miles south of Vera. A young man by the name of Chris Jones spotted a motorcycle traveling south at around 2:00 or 2:30 AM."

Wally interrupted, "What was he doing up at two in the morning?"

"Says he was checking on his chickens. Heard them squawking so he went outside to investigate."

Wally nodded and asked Tom to continue.

"Second sighting was twenty miles north of Meacon. Rider was seen by a mister and misses Jackson." Tom quickly added, "Both of them work the early shift at the munitions factory. They were getting into their car when the bike passed. He said he noticed it because the engine was exceptionally loud, and it was unusual for a motorcycle to be on the road that time of day."

Wally agreed, "He's right. Not unheard of, but unusual."

Tom didn't wait before he continued, "Last sighting was five miles north of town. The young boy I talked to said it was three thirty this morning when the motorcycle passed his farmhouse."

Wally squinted his eyes, "Three thirty?"

Tom explained, "He said his father makes him milk all three of the family cows and he has to start before three thirty each morning."

Jesse asked, "Why that early in the morning."

Tom explained. "School. He milks all year round, but when the school year starts, he has to be done before the school bus gets to his house."

Wally couldn't help but smile. He asked Tom, "Why did the boy notice the motorcycle?"

Tom explained, "Loud muffler and he said he was jealous. Said if he had a motorcycle, he'd bug out early in the morning too."

Wally turned to Jesse. "You found nobody in town that noticed a motorcycle this morning?"

"No. And I should have. The two early shifts at the factory start at four and five, so people are up and about. If he had passed through town, someone would have seen him."

Wally sat silently for a moment. Jesse and Tom saw Wally stiffen his posture and then he immediately spoke up, "The son-of-a-bitch turned off Highway Nineteen! He's taken Farm Road 1380 towards the Papago Reservation! Son-of-a-bitch!"

Jesse was on his feet immediately and headed for his squad car. Tom Weavers was right behind him. Wally stomped to Allie's desk and said, "Call the Ohdam Station! Tell Marc to get hold of Chief Brigswall and get some men looking for a blonde motorcycle rider somewhere along FM 1380!" Wally sounded frustrated as he half-shouted, "The sum-bitch is probably halfway to Mexico by now!"

Jo Ann was about to walk through the front door of the Sheriff's Office, but she had to pause and hold the door open so that Jesse and Tom could rush outside to their vehicles. She watched the two run to their squad cars and then went into the lobby. She saw Wally standing at Allie's desk and she heard the words *sum bitch*! She held up a paper bag so Wally could see it and asked sheepishly, "Bad timing for a burger?"

Gary Elkins was in his small pickup truck that had four-wheel drive. It was close to four o'clock in the afternoon and he sat on top of a valley rim at the northern end of his property. He was looking across the landscape and his attention had been drawn to the sight of circling buzzards. He sat behind the steering wheel of his truck and shook his head as he muttered aloud, "God…I hope not. I really hope not!"

He put his pickup into first gear and eased off of the valley rim and steered it around a jutting set of rocks. He was moving less than five miles an hour as he steered his way around bushes and cactus. The closer he got to the circling buzzards, the more he wished that it was someone else that had spotted the scavengers. Once again he tried to tell himself, "Maybe the boys just hurt." Then he shook his head and admitted to himself, "Buzzards don't circle anything alive." He sniffled and choked as he muttered, "Please God…let it be one of my cows." He didn't notice the tear form in his right eye as he spotted the four wheeler and half-shouted, "Shit!"

He was close enough to the body to see the buzzards, but he couldn't see exactly what they were feasting upon. He had his pickup in neutral and the engine was idling as he sat behind the steering wheel simply watching the movements of the buzzards.

After a very long moment, he turned his ignition key to the off position and gently placed the transmission shift lever into reverse. He was sniffling as he opened the driver's door and eased himself outside of the vehicle. The buzzards jumped to their left and right out of agitation and a few of them squawked their displeasure. Gary forced himself to take steps towards the ATV and his gait was very awkward. His arms hung limply to his sides as he made his way to the scene of the accident. Somewhere between his pickup and the four wheeler he told himself that the boy had had an accident and he just needed to just check to see how bad he was hurt.

Ten feet from the four wheeler he stopped walking and started crying. He had scared the buzzards away and he could plainly see that the body and head had been separated. The boy's torso was mangled and it was missing some limbs and that sight made Gary's head swoon, along with turning his knees so weak that he couldn't stand. He fell to his knees and muttered, "Oh…that poor child…that…poor child."

Gary couldn't pull himself upright. He turned on his knees away from the torn and mauled body of Hershel Span and then crawled towards his small pickup. Twenty feet later, and ten yards away from his vehicle, he coughed and spit phlegm upon the ground. He brought one knee up to his chest and rested his right elbow upon it. He forced himself to take deep breaths and he tried to clear his mind of the vision that he'd just seen.

It took almost a full minute, but he was regaining his composure enough to start rationalizing what his next responsibility was to the situation. He used the arm resting on his knee to force himself upright and then he staggered to the small truck. He leaned against the hood with his elbows and looked at the open land in front of him. He had a sudden thought. "I need to cover the...body." He tried to think of something that he might have in his pickup to cover the dead boy with, but he was having trouble remembering. His mind said, "Blanket... no...not in the truck." He suddenly stiffened and said out loud, "Poncho."

He moved to the passenger side door and opened it. He pulled a strap/latch on the back of the passenger seat and the backrest fell forward. He grabbed a plastic bag that was tucked under the back seat on the floorboard and tore it open. He flung the bag aside and inspected the rain poncho. It was dark gray and made of very thick and very flexible plastic. He grunted softly and muttered, "This will do." Then he remembered that there was a first-aid kit under the passenger seat. He was still muttering out loud as he said, "Oh, thank God Fanny made me buy that damn expensive first-aid kit! Thank the Lord for that!" He reached under the seat and pulled out a flat plastic box with snap type clips holding the lid closed. He flipped the two clips and sighed with relief when he opened the top.

His eyes fell upon a red aluminum flare gun and five flare shells lying beside it. His next thought was, "I hope I can figure out how to use it." He snatched the red pistol out of the case and pried a flare shell out of its clip. He inspected the handgun and saw a lever on the side, so he pressed it. The barrel of the piece fell forward and Gary shoved the shell into its breech. He snapped the barrel back into position and pointed it towards the sky. His small prayer was one word. "Please." He pulled the trigger.

There was a slight popping noise before the projectile

made a high-pitched whistling sound, and when the flare had reached its zenith, it exploded with a very loud bang. A mass of brightly colored chaff hung in the air for a very long moment. Gary was instantly relieved. He muttered his thanks as he said, "Thank you, Lord."

He took the poncho into his folded arms and held it close to his chest. He then started stumbling towards the butchered body of Hershel Span.

Jesse was driving his squad car along the dusty ruts that made up Farm Road 1380 and he was creating a lingering cloud of dust behind him. Deputy Marshal Weavers was behind Jesse and he had to keep a space of about two-hundred yards between his vehicle and Jesse's in order to be able to properly see the road.

Most Farm Roads in Arizona are either gravel topped or pavement, but FM 1380 was not one of them. It was basically a trail leading from Meacon to the Papago Indian Reservation and the only travelers were usually local residents. Once the road entered the Papago Indian Reservation, it became a gravel topped passage called the Gila River Route. The Gila River Route was fairly close to the Ohdam Station, so when Allie notified the Papago Dispatcher named Marc, he was able to dispatch the daytime deputy named Geoff.

As Jesse and Tom drove southwards on FM 1380, Geoff was rushing northward. Because Geoff was physically closer to the point of attack of biker Vince Amirah, he spotted the parked Harley on the side of the road and coasted to a stop directly in front of it. When he was completely stopped, he noticed the cloud of dust on the dirt road moving his direction and surmised that it was his friend Jesse headed his way. He took his radio microphone and called to Jesse, "This is Geoff, is that you making dust, Jesse."

Jesse snorted before he picked up his transmitter. He said out loud, "The Papago ain't much for correct radio procedures." Jesse answered, "Yes. Where are you?"

"Parked next to a dusty Harley Davidson. Doesn't look like anyone's around."

Jesse immediately tensed and he replied, "Geoff! Consider the owner armed and dangerous!"

Geoff answered almost nonchalantly, "I'll load my shotgun, but…like I said…the bike looks abandoned."

Jesse answered quickly, "Can you hold position until I get there?"

Geoff then sounded rather happy as he replied, "I kinda hoped you'd say that."

Jesse grinned and then keyed his microphone and said, "Tom? You get that?"

Tom Weavers answered, "Roger. Right behind you."

Allie was sitting in her chair very rigidly and listening to every syllable of the conversation. She removed the headset from her ear and yelled to Wally, who was in his office with Jo Ann. "Sheriff Sand! You need to come here and listen to this!"

Wally knew Allie wouldn't call out like she did unless there was something important or urgent that needed his attention. He didn't respond verbally, but stood up quickly and walked briskly to her desk. Jo Ann followed him out of curiosity.

Allie turned her headset off and removed the male plug connector from the radio console. That action sent the radio transmissions to the speakers and filled the room with chatter between three deputies.

Everyone heard Jesse announce his arrival, "Geoff! You loaded?"

Geoff answered, "Shotgun and sidearm!"

Tom Weaver's voice came across the speakers, "Jesse. Let me pull between you two before anyone gets out."

Jesse simply said, "Roger." Then he spoke to Allie, "Base this is unit three."

Allie replied, "This is base, go ahead."

"I'm at mile marker twenty-four on FM 1380, over."

"Roger unit three. Copy mile marker twenty-four.

What's the sitcon? Over." (Situation/Condition)

"Found parked Harley Davidson matching description of suspects' vehicle, over."

"Roger, unit three. Unit one wants to know if suspect is in sight, over."

"Negative. Putting officers in position to investigate, over."

"Roger. Base standing by."

All of the police cars had their engines stopped and the dust from the tires had dissipated. Jesse opened his car door and the other two men did so simultaneously. They all stepped outside of their vehicles cautiously with a weapon held at the ready.

Jesse realized immediately that the scene was entirely too quiet and the abandoned motorcycle was unnerving. He saw that there were a group of small trees next to a small gulley, and that stood out as a possible place of concealment. He motioned his two companions with his left hand and they moved away from him and left him in the center position. He began to advance towards the motorcycle slowly with his pistol pointing at the trees.

Geoff had his shotgun pointed at the gulley and Tom had his pistol pointed in the same direction. Geoff's line of sight was much different than Jesse or Tom's. He could actually see slightly beyond the trees, while Jesse's sight was blocked by the motorcycle and Tom could only see a clump of rocks and dirt in front of the gulley.

Suddenly Geoff called out, "Hold! Got a body!"

Everyone froze in place. Jesse yelled out, "Talk to me, Geoff!"

"Definitely a body! No movement!"

Jesse took a breath and yelled, "Police Officers! Come out with your hands over your head!"

Everyone waited for the standard three seconds to see if there was a response. Jesse called to Geoff again, "Talk to me, Geoff!"

"No movement! Nothing!"

Jesse hated this part. He took another deep breath and gave the order, "You two move to the flank. Follow me to the tree line!"

The three men approached the shadows of the small trees very cautiously and slowly with their weapons pointed at the spot indicated by Geoff. Jesse stopped walking when he could see the body and he knew immediately that the man was dead. It was lying in a twisted heap and he saw a severed arm not far from the torso. He dropped his weapon to point at the ground and spoke loud enough for his partners to hear him, "It's clear! Suspect is deceased!"

Geoff and Tom lowered their weapons and approached Jesse. Geoff looked upon the mangled body of Vince Amirah and commented with a voice that was barely audible. "Armed and dangerous? More like dead and dismembered. Looks like your fucking wolf has struck again, Jesse."

CHAPTER EIGHT

Gary Elkins was leaning against the tailgate of his small pickup truck and staring off into the distance. He was trying to discover any sign of anyone answering his emergency flare, and he was very concerned that several minutes had passed and he had heard nothing or seen any signs of anyone approaching. He had his arms folded and he sighed as he decided that he had better fire one more projectile.

The flare gun was on his pickup's passenger seat and the four remaining flare shells were still in the first aid kit, which was still on the floorboard and lay open. He opened the passenger side door, took his flare gun in hand and loaded another shell. He walked to the back of the pickup and faced towards the south. He pointed the pistol towards the sky and pulled the trigger.

The muffled popping noise was followed by a high-pitched whistle, and then he heard the loud booming sound overhead. He didn't look up. He knew that the flare chaff would be hanging in the air, so he lowered the pistol and watched for a sign that someone had noticed the signal.

It was very faint at first. The sound of a car's engine was coming from the south. He looked at the desert land stretched out before him and squinted his eyes in an effort to shield them from the heat waves dancing across the sand. His attention focused on a small dust cloud near the horizon. At first he thought it was just a small dust devil, (sand whirl) but it grew larger as the sound of an approaching vehicle grew louder.

Gary grew anxious as he kept his eyes riveted on the approaching dust ball. To him it was moving entirely too slow, but he had to admit to himself that whoever was coming had to drive cautiously. Just like he had to do beforehand.

He glanced at his right hand and saw that he was still holding the pistol and he considered sending up another flare, but realized that he would only be wasting a precious signal shell if he did so. Someone was coming and they would eventually get there.

Fifteen miles north of Hershel Span's body was the body of Vince Amirah. Like Gary Elkins had done, Jesse and his two deputy helpers had covered the body with a rubber blanket and they had put out wooden stakes with crime scene tape cordoning off the scene of the crime. Deputy Geoff was dispatched to Ohdam Station because that's where Wally's High Resolution camera was located. Jesse and Tom were guarding the scene and waiting for the arrival of the County Coroner and Wally.

The county coroner had spent the day working with the two bodies found at the Vera Bar, so he was tired and somewhat agitated when he received the call concerning the body close to the Papago Reservation. None-the-less, he gathered his helpers and made one of them drive him to the reported position.

Jo Ann was still at the courthouse when Wally had obtained the information regarding his suspect, so he was gathering his investigative kits and preparing to leave when Jo Ann spoke quietly to him. "Wally?"

He was opening plastic cases and checking equipment when he replied, "Yeah?"

Jo Ann took a breath and said, "Hon...I know you're stressed, and I know that you handle stress better than anyone, but..."

Wally stopped what he was doing and looked at his wife. He replied, "But?"

"Honey, I don't like the color of your skin. It seems...I don't know...kinda *jaundice* like."

Wally was stooped over one of the open kits that was on top of his desk, so he stood up straight and asked, "Jaundice?

You mean…yellowish?"

Jo Ann was very serious as she replied, "More greenish, hon."

Wally closed the lid of his test kit and picked it up with his right hand. He simply replied, "I don't have time right now, hon."

She smiled and replied, "I didn't think so. Come here and let me feel your forehead."

He obeyed, but he was obviously anxious to leave. She put her palm on his forehead for a second and said, "You have a fever. Not much of one, but you definitely have a fever."

Wally replied, "I have to go, hon."

"Yeah. I know. But I'm making you a doctor's appointment for tomorrow."

He leaned forward and gave her a quick kiss and then walked out of his office. As he passed Allie's desk he remarked, "I'll need you to stay late today, Allie."

She answered as he walked towards the front door, "I already figured that out."

The front door of the courthouse closed behind Wally as Jo Ann appeared beside Allie's desk. She remarked to her friend, "Men! I swear!"

Allie looked at Jo Ann and half-smiled as she said, "Hey…I need to thank you for the advice about introverts."

Jo Ann stared at Allie for a second, then realized what she had said, "Oh…you mean Bob…you and he are…"

"Dating" Allie answered quickly.

"Wow. You cornered and captured him, huh?"

"He's…very…compatible to me."

Jo Ann turned her head and looked at the front door as she replied, "I know the feeling."

Both women saw two new deputies walking through the entrance door, and Allie said to Jo Ann, "Ah…that's the Casa Grande deputies. Excuse me a second while I give them their assignments."

Gary Elkins was beginning to feel a sense of relief. He could now see two pickups moving towards him and although he had no idea who the people might be, he knew that they were part of the group working with the Span's. His only dread was the fact that he had to tell them about the boy's horrific demise. He also knew that once he had shown these people what had happened, the Sheriff's Office had to be contacted.

While the two pickups made their way towards him, he pondered that dilemma and thought to himself, "I'm more than half of an hour...no...almost an hour away from the house. I have no way to contact Fanny from out here...I'll have to drive to the house and call the Sheriff." He considered that predicament for a moment and then made himself a vow. "I could be hurt out here or one of my hands could have an accident...I need to set up a two-way radio so Fanny can talk to me if I need her to."

The two pickups coasted to a stop in front of him, and four people got out of the cabs.

Wally had just turned onto FM 1380 when he heard the radio transmission from Allie, "Base to unit six."

There was a long pause before Wally heard, "This is unit six."

Allie then asked, "Unit six, what's your twenty?" (Location)

There was another long pause as Bob had to question Jeff as their approximate location. Finally, Bob answered, "An hour and a half away from the Watkins Ranch house. The twin plateaus are about a mile to our right."

Allie looked at a topographical map spread out over her desk and spoke to Bob once again, "Roger, six. You're in the Watkins' northwest pasture. Can you tell me which end?"

This time, the response was quicker. Bob replied, "Close to the north end."

Allie studied the map again and called to him, "How

close would you be to FM 1518?"

Another pause as Bob looked at Jeff for an answer, then he replied, "Four miles."

Allie was smiling as she replied, "Roger that, six. I need you to make your way to FM 1518. I'll have a unit pick you up in twenty minutes. Over."

All of a sudden Bob realized what was going on. He turned to Jeff and simply said, "Jeff?'

Jeff replied as he turned his horse northward, "Tell her we'll be at the feed troughs!"

Bob spoke into the radio, "Base, I'll be at the feed troughs next to the road. ETA, ten to fifteen minutes." He and Jeff sharply kicked their horses in the ribs and they began a slow run towards FM 1518.

Wally was smiling as he drove towards Jesse's location, "Good girl, Allie! Good girl!"

Two men and two women had gathered around Gary Elkins. He nervously explained to the people that the Span boy was dead and that he had covered the body. He also made it a point to tell them that they shouldn't venture too close as the Sheriff would certainly want nothing to be disturbed.

A young woman clung to a young man who was obviously her husband and spoke to Gary, "We'll stay with the body. Are you going to go call the Sheriff?"

Gary answered, "It'll take me almost an hour to get to the house, but I'll try to make it quicker."

The woman's husband then said, "We have walkie-talkies, but their range is less than five miles. We don't know where Andrew or Melissa are right now."

His wife offered, "They headed south from Mister Elkins' house, so they're probably a long way from here."

The other woman spoke up, "We...we can head south and try to get them on the walkie-talkies, but...it's getting late. Surely they'll be headed for Mister Elkins' house soon."

The first woman spoke directly to Gary and asked,

"What do you think, Mister Elkins?"

Gary cleared his throat as he replied, "I think you better try to find them. They need to know about this as soon as possible. Meanwhile, I'll get to the phone as fast as I can."

Gary took the first aid kit and the flare gun out of his truck cab and gave them to the first couple that would remain on site. The woman took the kit and gun without comment. Gary simply got into his vehicle, started the engine, and then drove towards his house. The other couple were immediately behind him and making their way towards the south.

The two horses were sweaty and breathing hard when Jeff and Bob arrived at the feed troughs. Bob dismounted immediately and handed his horse's reins to Jeff. Jeff remained in the saddle and said, "I'll wait here until your ride arrives."

Bob heard the sound of a car's engine as he remarked to Jeff. "Sounds like you won't have to wait long." He untied his rifle from the saddle straps and said, "I don't know if I need this or not, but I'll take it with me. Along with the radio."

Jeff replied, "I'll get the horses home and I'll make the kids put your other rifles in the saddle house for safe keeping." He thought for a moment, then asked, "What about your Jeep?"

Bob considered that for a second and replied, "I don't know. Let me ask." He put the radio to his mouth and pressed the button on the side, "Base this is six."

Allie answered, "Go ahead six."

"My Jeep is at the Watkins Ranch House. Do I need it brought to Meacon?"

Allie answered quickly, "Roger that, six. Have someone bring it to the courthouse."

Bob looked up at Jeff and Jeff simply replied, "You mind if one of the kids take it to town?"

The police car was coming to a stop on the other side of the fence where Jeff and Bob were talking. Bob quickly asked, "Can I choose the driver?"

Jeff replied, "I was going to let Becky do it. She's the

toughest."

"She's the one I was going to ask for." Bob leaned his rifle against a wooden fence post and pushed a barbed wire strand downwards so he could work his way through the fence without cutting himself or his clothing.

Jeff watched him pick up his rifle and get into the police car with the deputy, and then he turned his horse towards his house and headed home again.

Wally was standing next to Jesse and they were both discussing the scene. Jesse had his notepad in hand as he was sharing his thoughts with Wally, "He was attacked from behind. Footprints showed him being pushed forward and I have to tell you...that's one big bastard lying there. Our wolf has to be a monster to knock a man down his size and then tear him up like that."

Wally nodded slowly and asked, "You found a gun?"

"Forty-five. It was six feet from the body. I've bagged it. The marker number on the ground for it is number sixteen."

Wally walked slowly around the scene, and kept himself on the outside of the established circle marked with yellow plastic tape. Jesse stayed at his side and watched the Sheriff studying the scene.

The body was covered and there was another smaller plastic sheet laying a few feet from the dead man. Wally pointed at it and asked, "That the arm?"

Jesse spoke with a slightly nervous sound in his voice, "Sheriff, that arm was bit through and ripped from his body. I can't imagine the force that it took to do that."

Wally paused to consider the words, then took a few more steps. He pointed to the motorcycle and asked, "Have you called for a wrecker?"

Jesse answered, "Tom made the call. The wrecker's coming from Vera."

Both Jesse and Wally turned to look at the dirt road and saw an approaching police unit. Wally said, "Ah...here's our game warden." He then turned to Jesse and said, "I'm going to have him wait here until the coroner arrives. He knows the drill. My camera should be here in a minute, so he's going to have to take his photographs and you'll have to take the crime scene pictures."

Jesse understood perfectly. He asked Wally anyway, "You want me to take the film to Tucson, don't you?"

"Just as fast as you can get it there. Along with that pistol. I'm sorry. You'll have to put some overtime in on this one, Jesse." (There were crime labs in both Tucson and Phoenix, so Wally was sending his evidence to be processed at the one in Tucson.)

Wally watched Bob step outside of the police cruiser and then he heard another vehicle approaching from the north. He sighed and remarked, "And here comes Geoff."

At five-forty-five this afternoon, Allie's phone rang. Jo Ann was still at the Sheriff's office, and she had merely been talking with Allie before she had to leave and go home. She had let time slip away from her, and she was about to excuse herself when the phone rang.

She listened to Allie speak, but she couldn't hear the other person on the line. Allie answered, "Sheriff's Office, this is Allie Thompson, how may I help you."

Jo Ann saw Allie's face and shoulders suddenly sag and she knew something bad had just been reported. She heard Allie say, "Oh my God!"

A few seconds passed and she heard Allie say, "Oh my God, Mister Elkins! Can you tell me where you found him? I'll need to contact the Sheriff! He's out on a call right now!"

Jo Ann saw Allie grab a pencil as she tucked the phone receiver between her shoulder and ear, and she started scribbling on her desk blotter. She spoke as she wrote, "Uh-huh...uh-huh...got it...I need to pinpoint it, though." Allie grabbed the topographical map and had it in front of her as she spoke again, "Okay...north end of your property...I need a prominent feature…I show a small plateau and a rock formation…which one is the closest?" She moved her finger along the map surface and held it at the rock formation. "Rocks…gulley…got it!"

Allie glanced at Jo Ann and whispered, "Hershel Span!" She then spoke to Gary Elkins, "Mister Elkins…has Mister Span and Melissa been informed? You don't know? Oh…I see. No…no…I'll contact Sheriff Sand now…please stay by the phone for us, okay?" She put the phone receiver down softly and whispered, "Damn!"

Jo Ann watched Allie copy a grid number off of the map onto a blank space on her log book, then Allie used the radio to call Wally, "Unit one, this is base, over."

Wally was talking to Bob while they were close to the crime scene tape, but the car radio was on the vehicle's external speaker so they heard Allie call. Wally looked towards his car and muttered, "Now what?"

Allie waited a few seconds and then called again, "Unit one…this is base…pick up, please, over."

A few seconds later, Allie and Jo Ann heard Wally, "This is unit one, over."

Andrew Span and his wife were dejectedly returning to the Elkins Ranch House and they were almost five miles away when their walkie-talkie sputtered to life. A crackly voice filled the cab of their pickup and they heard, "Andy! Melissa! Please pick up!"

Melissa snatched the small hand-held unit off of the seat and replied, "This is Melissa!"

The voice answered, "Melissa! Where are you?"

Melissa had to answer honestly, "I don't really know. Is this Judy?"

"This is Judy…are you headed back in?"

"Yeah…we're on our way…don't know how long we'll be, but we're headed for the Elkins house…why?"

Judy's husband grabbed her hand that was about to key the walkie-talkie and he shook his head at her. She understood immediately as she spoke to Melissa again, "Me and John are almost at the Elkins house. We'll see you when you get here."

It was six-thirty in the late afternoon. The beast was lapping water out of the mossy stream and he had his ears alert for any unusual or interesting sounds. He was thirsty, so he was lapping loudly at the surface of the trickling tributary.

He stopped drinking when he heard the sudden flutter of wings and turned his head towards the south end of the cut. It was the dead end of his ravine and he'd explored it before, so he knew that some small birds used it for a place to roost and lay eggs. They were of no particular concern to him. He had tried chasing birds when he was much younger, but the irritating little creatures always flew away before he could get close enough to possibly sample a bite. He lowered his head and drank some more.

The chasm where he made his residence had grown dark from the shadows of the sinking sun, and this was his que to leave the confines of the cut and go hunting. He stretched his front legs and leaned back on his hind quarters for a second, then shook himself to remove any dust or twigs from his fur. He sniffed the air and looked towards the sky, then trotted his way towards the north end of the gulch.

The entrance into the gully was a wide and gentle sloping path, whereas his den was located at the narrowest portion of the gorge. His instincts told him that it was a perfect lair when he discovered it, and so far his instincts had proven him to be correct. He had managed to feed himself each and every night since he had moved into his refuge and he didn't have to share his space with any other creatures.

At first, there had been a few stray wolves and wild dogs about, but they had all vacated his territory and left him free to hunt without competition. It was a good place to live. He stopped at the mouth of his ravine and sat on his haunches. He used his ears once again to try and hear anything that would indicate a possible meal. After a long pause, he grunted, and then stood up on all fours.

Far off towards the north, he knew that there were strange dwellings and strange creatures gathered in abundance. He had no particular designation to give to the creatures, but he'd killed them and eaten them, and in spite of being sparse in meat, the creatures weren't that bad of a meal. Antelope and bovine were his favorites, but they seemed to be scarce most of the time.

He looked towards the direction of Meacon and remained silent and still as if he were considering something important. Suddenly, he sniffed the air and made a soft woof noise, and then trotted up a long sloping hill headed northward.

Wally had left the site where Vince Amirah lay dead and awaiting the arrival of the coroner. He was traveling to the Elkins' Ranch and he was frustrated that he'd have to drive almost all of the way back to Meacon before he could cut across the desert and make his way to the gravel road leading to Gary and Fanny's house. He had both hands on the steering wheel as he was traveling over soft sand and he was driving slightly faster than would be considered a safe speed.

He had left Jesse and Bob behind to take pictures of the crime scene and he put Tom Weavers in charge of keeping the area secured. He was very stressed by the enormity of all of the death surrounding a beast that he had recently discarded as a simple game warden issue. He cursed himself for that oversight and sped his vehicle up slightly.

Before he had left Bob and Jesse, he had instructed Allie to take Bob's Jeep to him as soon as it was delivered to the courthouse. Allie had called Horace Fannin and told him to report to work early so she could comply with his orders. As she waited for the Jeep, she grew a little anxious and slightly thrilled at being used in an official capacity outside of her desk job. Wally had never called upon her to be part of an investigation before, but she quickly surmised that Wally had never been faced with this many deaths at one time before, either. He was short-handed and she was an employee of the Sheriff's Department. He was simply making the best use of his personnel under trying circumstances.

At five minutes to seven, Becky came walking through the courthouse front door and she had Bob's keys dangling from her right hand. Horace Fannin was already sitting at the dispatcher's desk when Allie saw Becky and quickly met her in the open lobby.

Becky was still dressed in her lineman's clothing with her sweat stained straw hat and she smiled at Allie as she handed her the keys. "Mister Watkins said to give you these as quick as I could."

Allie took the keys from her hand and said, "Thank you. Do you need a ride somewhere?"

Becky indicated the front door with the thumb of her right hand and said, "Nah...I got a ride with my friend Karen."

Allie smiled at Becky and said, "Thanks again. I need to get on my way, then."

Becky stopped her as she said, "Hey...it needs gas. I was gonna stop and fill it up, but Mister Watkins said to get it to you as quickly as I could."

Allie moved to the front door and pushed it open. Becky followed and Allie said to her as they left the building, "Thanks...I'll take care of it."

Wally had met a very angry Andrew Span and a very distraught Melissa Span at the home of `Gary and Fanny Elkins. It took all of Wally's interpersonal training and experience to convince Andrew to take his wife to the hospital and not go to the scene of the animal attack. She was obviously on the verge of a nervous breakdown, and she needed medical attention as quickly as possible.

While he was trying to console the man and his wife, two deputies from Casa Grande arrived at the Elkins' home. They had been dispatched by both Allie and Horace to assist with the investigation. They were chosen primarily because they had a four-wheel drive utility vehicle that would allow them to drive over rough terrain. Plus, their vehicle could carry some night lights and a small generator.

Wally's police car was a cruiser and unable to traverse the rough ground between the Elkins' house and the body of Hershel Span. Wally had to ride in the deputies' vehicle and leave his own car in Gary's front yard. Fanny made her husband drive his small pickup back to the accident scene so he could lead the deputies to the exact spot. It was very reasonable for Fanny to insist that her husband lead the officers because sunset that day was going to take place at seven-fourteen PM. It was ten minutes after seven when Gary started leading Wally and his deputies to the site of the boy's body.

Gary was very insistent about one thing. He was perfectly willing to take the officers to Hershel's body, but he wasn't going anywhere near the boy. He told Wally that he didn't even want his poncho back. Wally understood the man perfectly.

The beast was four miles north of his lair and he was sitting on top of a plateau while he looked at the distant glow of lights that was the town of Meacon. He was a little over ten miles from the town and that was nowhere near the people and the traffic for him to be able to hear or smell anything related to the town. The flickering glow if lights fascinated him, but it didn't lure him towards it. He was far more interested in locating a meal than satisfying a curious instinct.

He turned his attention to the west and sniffed the air. He woofed softly when he caught the faint scent of a bovine and stood up on all four of his legs. He tested the air again, and judged that the smell was quite a distance away, but definitely coming from the western direction. He bounded off of the plateau and made his way down the gentle slope and started trotting towards the scent.

He heard the lowing of cattle. It was still a very long distance away, but his keen ears heard the sounds of a small herd making their way towards a watering hole. Or so he reasoned in his mind. Water attracted game, so he naturally assumed that he had located some game animals headed for water.

What he had actually stumbled upon was a line of five milk cows and a bull slowly walking towards a barn that was near a farm house. They were trained to graze in the pasture during the day, and then return to the safety of the barn at night. They were trained by an elder gentleman who raised Jersey milk cows and Border Collies.

His name was Perry Vanhorn and he was retired from the munitions factory. He lived alone on a small one-hundred-acre farm where he grew field grasses for his herd and raised chickens for their eggs. The only reason that Perry had five milk cows was that he was a very religious man who donated the milk from his cows to several elder families that were members of his church. He did not milk his herd by hand. He was far too lazy for that. He had bought a small milking machine several years ago, and he had his herd trained so that they came in at night so he could have them milked within an hour's time after their arrival.

Getting cows to march into a barn every day wasn't much a chore, but to get them properly positioned so that the milking could be done, that was much trickier. That's where the Border Collies came into play. He had three of them, all females, that were very proficient at parking a milk cow into a wooden stall. All Perry had to do was close a wooden bar at the back of the stall and then hook up the milking cups to the cow's udders and let the machine do the work.

He collected the milk in two-and-a-half-gallon galvanized containers, which he placed directly into a walk-in refrigerator. The next morning, he took the containers to his friends' homes and exchanged the full ones for empty ones. He was always invited into the homes for coffee or tea and then provided with a half-hour or so of simple visitation. It pleased Perry to do this for his friends. He never charged them for the milk or asked them for any donations to help pay for the gasoline that he had to use in order to make his deliveries.

The cattle were not quite a half of a mile from the barn and the sun was sinking below the western horizon. Perry was cleaning the teat cups on his milking machine while his three dogs sat at the barn's entrance. They would wait there until they saw the line of cows appear at the corral, then they'd trot out to herd them into the barn. They had done this so many times that they didn't even bark at the cows in order to get them into the confines of the building and then into the stalls.

The beast launched his attack when he was a little under a quarter of a mile from the cows. He growled as he burst into a dead run and kicked puffs of dirt behind him as he took tremendously long strides towards the bovine. The bull heard the roar of the beast and bellowed loudly in response. The cows scattered off of the well-worn path and started snorting as they swished their tails excitedly.

The bull bellowed again and turned to face the charging beast. The scattered herd was two-hundred yards from the barn, and the three border collies started barking and racing towards the herd. Perry stood motionless inside of the barn and muttered aloud, "What in the name of tarnation?"

The bull bellowed again as the beast pounced upon his back and sank his teeth into the neck muscles. The cows had scattered in five different directions and they were all crying out in fear. The border collies had created a chorus of barks and howls as they raced to the aid of their charges.

The beast used his jaw muscles to sink his oversized canines into the bull's neck and one of them penetrated the spinal cord. The bull bellowed again as he dropped to his front knees. He kicked his hind legs at nothing but air and then rolled to the ground.

The beast released his bite from the bull and spun to face the charging dogs. He growled again and this time his growl was more of a roar and the sound made it to Perry's ears. Perry heard one of the dogs cry out in pain while the other two were barking and howling furiously.

Perry raced out of the barn and ran as fast as he could towards his house. His house was almost a hundred and twenty feet from the barn, so he didn't have far to run, but he was a man in his late sixties. He was not able to move at a fast clip.

As he burst through his front door, he flipped a light switch and dashed towards a double-barreled shotgun that he kept leaning against the far wall of his living room. There was a flashlight lying on a coffee table, so he snatched the flashlight and the shotgun into his hands and charged towards the open door again.

As he ran out of the house, he heard another dog yelp and then all he could hear was one of them barking at something. His mind shouted as he made his way towards the commotion, "Something's got my dogs! What in God's name has got my dogs?"

The last dog yelped and the night air became silent. Perry stopped running and turned on the flashlight. He walked nervously towards the place where he had heard his dogs either attacking something or getting attacked themselves. He tried calling to his pets, "Jen! Ranger Girl! Bolette!" He received no answer.

He pointed his flashlight along the dirt path and when the beam of light struck the beast in the face, a roaring shriek filled the air. Perry was twenty feet from a dark and shadowy creature with glowing eyes. The shock of seeing such a large creature made Perry drop the flashlight and he cried out as he pulled the shotgun into his shoulder, pointed it into the darkness and pulled both triggers.

Perry saw the muzzle flash the instant the gun's blast echoed around him. He heard the cry of a wounded animal, which immediately turned into a cry of an angry animal. He immediately wished that he had more shells to put in his shotgun.

He remained motionless as he heard the baying sounds of a snarling beast, which alternated between a wail and a yawp. The sounds were moving away from him and they were moving very rapidly. He started to breathe again when he could no longer hear whatever it was that he had shot.

He looked at his feet and saw the flashlight still shining a beam of light across the ground, so he picked it up and pointed it at the path again. He started crying as his light shown upon the torn carcasses of his beloved dogs and the dead body of his bull.

He wanted to grieve over his loss, but somewhere in the back of his mind, a sobering thought filled his brain. He spoke to himself, "You just shot something capable of killing a full grown bull and three dogs. You need to get your ass back into the house because you didn't kill it!" He paused for a second and then added, "Stupid!"

Allie pulled Bob's Jeep onto the side of the road behind the cruiser driven by Jesse. The Coroner's van was parked on her other side. She had the headlights on, even though it wasn't quite dark yet, so she switched them off before she turned the ignition key to the off position. She saw Jesse and Deputy Tom Weavers standing next to each other, but she didn't see Bob.

She left the keys in the ignition and stepped out of the Jeep and made her way cautiously towards Jesse and Tom. When she was only a few feet away from Jesse, she saw Bob kneeling next to an uncovered body and he was obviously taking some pictures. She averted her eyes and turned so that she could face Jesse without looking at the dead man.

She whispered a greeting, "Jesse...Tom..."

Jesse replied, "Hey Allie. I've got to head to Tucson as soon as Bob and the Coroner are done. You taking Bob to the Elkins' place?"

She whispered again, "Uh-huh."

Jesse teased her, "You don't have to whisper, Allie. The man's dead. You won't disturb him."

Allie felt like punching him in the arm, but she refrained as she replied, "Don't be an ass, Jesse."

She could hear Bob talking to the Coroner, but she couldn't make out any words. She folded her arms across her chest and spoke to Jesse again, "Is he gonna be much longer?"

Jesse shrugged as he replied, "I hope not."

The coroner was kneeling next to Bob and he waited for the game warden to snap two more pictures. He asked quietly when Bob was done, "You got a name for the animal that did this?"

Bob shook his head in the negative, then as he stood slowly up he had a thought. He asked the coroner a question, "You have to put something on the autopsy report, don't you?"

The coroner was tired and aggravated as he replied, "And the death certificate." He was brushing his pants legs at the knees as he spoke.

Bob suggested an answer for the doctor. "I know it's a wolf, but I can't tell you what kind. How about if you call it a D-Wolf until I complete my investigation?"

The coroner looked surprised as he asked, "D-Wolf?"

Bob tried to act as serious as he could when he said, "The D would stand for deformed…for now."

As the coroner was very tired, and he readily agreed. "Yeah…okay…why not." The two of them turned and walked to the group of people standing outside of the ring of yellow tape. As they passed the two assistants of the coroner's, the doctor simply said as he walked by. "Bag him. Take him straight to the morgue. I'll deal with him in the morning."

The two assistants didn't reply. They were also tired, so they just stepped over the crime tape and made their way to the body.

Bob's mood improved significantly when he saw Allie standing next to Jesse. He walked towards her and said cheerfully as he approached, "Hi there."

She turned her head and smiled at him. "Hi there yourself."

He stopped in front of her and then spoke to Jesse as he removed a roll of film from the camera. "You're going all the way to Tucson tonight, huh?"

Jesse answered flatly, "And driving right back here for

the morning shift." He took the roll of film from Bob and dropped it into a small leather case. He then spoke to Allie, "You're taking him to the Elkins' place and Sheriff Sand wants you to take him directly to the accident site."

Bob interrupted, "She's taking me?"

Jesse couldn't help but smile as he answered, "Do you know how to get there?"

Bob had to admit, "Uh...no."

"Then she's taking you."

Jesse then turned to Allie and said very seriously, "Allie, honey...this is some nasty business. When you get Bob to the Elkins' site let him and the Sheriff take the pictures. I've talked to Sheriff Sand and he says it's an ugly scene. No need for you to have to look at it."

Allie felt immediately grateful to Jesse. She said, "Thanks, Jesse. That's good advice."

Jesse then spoke to Bob, "When you're done, Allie will bring you and the Sheriff out. The Casa Grande boys are going to bag the body and take it to the morgue in Vera. Sheriff's orders."

Allie offered, "This is all a little overwhelming."

Bob agreed, "I never thought I'd have to do this with deceased humans. I've done it a few times with dead animals, but this...this is almost too much."

Jesse handed Bob the plastic case for the camera and then said to him and Allie, "You two need to get going. Sheriff's waiting on you."

Four miles south of where the beast had been shot, he stumbled upon a watering tank and staggered towards the smell of fresh water. He had coughed loudly several times before he made it to the trough, and then he started lapping greedily at the cool liquid.

Half of his right ear had been torn off by shotgun pellets while some more of the small, round, balls had furrowed under the skin of his right rear leg. He favored the leg when he walked and he was growing angry at the pain that was throbbing in his haunch. His anger had driven away the feeling of hunger for the moment, and he had but one thought. That thought was *shelter*. He was making his way towards his lair, but he wasn't able to travel very fast.

When he raised his massive head out of the water trough, he coughed again and then produced a sound that he'd never made in his life. He whimpered.

There were no short-cuts to the Elkins' place. Allie had to drive the Jeep almost all of the way back to Meacon before she could turn off onto a dirt road that skirted the town and then joined with another county road that led to the Elkin's ranch.

It was dark and therefore it meant that the driving speed was significantly lowered. It took Allie and Bob a full hour before she turned the Jeep onto the Elkins' land and she didn't stop at the Ranch House to let the owners know that they were there. It was almost nine o'clock at night when she spotted the flood lights and made her way across the rough ground so she could park next to the white SUV driven by the Casa Grande deputies.

It was a somber trip. She and Bob spoke very little during the journey, but they did speak to each other. At one point during the drive, she commented without much enthusiasm, "Not much of a third date, huh?"

Bob readily agreed, "No…not much."

Allie started to comment, "Speaking of which…"

He stopped her in mid-sentence and added, "Speaking of which…tomorrow is Friday. I want to take you to dinner tomorrow night."

The Jeep bounced over a small bump as she replied, "Oh, that sounds so good!"

She killed the Jeep's engine the moment that she parked beside the white SUV. Bob stepped out of the Jeep and walked towards the flood lights. He stopped when he was standing next to Wally and Allie stayed in the driver's seat watching the two of them talk. She was taking Jesse's advice. She told herself firmly, "There's no need for you to even get out of the vehicle. Your job is *chauffer*, so *chauf* and shut up."

To her surprise, both Wally and Bob made their way down the small sloping hill and out of her line of sight. She sat behind the steering wheel and noticed that the two deputies never once looked in her direction. She had a thought about that. She said to herself, "I wonder if they even know I'm here."

Ten minutes later she saw Bob and Wally step back into the glow of the floodlights and she watched Wally speak to the two deputies. The deputies moved immediately towards the body while Wally and Bob made their way to the Jeep.

Wally never said a word to her as he climbed into the back seat, and he settled into place as Bob stepped into the passenger seat. She sat motionless as Bob turned to her and said, "All done. We can go."

She kept her eyes on him as she turned the ignition key and let the engine spark to life. Before she put the Jeep into gear, she decided to ask, "That was fast. Are you really done?"

Wally answered her, "We're done. Take me to the Elkins' house, please."

She put the Jeep into first gear, then let out on the clutch slowly and drove the vehicle away. The small Jeep bounced over the uneven ground so she focused her attention on the land under the headlights as an effort to try and dodge any unnecessary bumps or ruts. It was an exercise in futility. There was no trail. Only rough and patchy ground.

Wally spoke to Bob while she drove away. "I want you in the office first thing in the morning." Allie thought he was talking to her, so they both answered at the same time. "Okay."

Wally chuckled under his breath as he clarified, "I was talking to Bob, but…I need you there also."

Allie was slightly embarrassed as she said, "Oh…okay."

Bob turned his head towards the back seat and asked, "You want me to get the film developed first?"

"No. Just drop it off and see me first thing in the morning." There was a moment of silence as Wally had another thought. He then spoke directly to Allie, "Allie…when we get to the Elkins' house…can you use their phone to call Jeff Watkins for me? I don't have his number."

Allie grimaced as the Jeep bounced again, but she answered him, "Sure. You have a message for him?"

"Tell him I need him and…I don't know…six or seven hands to meet me at the courthouse first thing in the morning. Tell him to bring at least nine horses and a couple of trailers."

Perry Vanhorn sat alone in the dark of his living room. He had locked the front door and the back door and he sat silently on his big cushion chair and stared into the blackness of the room. His telephone was at his right side, but he was not about to pick it up and make a phone call. His double-barreled shotgun was loaded and laying across both of his knees.

He sat in the dark and talked to himself. Most of his conversation was spoken out loud. "Can't call…who'd I call? Sheriff? No! Game Warden! I need to call the game warden! I shot something dangerous…bad dangerous!" He sniffled and rubbed his eyes as he shed a tear. "Killed my damn dogs! They never had a chance! Killed the dogs and killed my bull!"

He took an uneven breath and muttered to himself again, "Can't call…it's dark out. Gotta wait until daylight. Yeah. Gotta wait until daylight. I'll call the Game Warden come daylight."

It was ten o'clock at night when Wally left the front yard of Gary and Fanny Elkins. As he drove away, he had a thought that he couldn't shake. He said to himself, "Fanny and Gary are fine people. Solid folks. I hate that something like this has come upon them. I truly do."

He steered his vehicle out of the long driveway and across the cattle guard and drove slowly towards Meacon. He wanted to be with his wife. He was bone weary and very sad. He had an overwhelming urge to be near her. He had long thought of her as his strength and he needed her.

CHAPTER NINE

It had taken the beast five hours to work his way back to Quail Cut. His bloody and ragged ear caused him to bark sharply every time that a slight breeze blew across the open wound. For some reason, it wouldn't stop bleeding, and a rivulet of blood kept pooling into his ear canal. This caused him to violently shake his head to dispel the blood and the flopping of his torn cartilage caused him to bark in frustration and pain.

The buckshot embedded into his right hip made him limp and favor the leg. Six times, he stopped and tried to chew on the hip wounds to relieve some of the pain and the itching, but his deformed mouth wouldn't let him properly bite at it. After four hours of fighting with the painful ear and nagging hip wound, he forced himself to stop walking. He turned his head to the sky and produced a loud and mournful howl that was meant to express his anger and frustration. He was miles from any living creature, so his anguished cry echoed across dry land and fell upon no other ears than his own.

It was after midnight when he limped up the gentle slope leading to his hidden lair. He whimpered loudly when his wounded ear brushed against the thick bush covering the opening of his cave, but he pushed himself inside and fell to his stomach.

It was half of an hour past midnight when Wally finally made it to his bed and lay down next to Jo Ann. She let him stretch out after he had taken a shower and then crawled into bed beside him. She rested on her left elbow as she took his right arm and moved it to that it stretched across the mattress.

She lay next to him and rested her right knee over his right leg as she put her head down upon his arm. She then put an arm across his chest and squeezed him gently.

He said nothing to her. He was about to tell her that he loved her, but he fell asleep from exhaustion first. She simply lay next to him and felt his body against hers and breathed softly.

She didn't close her eyes. She lay there with her arm across his chest and had a very concerned thought. She opened the palm of her hand and held it against his rib cage and waited for a few seconds. After that short period of time, she moved her hand to his face and felt of his cheek.

Jo Ann took a deep breath and let it out slowly. She said to herself, "You have a fever. I might let you go to work tomorrow, but I'm definitely making you a doctor's appointment. I've been watching you for years, looking for any possible sign. And with that thought, she let her right arm go limp and fell to sleep herself.

It was after eleven thirty when Allie and Bob arrived at the courthouse. She had driven his Jeep all the way back to Meacon from the Elkins' ranch and for some reason, the mood in the vehicle had changed slightly. Perhaps it was due to the fact that the worse part of the ordeal of this day was behind them, or it could have been the fact that they were forced to interact with each other on a professional level and that part was now completed. At either rate, she and Bob both were more relaxed during the trip to Meacon than they had been during their trip to the Elkins' Ranch.

She drove a little slower than she needed to during the ride to Meacon. At one point in the conversation she remarked to him, "This was really a shitty date, you know that, don't you?"

He snickered and replied, "You considered this a date?"

He was looking at her and she kept her eyes on the road, but she was smiling as she replied, "Yes! I consider this a date.

It's me and you together in one vehicle, so it's a date."

He shifted his sitting position so that he was looking more directly at her as they traveled along. "Well...I guess if you consider it our third date, then I'll consider it our third date, also."

She kept her eyes on the road and quipped, "I like a man that agrees with me."

He tried to compliment her as he said, "You are a fascinating person."

She stole a glance at his face and answered, "Shouldn't that have been pretty fascinating? You think I'm pretty...you think I'm fascinating...I'm reasonably certain you should call me *pretty fascinating*."

He answered quickly, "You'll get no argument about that from me."

She stole another glance and gave him a huge grin. She reminded him, "And don't forget...you have to be at the courthouse early in the morning, so you get to see me again. If we spend five minutes together...I'm calling it our fourth date."

She pulled off of the gravel road and onto the paved highway leading into Meacon and steered the Jeep towards the courthouse. They remained silent for those few minutes until she pulled into the parking lot and stopped the Jeep next to her personal vehicle. She put the Jeep into neutral and depressed the emergency brake pedal with her foot and left the engine running.

She turned to him and said, "Follow me home. Boyfriends make sure their girlfriends get home safely."

Bob started to reply, but he couldn't think of anything cute or witty so say, so he simply got out of the cab and walked to the driver's side opening. She had already slid into her car and started the engine as he popped the parking brake and backed up slightly. She drove a few feet in reverse and then steered out of the parking lot.

Ten minutes later, he parked beside the curb in front of her house and watched her pull her car into the driveway. She opened her car door, and called to him as she shut it behind herself. "Well, come on! Walk me to the door and kiss me goodnight!"

He didn't hesitate for an instant.

At five o'clock sharp Friday morning, Wally jerked madly as he woke up suddenly. He startled Jo Ann, who immediately yelled, "Shit! What?"

He coughed and tried to explain himself. "I had a dream!"

"I was dreaming too, Crazy Horse! Damn!"

He swung his legs over the side of the bed and started to explain, "No! It wasn't a dream...I just realized something!"

She complained as she moved to the opposite side of the bed and took her robe off of a small chair next to an end-table. "I hope you just realized that you scared the shit out of me!"

He apologized, "I'm sorry, hon...I have to get to work!"

She held up her right hand and raised her voice, "Whoa! Hold on there, Tonto! The Lone Ranger's not even out of bed yet! You need to eat some breakfast before you go galloping off to the fort!"

Her sarcasm stopped him cold. He said sheepishly, "You may be right!"

She put her robe over her shoulders and put her slippers over her feet as she replied while walking out of the bedroom. "Never argue with the squaw that feeds you!" She then called to him from the kitchen, "Go clean up and get dressed! I'll scramble you some eggs or something!"

He called to her from the bathroom, "And some bacon? Coffee?"

"Don't push your luck, Geronimo!"

She was utilizing the most effective weapon that she had and that was sarcasm. She knew how to pull Wally back from being impetuous or overly excited and she was very good at grounding him into reality when she had to. This wasn't the first time that he'd jerked himself out of a deep sleep with the intent of heading straight to work. She may have been working the scenario pretty hard this particular morning, but she knew that he was getting sick and she knew that she had to keep him nourished so he wouldn't get weak. Besides, she was going to go visit their family doctor later and make him an appointment, anyway.

Allie arrived at the courthouse parking lot at exactly seven thirty on Friday morning. She had a Styrofoam coffee cup with a lid on it in her left hand as she walked through the front door of the building and called to her friend Horace, "Hey, Bubba! You need some relief?'

He called back, "You're a little early this morning."

She took a drink of coffee and replied, "A little. I called you in early yesterday, so I thought I'd repay the favor."

He removed the radio headphones from his head and lay them gently on the desktop. He made a short entry into the official log and then stepped away from the desk. He asked her as she took a seat, "Did you get to run this morning?"

She answered him with a quick response, "Three miles. Same as every morning."

He nodded his head in approval and offered, "I used to do that myself. When I was younger, that is."

She took another drink of coffee and replied as she took a seat in the office chair, "You never were young, Bubba. Don't try to push that lie on me."

He chuckled and left the front desk to make his way to the locker room in order to change his shirt before going home. Allie was looking out of the glass front door and noticed two horse trailers pulling into the parking lot. She whispered out loud, "Damn! Jeff Watkins gets around early for an old man!" She called to Horace Fannin, "Hey Bubba!"

She heard a muffled call answer her, "What?"

She teased him as he was changing clothes, "You should get around like Mister Watkins! I asked him to be here at eight, and here he is at seven forty!"

Horace came out of the locker room buttoning his shirt as he replied, "Why'd you bring that up?"

She teased him again, "He's older than you, right?"

"Yeah...so?"

"I'm just saying that he gets around a lot earlier and faster than you do...that's all!"

Horace was still buttoning his shirt as he and Allie heard some vehicle doors opening and closing in the parking lot. Allie turned to him and teased him again, "Damn, Bubba! You need help with that shirt?"

Horace replied with a remark, "Wow...you're sure in a good mood this morning."

Allie answered him somberly, "Yeah...yesterday was pretty rough on all of us, Bubba. I'm trying to put that sadness behind me for the moment."

Horace answered, "Good plan. This office could use some cheering up." And with that, he walked out of the front door.

Horace held the front door open as a file of teenagers walked in followed by Jeff Watkins. Allie was watching the procession and the first thing that she noticed was that as each young person walked through the open door, they immediately removed their cowboy hats. She remarked to herself as they did that, "Wow...manners...who'd of thunk?"

She then watched all of the teenagers step aside and let Jeff walk straight to her desk. He spoke as he approached, "Good morning. Sheriff called for us."

Allie smiled at him and replied, "Good morning Mister Watkins. Actually it was me who called last night. Do you remember me?"

"Of course I remember you, Allie. You were one of my lineman girls. You worked with Beth Williams one year and Judy Flanders the next."

Allie was impressed as she complimented him, "Wow. Good memory. That was almost five years ago."

Jeff nodded and indicated his crew with his left hand, "Sheriff Sand wanted seven of us, so here we are."

Allie explained, "The Sheriff and Deputy Blount aren't here just yet, but they will be any moment now. Why don't you guys go have a seat in the meeting room and wait for them."

Allie had to chuckle when Jeff whistled softly and waived his arm at the kids standing behind him. They followed him to the meeting room and each of them muttered to her as they passed her desk, "Mornin'."

Perry Vanhorn had slept while sitting up in his big cushioned chair and he jumped slightly when he heard the crowing of his rooster. He almost dropped his shotgun and immediately felt embarrassed with himself. He muttered out loud as he tried to stand up. "Danged old fool! Spent the night in the living room scared out of your britches…shame on you."

He was having difficulty standing as his limbs had grown stiff and sore from the unnatural position that he had been in for several hours. His knees popped when he finally made it to a standing position and he groaned at the sharp pain. "Ouch."

He leaned the loaded shotgun against the arm of his chair and walked stiffly towards the bathroom. He muttered out loud all of the way, "I need to brush my teeth and wash my face." He walked a few more steps and changed his mind as he muttered aloud again, "No…I need to shave and take a shower after I brush my teeth. Maybe I'll feel like eating something after that."

It was six thirty in the morning and full daylight outside. Early morning shadows formed around the dead bull and the three deceased dogs still lying around the dirt trail. His five milk cows were scattered throughout his grazing pasture and although they had no memory of the fearsome incident from the night before, they had no inclination of moving towards the barn either.

Perry spent much more time in the bathroom this

morning than he usually did. He didn't admit it to himself, but he was quite nervous about opening his front door and walking outside. Three times while he was in the shower, he had a memory flash of the shotgun blast and the most frightening animal roar that he'd ever heard or could imagine, and he shuddered involuntarily.

Normally, Perry dressed himself in overalls and work boots, but this morning, when he went to his closet in the bedroom, he pulled out a pair of jeans and a white tee shirt. He slipped the jeans and shirt on, then pulled a white pair of socks over his feet and put his high-topped shoes on. He bent over and slowly laced them and then tied a double-loop knot in each one.

He was sitting on the side of his bed and simply staring at the wall in front of him. Then, as if he'd suddenly regained his senses, he stood up quickly and grabbed a worn, red, ball cap off of his nightstand. He pulled the hat over his head and marched quickly to the living room. He didn't break his stride as he marched past the cushioned chair and snatched the shotgun off of the floor.

He kept marching as he flipped the lock mechanism on the door and pushed it open. He stomped across the wooden porch and down the two steps leading into his front yard. He ignored the pecking and scratching chickens as he moved straight for the animals that he loved and cherished and he didn't notice the small tear forming in his right eye.

Allie had sat down in her high-backed office chair and had one leg crossed over the other as she was staring at the topographical map spread across the desk. Her attention was drawn to the two grease pencil marks that she had put on the map herself. She put a very serious look on her face as she leaned her right cheek against the palm of her right hand and didn't hear herself mutter aloud, "Uhm..."

She glanced up when she heard the entrance door open and she saw Wally and Jesse walking in together. She took her face off of her hand and spoke to them both, "Good morning...

you two have visitors in the meeting room."

Wally explained as he passed her desk, "Bob Benoit should be here shortly. Send him straight to the meeting room when he gets here."

Allie returned her gaze to the map and simply answered, "Okay."

She absent-mindedly picked up the black grease pencil with her right hand and held it over the map. She put a circle around the check mark indicating the spot where Hershel Span's body was found. She did the same with the check mark that she'd made the day before indicating the location of the biker's body. She muttered to herself again, "Uhm…" and tapped the butt end of the pencil against her table top. She was having a thought, but it wasn't coming to her very clearly.

She didn't hear herself mutter aloud again, "The photographer…he was on Papago lands…this map doesn't show that…but…it was over thirty miles south of the biker…" She let the thought drop when her desk phone rang.

She dropped the grease pencil and picked up a lead pencil as she answered the phone, "Sheriff's Office, Allie Thompson speaking, how may I help you?"

The chatter from the meeting room was growing slightly louder as the young people visited among themselves. Wally and Jeff had left the room and had moved to his office while Jesse was still in the meeting room with the teenagers.

Karen spoke directly to Jesse, "Hey, Deputy Blount…are we gonna be deputized?"

"What? No! Why'd you ask that?"

Karen smiled and explained as she pointed at a young boy, "Bill Ivers over there…who's a doofus, by-the-way…he said we was all gonna get deputized this morning."

Bill retorted, "Hey!"

Jesse couldn't help but grin as he answered, "First of all, you have to be eighteen years old in order to be deputized. And, you can only be deputized when there is a need to help make and arrest…so…no, none of you are going to be deputized."

A groan filled the room and Jesse shook his head.

Allie had put another grease pencil check mark on her map as she was talking on the telephone. She saw Bob entering the building and she immediately became excited, "Ooh! Ooh, Mister Vanhorn! Wait a second! The Game Warden just walked in!" She put the phone receiver against her shoulder and called to Bob, "Bob! Go to the meeting room right now! I've got a phone call that I'm going to transfer in there and you need to hear this!"

Bob whispered to Allie as he walked by her desk, "And good morning to you too."

She snorted and spoke on the telephone again, "Mister Vanhorn, listen, this is important! I'm going to transfer your call and you'll be speaking with the Sheriff and the Game Warden at the same time!" She put her telephone on hold and moved to Wally's office. She stuck her head in the door and saw him staring at a map with Jeff Watkins as she said loudly, "Sheriff! Go to the meeting room! I'm putting Mister Vanhorn on speaker phone in there and you have *got* to hear what he has to say!"

Wally stared at her for a second and she frowned at him when she said firmly, "Right now!"

Jeff took Wally by the elbow and laughed softly, "Come on, Sheriff...She means business!"

Allie was indeed excited as she rushed back to her desk and picked up her phone receiver again. She spoke to Perry quickly, "Mister Vanhorn! You still there? Okay! You hold just for a few more seconds while I round everyone up for you!" She put her desk phone on hold again and ran to the meeting room.

As she was making her way through the crowd she shouted at the teenagers, "Everybody be quiet! This is important!"

A lone boy's voice replied, "Who says?"

Allie didn't even look in his direction as she replied, "Shut it, Joe Wills! I'll have Becky kick your ass in front of everybody!" She picked up the meeting room telephone receiver as she heard soft giggles around her. She spoke into the receiver, "Mister Vanhorn, I'm putting you on speaker now!" She sat the phone receiver on the desk and punched a red button on the base. "Can you hear me?"

Perry's voice answered, "I can hear you."

She replied, "I have Sheriff Sand, Deputy Blount, Bob Benoit, and a host of other people listening to you. Please tell them what you told me!"

Perry started repeating his tale of shooting a black animal the night before as Allie left the room. She returned to her desk and looked at the map again. Once again, she muttered, "Uhm..."

She then spoke to herself in her mind. "There was something Professor Wilcox said. I can't remember all of it, but...it was something about wolf habits." She sighed and sat down in her chair and stared at the three check marks on her map.

As she sat there, she drew a very faint line between the mark indicating Hershel and the mark indicating the Vanhorn ranch. She then drew another faint line between the dead biker's mark and the Vanhorn ranch.

She was trying to work out a puzzle in her brain, but the answer was evading her. She shook her head and drew a thin line between the biker's mark and Hershel's mark.

The very instant that she drew that last line, she dropped the grease pencil and pushed herself to a standing position. She almost shouted as she said, "Oh my God!"

She grabbed the map with her right hand and ran towards the meeting room.

The beast was lying on his left side and he was wheezing slightly as he breathed. His wounded ear had let a stream of coagulated blood run from the missing section down his neck and throat. His right rear hip had swollen slightly during the night and it was burning his sensitive nerves. He had slept very little during the night. Every time he started to doze off, a sharp pain from his wounded hip woke him up and made him snarl with anger.

A slight breeze moved through the bush covering the entrance and rattled the leaves and stems. It made the temperature in the cave much cooler than the outside air, so the beast took another deep breath, and then let out another whimper. He closed his eyes and wished for sleep.

Allie jumped through the meeting room door and stood on the carpet facing Wally. She heard him say to Perry Vanhorn, "The Game Warden will be there soon, Perry. Don't disturb anything until he gets there, okay?"

Allie watched Wally punch the red button of the phone base and terminate the call. She held her map above her head and pointed at it. Wally furrowed his brow and said, "Allie?"

"You need to see this!" she almost shouted.

He motioned for her to join him, so she pushed her way to the table and sat the map in front of him. Bob and Jesse was looking at it also as she pointed to the triangle that she had drawn on the map. She sounded very proud of herself as she said suddenly, "Triangulation! We needed three points on the map in order to triangulate a position!"

Bob was the first one to react, "Oh, shit! She's right!"

Wally suddenly understood and he spoke up, "He operates in a hunting field. Always circling outwards! Jesus, you're right!"

Jeff was standing next to Allie as he shrugged his shoulders and asked, "You want to let the rest of us in on it?"

Wally held an open palm to Allie and said, "Allie...explain it to the people."

Allie spoke quickly, "You need three points on a map to triangulate a position. If you look at the three places checked, you will see that they form a triangle and the area inside of that triangle is a place where we can possibly find the lair."

Bob couldn't help himself as he added, "And inside of that area, there will be everything that it needs. Water. A cave. Sanctuary!"

Allie teased him, "Yeah! I just said that!"

Bob answered, "Oops...sorry."

Wally took the map off of the table and held it close to his face. He let his hands drop after a few seconds and then he spoke to Jeff. "The only source of water in this triangle is the place called Quail Cut."

Jeff frowned and replied, "Sheriff, that's public land and it used to be a park where people camped. Of course...that was a long time ago...there used to be a creek at the bottom of the gorge, but it's nothing but a trickle now."

Bob interjected, "I'm not familiar with the place, but a trickling stream sounds like a good source of water for our wolf to me."

Jesse added, "And you can't drive a normal vehicle to it." He looked at Bob and said, "Maybe your Jeep, but nothing we drive can get us close."

It was Jeff's turn to offer a suggestion, so he said, "We can get the horse trailers to the old roadside picnic area. That's about five miles from the gorge. The rest of the way would have to be by horseback."

Wally realized that it was time to put a plan into place. He pushed the map away and told Allie to take it. He turned to Jeff and said, "Bob is going to go see Mister Vanhorn and I need you to ride with him." Jeff looked slightly confused, so Wally explained, "Mister Benoit isn't from around here. He doesn't know his way through the desert like the rest of us. You go with him to see Mister Vanhorn and then make sure he can get his Jeep to Quail Cut."

He then turned his attention to the teenagers and said, "You six will go with me and Deputy Blount to the old picnic area. We'll unload the horses there and then *possibly* go to Quail Cut."

The voice of Joe Willis was heard to say, "Possibly?"

Wally never changed his facial expression as he raised his voice and said, "Becky. Please smack him!"

A slapping sound filled the room as Joe yelled, "Ouch!"

Wally continued, "You all heard Mister Vanhorn say that he was sure that he shot the animal last night. We don't know how bad its hurt. It could be dead for all we know, so that's why Mister Watkins and Mister Benoit are driving from the Vanhorn place to Quail Cut. If it died trying to make it to its lair, then they will find out and tell us. If they tell us that it's still alive…possibly…then we can go to Quail Cut."

Wally looked around the room and realized that he was enlisting the help of six adolescents, but he also realized that Jeff Watkins placed a lot of trust, faith, and confidence in his hired hands. He knew that they might be young, but they all knew how to use a fire arm and that was important for this particular job. Finally, he took a breath and addressed them like grownups, "All of you listen. If we are going after a wounded animal, then each of you know full well that a wounded animal is a dangerous animal. I've asked for your help because I know you're all good kids and you follow instructions. I'm trusting you to help me rid this town of a very bad animal so…understand me when I tell you that I could have asked for help from a number of different places…but…I chose you…on purpose."

The room went silent. Allie sensed that the meeting was about to end, so she took her map off of the table and turned to leave the room. She smiled at Becky and pointed at Joe as she said, "Good job."

"Thanks."

The beast had dozed for about an hour, but he woke up with a burning sensation in his throat. His need for water was overpowering and he had to act upon it. He forced himself to his feet and tried to put weight on his rear leg. He snarled at the stabbing pain that he experienced when he tried to push himself with his paw. He raised it slightly and used his three good legs to limp out of the cave and past the rustling bush.

He continued to limp as he made his way down the gentle sloping rock trail and he grunted with almost every step. Once he was at the bottom of the trail, he moved as quickly as he could to the stream and began lapping at the water wildly. His tongue splashed water over his lips and his throat swallowed greedily. He lapped water for a full minute, then paused to lick his lips, and began drinking once more.

He heard a fluttering noise coming from the south end of the gulch and he knew instantly that it was the pesky birds moving about. They were feeding and drinking water and irritating him slightly. He suddenly had a strong urge to be alone and nurse his wounds. He growled at the unseen quail, then limped his way back to his den.

Everyone was leaving the courthouse lobby except Wally. He had stopped at Allie's desk and he was about to give her the instructions about the coroner's office. She noticed Bob passing her desk and whistled loud enough to make him stop in place. Wally chuckled as he heard her say, "Come here, big boy! Gimme that radio."

Bob unclipped the hand-held radio from his belt and gave it to her. She took the unit and pressed a lever on the bottom. The battery slid off into her hand and she then pulled another one out of her desk and slipped it into place. She handed him the unit and said, "Now...keep in touch."

Bob could do nothing but grin in return. Jeff called to him from the front door, "Come on...big boy!"

Bob hung his head and half-shouted, "Jesus!"

Wally was close to laughter as he asked Allie, "What was that?"

Allie was watching Bob leave as she answered, "Date number four."

"I'm sorry?"

She smiled at Wally and replied, "Never mind. I'll bet you were about to tell me to get all of the information that I can from the Coroner in Vera and the Crime Lab in Tucson, huh?"

"Yes...as a matter of fact, I was just about to say just those words..."

She continued, "And you were about to tell me that you

want the coroner's report faxed here and then you want me to fax it to…" she paused and looked at the log book on her desk and then continued, "Lieutenant Borden."

Wally squinted his eyes and folded his arms across his chest. He then whispered, "What about Shane Owens?"

Allie was slightly taken aback. She replied, "Bob's boss?"

Wally explained, "Mister Benoit needs to give his boss an update. I haven't given him time to do that…so…"

She nodded her head and said, "Oh…alright…I'll call Shane Owens and tell him what Bob's up to."

"I knew I could count on you." Wally turned away from the desk and walked quickly out of the lobby.

Not a soul in that courthouse had realized what had just happened. When Perry Vanhorn called and gave the news about having come face-to-face with an animal that had killed three human beings and then shot it, the overwhelming sense of dread associated with that beast was suddenly dissipated. It was no longer a mystical entity that murdered indiscriminately and spread fear among all that sought it.

Although the words were not spoken, a new feeling was felt among them all. That feeling was that if it could be wounded, it could be killed. There was nothing unearthly about it anymore.

The teenagers were climbing into two large pickup trucks that had horse trailers attached to them. Wally and Jesse had decided to use Jesse's cruiser to drive to the place referred to as the picnic area, and the kids were to follow after them.

Jeff and Bob had left the parking lot and were driving towards the Vanhorn Ranch. Bob looked at his gas gauge and saw that it was less than half full. He asked Jeff if he needed to fill up the fuel tank before they left Meacon and he replied, "You'd better have a full tank for this. I'm too old to be walking across the desert when you run out of gas."

Wally, Jesse, and the teenagers would be at the picnic area within less than an hour's travel time. The two drivers of the pickups pulling the trailers were Becky Simms in one pickup and Elliot Johnson in the other one. Both of the kids were excellent drivers, so they knew how to move a trailer full of livestock over a rough road without any risk to the animals that they were hauling.

Keeping the vehicle and trailer tires in the middle of a gravel road that was rutted wasn't always a good practice. The road had to be closely watched so that any pot holes or surface breaks could be avoided. This meant that a good portion of the driving time was spent driving the vehicles fairly close to the road's shoulder.

Becky's passengers were Karen Higgins and Sam Linden. Sam was seventeen years old like Karen was and this would be his last year working on the ranch before he went off to college. He and Becky were acquaintances, but hardly more than that. He didn't consider her to be exceptionally pretty, but he did like her figure and her face was attractive. It was almost the same with Karen, but he thought that the smaller girl was very beautiful and therefore he thought that she'd never talk to someone like him.

In other words, Sam Linden didn't say too much. As they drove along, Karen tried to engage him in a conversation. He was riding in the back seat, so Karen turned to him and asked, "When we park the truck, you want to be the one that unloads the horses, or do you want us to do it?"

He answered with a soft voice, "I don't mind feeding and watering them if you girls want to take them off of the trailer."

Karen turned to Becky and asked, "What do you think, Becky?"

The pickup bounced and the horse trailer rattled as Becky replied, "Yeah...lets me and you get them off of the trailer. Sam can unload the grain bags and the water cans, and then we'll help him feed and water the horses."

Sam answered quietly, "Wow."

Karen turned to face him and asked, "Wow, what?"

Sam shrugged his shoulders and replied, "It's just...I didn't expect you guys to be so..." his voice trailed off.

Karen pressed him, "Be so what, Sam?"

Sam was obviously embarrassed, but he answered her anyway. "Friendly. I didn't expect you to be so friendly."

Becky was listening to the conversation and became extremely curious as she asked, "Why would you think we'd be unfriendly, Sam?"

Sam decided that honesty was his best policy to answer that particular question, so he said, "You are the two line riders. You get to the ranch every morning before any of us and most of the time you get back to the barn after all of us are gone. We never get talk to either of you."

Becky answered with a grunt, "Humph..."

Karen continued the conversation as they rolled slowly along the gravel road, "Sam...just out of curiosity...do you have a girlfriend?"

Sam answered quickly, "No. I don't."

Becky chimed in, "Have you ever had a girlfriend, Sam?"

Sam looked at the floorboard as he answered, "Uh...no...I guess not."

Karen fairly squealed as she said, "I knew it! Shy!"

Becky was chuckling as she joined in, "What makes you so shy, Sam?"

Sam suddenly felt a little more at ease as he replied, "Well...I'm skinny...and girls are hard to talk to..."

Becky stopped him instantly, "Whoa...hold on there, there Sam!" She spoke to Karen, "Karen...make Sam give you his hat."

Karen held out her hand past the back of the seat and said, "You heard Becky! Gimme the hat!"

Sam had no idea what was going on, so he simply handed Karen the cowboy hat and held his eyes wide open in anticipation of what would happen next. He didn't wait long because Becky then asked, "Karen, is he skinny?"

"Nope."

"Is he fat?"

"Nope."

"Is he cute?"

Karen turned to Becky and asked, "What's above *cute*?"

"Handsome."

Karen then asked, "Okay...what's below handsome?"

Becky chuckled and replied, "Hunky."

Karen then smiled at Sam and said, "Let's go with *hunky*."

Sam tried to complain, "Hey...you guys are embarrassing me..."

Karen teased him again, "Yep...definitely hunky...you got dark brown hair...dark brown eyes...we love your cheekbones...can we look at your arms?"

"What?"

Becky jumped into the conversation, "Yeah! Show us your arms!"

"What? No!"

Karen turned around in the seat and faced Sam directly. She smiled and said, "Gimme your shirt sleeve!"

He slowly raised his arm and she opened the snaps that held his shirt sleeve cuff together. She pushed the shirt sleeve up past his bicep and said to Becky, "Oh, Becky! You should see this! Hunky face and hunky arms!"

Sam snatched his hand away from Karen and pulled his shirt sleeve down. He muttered, "That was a little too far, Karen."

Becky quickly replied, "No it wasn't, Sam! Me and Karen want you to work with us today! We want you to be our partner! We really do!"

Sam didn't believe her as he replied, "What's with all the hunky stuff, then?"

Karen answered, "We think you're hunky, Sam. We both do. As a matter of fact, we talk about you a lot...well...maybe not a lot...but...sometimes."

Sam glanced back and forth between the girls and

paused for a long moment. He then asked, "Really?"

Karen and Becky answered simultaneously, "Really."

"Wow."

Perry Vanhorn had led Bob and Jeff to the trail so his bull and dogs could be inspected. He kept his back turned away from the two men as they looked the dead animals over and discussed the carcasses.

Bob pointed at one dog and stated flatly, "She wasn't bitten. None of the dogs were bitten."

Jeff agreed, "Looks like our wolf just swatted them aside. Never seen anything like it."

Bob added, "Broke their spines. Poor dogs died almost instantly." He turned to the bull and pointed at the deep punctures on the neck. "Not so with the big bull."

Jeff put his hands on his hips and asked Bob a question that he was wanting to ask previously, "Bob? Is your Dire Wolf a saber tooth?"

Bob jumped slightly at the question and replied, "What? No!"

"Well..." Jeff was pointing at the deep puncture wounds, "What do you call these, then? Stab wounds?"

Bob realized Jeff's misconception, so he explained, "Mister Watkins...a saber tooth is...much bigger."

Jeff asked disbelievingly, "How much bigger?"

"More than twice the size of these wounds."

"Shit! Really?"

"Yeah."

"Damn! That'd be a big-assed tooth!"

Bob had to agree with the man. "Yeah...our wolf has big-assed canines...but he's not a saber tooth." Bob then paused as he walked around the bull. He pointed at some pellet holes in the bull's skin and replied, "Our wolf was standing on top of the bull when Mister Vanhorn shot him. Got pellets scattered on one side of the carcass."

Jeff mused, "Didn't get him head on, huh?"

Bob answered soberly, "He'd be laying here with the bull if he had been." He then added, "And it's not the wolf's canines that are his fiercest weapon. His jaws are what makes him deadly."

Jeff kept looking at the dogs and then offered, "Well… I'm gonna have to add *feet* to that list."

Bob sighed and replied, "Good point."

The beast woke himself up coughing. He was hacking and choking and he felt like something was stuck in his throat. It was beyond his comprehension to realize that the pure lead buckshot lodged within his muscles would start poisoning his blood and start causing him to have reactions like he was experiencing. He was an animal that was hurt. He wasn't suffering just yet, but the seizures and diarrhea weren't that far away.

He had been a powerful creature that knew no fear. He was faster and stronger than anything that he had ever met. He could kill any animal that crossed his path and for the most part, he had done just that his entire life. This new feeling that was creeping up on him was beginning to irritate him. He'd never experienced *fear*. He didn't like it.

He coughed again, then whimpered, and tried to go back to sleep.

The old picnic grounds had once been a well-cared for grove of desert willow trees providing shade for a dozen picnic tables. The trees could have reached a height of thirty feet had they of been properly attended to, but they now stood a mere fifteen feet high and their leaves and branches were nowhere near as thick as they should have been.

The picnic table tops had rotted away decades ago, so the ground between the trees was mostly the remains of a concrete stump here and there. The kids discovered quickly that the old concrete stumps made a good place to put a feed bucket for their horses, so that's what they did.

Joe Wills and Bill Ivers carried canvas water bags to the

horses and made sure that they were all hydrated after eating a bite of grain. Becky and Karen had Sam assisting them by loosening all of the saddles. The horses weren't being worked or ridden for the time being, so it wasn't good to leave the saddle girths tight around their chests. Loosening them up a few notches and then letting the horses lounge under the shady branches of the trees was the best way to treat the animals. They were tending to nine horses, so the work was fairly demanding, but not overwhelming.

None of the people at the picnic area even knew for certain that they would be using the horses that day. Everyone was waiting for Mister Watkins and Bob Benoit to arrive and let them know if their wounded animal had died during the night. And the truth of that matter was that none of them cared much for another wolf hunt anyway. It was sort of the unspoken wish that the animal had perished in the desert and they could all go home after a fun day on the road.

Wally had called Allie on the radio a half-hour earlier and got an update on his forensic tests being conducted in Tucson. She let him know that the forty-five pistol had been conclusively determined to be the murder weapon in Vera, but that was no surprise to him. She had no autopsy reports from the coroner's office as of yet, so he told her that he'd check back later.

The minutes had turned into hours and the kids had started to lounge around the trees simply chatting with one another. Jesse and Wally stood about fifty yards away from the kids so they could discuss matters in private. It was an unspoken rule. Never discuss misgivings around teenagers. And that meant yours or anyone else's too.

Jesse finally worked up the courage to say it in front of Wally. "This has been a cluster fuck, huh?"

Wally agreed immediately. "And then it got worse."

Jesse then offered, "You know Andrew Span will be at the courthouse today. He'll want answers that we can't give him."

"He hasn't shown up yet. Allie will let me know if and when he does."

Jesse smiled, "You'll deal with it then, huh?"

"Yeah."

Jesse used his right hand to indicate the kids relaxing under the shade of the trees and remarked, "You put a lot of trust in those kids."

Wally looked at the young people and smiled slightly. "Mister Watkins turns good young boys and girls into respectable men and women. Yeah. I like working with them." He then paused and added, "You just have to overlook their hormones most of the time."

Jesse then pressed Wally on another matter, "You seem almost certain that this wolf thing is using Quail Cut for his lair. Who convinced you? Was it Allie or Bob?"

Wally shrugged his shoulders and answered, "Now that you mention it…I think it was Allie. Bob just agreed with her assessment, didn't he?"

Jesse chuckled, "You know…you're right…Shit! Maybe Allie should be the Game Warden!"

Wally simply answered, "She could be anything that she wants."

Jesse nodded and agreed, "Can't argue with you there."

Both men turned and looked in the direction where the sound of a gasoline engine was purring in the distance. They saw the dust cloud and the hood of Bob's Jeep coming at them from the north.

All of the teenagers heard the Jeep, so they stood up from where they had been sitting and lounging and watched the approaching vehicle as well. Not a one of them had a word to say, and that included Jesse and Wally alike.

Jo Ann was in the office of Doctor Barry Wilson. He was a general practitioner that had been her doctor and Wally's alike for over five years. He was an elder man with a lot of experience and Jo Ann trusted him. She had made an appointment to speak with him in person, rather than discuss her concerns over the phone.

He was dressed in a light blue set of scrubs as he sat behind his desk and listened to her explain why she was there to meet him.

Doctor Wilson had his hands folded behind his head as she spoke to him. "His skin color is pallid with a touch of green."

"Go on."

"He's running a low grade fever…I'm sure of that."

He shifted his chair and asked, "Any signs of shaking?"

"No."

"What about speech patterns?"

"Such as?"

"Has he started to stutter or have trouble remembering words?"

"No."

Doctor Wilson pulled his hands from behind his head and let them fold across his chest as he leaned back in his chair. He continued, "He's told you about his exposure to Agent Orange and he's admitted that it was a rather large amount of exposure?"

She sniffled and replied, "Yes."

He smiled and leaned forward, "Okay…here's what I think…outside of you being a worry-wart about him, it may be his liver giving the first sign of trouble symptoms. I don't think he's been affected neurologically. The speech patterns usually give that away."

"What do we need to do?"

"Give him a blood test. Specifically, I need to look for Porphyria Catania Tarda. If I find it, I can treat it."

She choked out a short cry as she replied, "Really?"

He smiled as he assured her. "Yes. Really. When can you drag him to the hospital and make him get a blood test?"

"When do you want him?"

He chuckled and answered, "Well…don't dawdle. I have to send the blood sample off for lab testing, so let's get him in as soon as we can."

      She suddenly felt very relieved. Somehow, the doctor's confidence in himself made her very happy.

CHAPTER TEN

Bob parked his Jeep next to Jesse's cruiser, then all four adults walked together to join the teenagers under the shade of the willow trees. The four boys and two girls instinctively formed a tight semi-circle and faced the four men.

Wally gave the instructions as soon as he was standing in front of the teens. "The game warden didn't find the body of our wolf. He said there were blood signs from the Vanhorn Ranch leading them towards here, but they haven't seen any of those in several miles."

Wally pointed towards the west and then continued, "Deputy Blount and I have discussed this, and we believe that the animal is holed up in one of the three gulches that are about five miles south of here." He explained, "He's more than likely in the one called Quail Cut, but there's a chance that he could be in any of the three. This makes our job a little trickier."

Every teenage eye was on Wally as he spoke. Their faces were held in rapt attention as he continued, "Deputy Blount and I will scout the Quail Cut, while the rest of you form a protective guard for us." Wally pointed to Jeff and explained, "Mister Watkins will take two people and post them at the sister gorges. Then, Mister Benoit and Mister Watkins will stand guard at the south end of the Quail Cut."

Wally purposely paused so that his instructions could be digested before he continued. "Deputy Blount and I need two people to guard us as we scout the ravine. I've already decided that my flank guards will be Sam Linden and Elliot Johnson." He spoke directly to the boys, "Elliot? Sam? Do you understand what I need you to do?"

Sam answered for them both. "You want me one side of the gulch and Elliot on the other side. We follow you and Deputy Blount and keep an eye on you from above."

Wally couldn't help but smile out of appreciation. "That's exactly what I need."

Wally turned to Karen and Becky and said, "I need you two to block the northern entrance. Don't let it slip out behind us, okay?"

Karen and Becky, once again, answered in unison. "Yes sir!"

Jeff Watkins knew that it was his turn to speak. They were his hired hands and the horses belonged to him, so he gave the instructions regarding the mounts. "Me and Mister Benoit think it would be best if we didn't ride the horses right up to the gorges. The animal is wounded and that means its unpredictable. Horses can smell blood from a long way off, and we don't want them to get spooked and then spook the wolf. That could cause us unnecessary grief."

Every teenager there knew this to be a true fact. Joe Wills offered, "Mister Watkins, there's another grove of trees about a quarter mile from Quail Cut. You think we could use them to tie off the horses." Jeff smiled and complimented the lad. "Good thinking. That's exactly where we'll stage the mounts."

Bob then gave his instructions. "I need the Jeep to be close to the gully's for safety's sake. Mister Watkins tells me that the northern end of the main cut has a long sloping hill leading down to it. That means I can kill the engine and then coast the Jeep to the entrance." He smiled at Becky and Karen and said, "You girls can guard the Jeep and the canyon, right."

Both girls rolled their eyes and remained silent.

Wally took over again, "Alright. Everybody get your rifles out of the trucks and load 'em. We'll ride out as soon as everybody's ready."

Nine horses and riders formed a line from side-to-side

as they rode slowly towards the triple canyons. Wally posted himself and Jesse in the middle of the troop and made everyone walk their mounts very slowly. Bob followed behind in his Jeep and kept over a hundred yards between himself and the rest of the group. His vehicle remained in first gear and merely idled along.

They had a little over four miles to travel and their current rate of speed would take them almost an hour to get to the designated tree grove. It was one o'clock in the afternoon when Wally tied his horse to one of the trees. He walked to Bob's Jeep and took the hand-held radio off of the front seat and checked in with Allie. He then told Bob that the radio needed to be turned off. He explained that it was a good idea to leave it in the Jeep, but he didn't want any surprise squelch noises to announce his arrival at the cut.

Bob turned the radio off and Jeff Watkins stepped into the passenger side. He took the radio and placed it on the seat in the back of the Jeep. Becky was standing next to him at the passenger side door and she handed him two 30-30 rifles. He said nothing to her, but he did smile in appreciation.

While everyone else gathered together, Bob drove him and Jeff to the gulch. They had to arrive first so they could walk to the southern end of the cut and be in position by the time the rest of the people arrived.

When Wally judged that he was about three hundred yards from Quail cut, he motioned for Bill Ivers and Joe Wills to separate from the group and go to their assigned places at the sister gully's. Everyone had their rifles resting on their shoulders and held the barrels pointing towards the sky.

Wally, Jesse, Karen, Becky, Sam and Elliot paused at the top of the long slope leading down to the southern entrance of the arroyo. They all spotted Bob's Jeep standing mute at the left side of the entrance. It was parked close to a shimmering trickle of water coming out of the valley and draining towards the west.

Wally motioned to Sam and Elliot. The two boys began

walking to the eastern and western side of the cut while him, Jesse, and the girls waited behind.

He let Elliot and Sam position themselves and saw them turn to face the remaining four. Wally whispered, "Okay. Our turn." And with that, the four of them marched to the narrow entrance.

When the four of them arrived at Bob's Jeep, Karen and Becky stopped and stood at the right side of it. Wally and Jesse continued walking into the gorge with Wally taking the lead position. Elliot and Sam began matching their steps and keeping pace.

Becky and Karen stared down into the abyss and they could see that the cut narrowed at a distance of several hundred yards, but they couldn't see beyond that. All they knew was that Bob Benoit and Jeff Watkins were on the other end. They kept their eyes on the two men marching into the ravine and they both felt a pang of worry as the men became smaller and their shadows blended with the bushes dotting the trail.

The beast woke himself up again with an uncontrollable coughing outburst. His throat was burning and his mouth was extremely dry. He rolled onto his stomach and positioned his injured leg so that he could try and stand up. He whimpered loudly when he tried to put weight on it, so he eased himself to a standing position on three legs.

He limped towards the cavern entrance and stopped when a slight breeze rattled the brush limbs in front of his nose. The breeze brought a familiar smell to his sensitive snout and it caused him to begin a low-pitched growl.

He dropped to his stomach and inched his way towards the opening as he maintained a warning snarl. His wounded ear brushed the low-hanging branches of the bush, and even though it caused a sharp pain to shoot through the right side of his face, he ignored the agony and pressed forward.

Jesse and Wally had passed a few of the rocky trails making their way up the sheer cliffs as they walked along the gully floor. They both visually inspected the rocky trails, but they couldn't see anything resembling a cave, cavity, or hollow at the cliffs. The trickling stream was on their right hand side, so they were mere feet from the high wall hiding the beast. They had arrived at the narrowest section of Quail Cut.

Wally was twelve feet in front of Jesse. Jesse was directly under the beast's lair. The beast had made his way to the edge of the rock trail and he was looking down at the big man standing below.

Anger and outrage overtook the beast. His sanctuary had been violated and his protective instincts took over his actions. He roared with all of his power and launched himself off of the side of the cliff.

Jesse snapped his head upwards and saw the gaping jaws of the frightful animal descending towards him. The beast's front legs were stretched out widely as he crashed into Jesse and closed his mouth over the deputy's head.

The instant that the beast slammed into Jesse, the rifle that he was carrying discharged and the bullet tore into Wally's right shoulder. Wally was thrown forward and the weapon that he was carrying was flung to one side.

Elliot Johnson was directly above the Sheriff and his Deputy, but the cliff had an overhang that blocked his view. He could hear what was happening, but he couldn't see anything. Sam Linden had witnessed the beast flying out of the cave and landing on Jesse. When Jesse's rifle discharged, he threw his own weapon into his shoulder and aimed it at the black beast. He shouted, "Oh, shit! Oh, fuck!" and kept his weapon aimed at the black animal.

This was a testament to his hunting skills and his ability to keep from panicking. He couldn't shoot while the beast was so close to Wally and Jesse.

The beast snapped his jaws together over Jesse's skull as the weight of his body forced the deputy to the ground. Jesse died instantly.

Wally had rolled himself into a sitting position and grabbed his wounded shoulder with his left hand. Blood was flowing out of the wound and between his fingers as he watched the beast in abject horror.

The deformed wolf dropped Jesse and turned towards Wally. He roared again and began limping towards the wounded man. He inched his way closer as Sam kept muttering above, "Move away! Shit! Please move away! I can't shoot with you so close!"

When the beast was three feet from Wally, he opened his mouth and let his lower jaw drop to its widest position. He was about to lunge forward, so he took a breath in order to growl.

Wally was unable to move due to shock as he saw the animal preparing to lunge. He saw the front legs of the beast stiffen and he was about to close his eyes to accept the inevitable, when the beast suddenly stopped moving.

A full two seconds passed and then Wally watched the animal close its mouth. The beast eased his nose closer to Wally and sniffed. It coughed and sniffed again and then growled at the man. It began to move backwards away from Wally, but kept his warning growl coming as he put several feet between him and the wounded man.

Sam had his rifle aimed at the beast's shoulder and he kept whispering, "Yes! Yes! A little more!"

The beast was halfway between Wally and Jesse when Sam's rifle discharged. It was a well-aimed shot, but the bullet cut a furrow across the beast's shoulder and ricocheted off of a flat rock.

She beast screamed and roared in pain and spun towards the opening of the arroyo. Sam yelled from above, "Fuck! Sights are off!" He operated the rifle lever to eject his shell and loaded another one into the breach. The beast began howling and running towards the northern entrance.

Because he was forced to run on three legs, his gait was extremely unsteady. Sam took aim again at the retreating beast and pulled the trigger. He cursed loudly as he saw the puff of dust kick up beside the animal and then he began to chase after it. It was outdistancing him.

Becky and Karen jumped in surprise when the first shot echoed out of the pass. They automatically took two steps away from each other and pulled the rifles into their shoulders. They had the barrels pointing towards the open space leading into the cut and Karen whispered nervously, "Becky?"

Becky answered immediately, "I don't know! Just be ready!"

They heard two more shots and both of them shouted together, "Oh, shit!"

Sam and Elliot were both yelling and chasing after to escaping beast. They were trying desperately to get into a position so they could take a shot, but the animal bounded his way towards the opening. He knew instinctively that the north end was his only avenue of escape.

Karen and Becky saw the approaching wolf at the same time. Karen repeated herself, "Becky?"

Becky half-shouted, "Aim for center mass!"

Both girls aimed their rifles straight at the approaching monster. They each took a deep breath and increased the pressure on the rifle's triggers.

The beast saw the two girls and he growled a warning as he tried to speed himself up for an attack. As he came closer and closer to the stationary teens, he let his mouth fall open in preparation for a lurch.

He was fifteen feet away and about to pounce when Becky and Karen pulled their triggers at the same time. The explosion of the two rifles filled the arroyo with an echoing thunderous roll as Becky's bullet smashed into the roof of the beast's open mouth. Karen's lead tore into the black chest and mushroomed before it ripped the carnivore's heart in half.

Becky's shell exited out of the wolf's skull at the base and pulled blood and brain matter with it. The two-hundred-pound beast was flipped backwards from the impact of two bullets and he was dead before his limp body slammed onto the dusty ground.

Becky and Karen let their rifles point towards the ground and stood in place as they stared upon the broken body of a once fearsome creature. They didn't look upon their handiwork for very long, because the yelling voices of Sam and Elliot were fast approaching.

Sam was the closest to the girls as he stopped to look upon the dead animal from his position above. The girls could barely hear him, but they saw him waving his free arm and his rifle and they listened intently to try and understand what he was saying.

Sam was literally screaming, "Sheriff! Hurt! Needs help, now!"

Karen whispered, "Becky?"

Becky leaped towards the Jeep and yelled to her friend, "Get in! Sheriff needs us!"

Becky jumped into the driver's seat and started the engine. Karen was on the other side of the vehicle immediately and she was still climbing aboard when Becky popped the clutch and sped down the slope and into the ravine.

Bob and Jeff had not witnessed the attack on Jesse and Wally. They both started running towards the north end of the cut, but Jeff was a man in his sixties. His ability to run didn't last long. He huffed after a few hundred yards and came to a stop. He waived Bob on and yelled, "Go! See if the kids need help!" He took a ragged breath and then added, "Too many shots, Bob! Too many shots! That ain't good!"

Becky slammed on the Jeep's brakes and slid to a stop. She and Karen leaped from the Jeep and ran towards Wally. They passed Jesse and both of them grimaced when they looked upon his crushed skull.

Both girls knelt beside Wally and saw him trying to hold his shoulder wound. He was very pale looking and they both knew instantly that he was in shock. Becky pulled his hand away from the bleeding shoulder and pushed her palm against it. She then saw that he was bleeding from both sides of his shoulder, so she clamped her other hand over the exit wound. She then yelled at Karen, "Get the first aid kit!"

Karen staggered to her feet and called out, "I think I'm gonna be sick!" She ran towards the Jeep as Becky called after her, "Karen! This ain't little girl time! Get the fucking kit!"

It was a large white box strapped to the right side of the back seat panel. Karen flipped the two latches holding it in place and ripped it away from the recess. She ran back to Becky and was tearing the box open as she fell to her knees beside Wally.

Becky yelled at her friend, "Coagulant! It's the big white plastic bottle!"

Both girls had taken first aid courses. Jeff Watkins made the classes mandatory in order to be employed at the ranch.

Karen twisted the cap off of the bottle and flipped a hinged cover on the lid. She exposed the small holes allowing the powder to be sprinkled over the wound and started shaking the container as Becky grabbed two clear plastic pouches. She ripped the plastic covering away from one and pulled out a thick cotton pad.

She brushed Karen's hand away, and pressed the pad onto the wound in Wally's upper shoulder on his front side. She then commanded her friend, "Hold this in place!" She clawed the other plastic bag open and pulled out another cotton pad. She pressed that one over the hole in the back of Wally's shoulder. Once again she yelled, "Hold it in place, Karen!"

Karen was squeezing her palms together over the now bloody pads as Becky was extracting a roll of gauze from the open box. She wasted no time as she unfurled the gauze and wrapped it around both wounds. Within less than a minute, they had Wally bandaged and Becky made a decision.

She moved her face close to Wally and said, "Me and Karen are gonna put you in the Jeep, Okay?"

Wally didn't respond. He only groaned as Becky and Karen pulled him to his feet. They half drug him to the passenger side of the Jeep and pushed him inside. Karen automatically jumped into the back seat and placed her hands over Wally's bandages.

Becky scrambled into the driver's seat and started the engine. She was turning the vehicle and speeding towards the north end within a few seconds.

Becky was shifting gears and racing the Jeep out of the gulley as fast as she could possibly drive. Karen was bouncing up and down in the back seat as she tried desperately to keep pressure on Wally's wounds. Her hands were blood soaked, but the blood was drying because they had doused the bullet holes with the coagulant. The dressing that they had hastily put on Wally was working. They had slowed the bleeding. He was still in shock and not able to speak, but his eyes were open and they both knew that this was a good thing.

Sam and Elliott were standing in the middle of the opening when Becky stomped on the brakes and stopped directly beside the two boys. She shouted immediately, "We're going straight to the hospital! He can't wait!" She shoved the shift selector into first gear and sped off again.

She drove up the long incline and threw dirt behind her with the wheels as she plowed her way to the top. She lurched over the top of the incline and made Karen bounce again. Karen lost her hold on Wally's shoulder and he groaned again. Bob's radio fell off of the seat and banged onto the floorboard.

Karen couldn't believe her eyes. She used her left hand to grab the unit and then she yelled at Becky, "Becky! Radio!"

Becky shifted the Jeep into fourth gear and pushed the fuel pedal to the floor. She was smiling as she replied, "Radio?"

"Yeah!"

Becky shifted into fifth gear and the Jeep gained momentum. She shouted, "Call Allie! She can help!"

Karen fumbled with the radio for a moment, then she figured out how to turn it on. There were no such thing as proper radio procedures from that point forward. She bounced as she squeezed the transmit lever and called out, "Allie! This is Karen! Can you hear me?"

Becky had to steer her way around the grove of trees and she made the horses nicker as she sped past them. Wally started to slouch forward, but Karen grabbed him by his shirt collar with her right hand.

Allie jumped when she heard the crackling voice call her name. She said loudly as she reached for the microphone. "What the hell?" She put the microphone to her mouth and asked, "Karen? Is that you?"

Karen's excited voice replied, "Allie! We're headed straight for the hospital! The Sheriff's been hurt!"

Allie jumped to her feet and called back, "Hurt? How?"

"He's been shot, Allie!"

Allie became apprehensive and forced herself to repeat the word, "Shot?"

"Is he alright?"

"He's awake, but he's in shock!"

Allie breathed a sigh of relief as she suddenly took charge of the conversation, "I understand! Where are you?"

"Headed for the picnic area!"

Allie understood and then gave Karen the instructions, "You must be in Bob's Jeep! The picnic area in on FM 1218! You turn right when you get there and make for the hospital as fast as you can!"

Karen sounded exasperated as she replied, "We know that!"

Allie then said the words that brought relief to both Karen and Becky at the same time. "Keep driving as fast as you can! I'll have an ambulance meet you before you get to Meacon!"

Karen then responded, "Oh, God! Thank you!"

Bob was standing between Sam Linden and Elliot Johnson. He was staring at the body of the dead wolf and listening to Sam explain the situation. "Becky and Karen drove out of here like a bat out of hell. They had the Sheriff with them and he was bad hurt."

Bob's eyes never left the limp body of the wolf as he replied, "Deputy Blount?"

"He's dead, Mister Benoit."

Bob spun his head around and glared at Sam. The boy simply continued, "Wolf got him before I could do anything. He's down the cut at the narrow spot before the quail's roost."

Bob simply groaned, "Oh, God."

Elliot expressed his sentiment in much the same way, but more openly honest. "Yeah…it got pretty fucked up."

Bob stared off into the open arroyo and then spoke softly to the boys. "I'm going to go be with the body. When Mister Watkins gets here, he'll have one of you go get some horses." He turned to the boys and asked sadly, "Would you bring me something to cover Deputy Blount with when you come back?"

Bob didn't wait for an answer. He shouldered his rifle and walked slowly down the path leading into the gulch.

An ambulance and two police cars met Becky and Karen on the gravel road about six miles from Meacon. Becky braked to a halt and jumped out of the driver's seat and rushed to help take Wally out of the Jeep. Two paramedics were immediately at her side and one of them said firmly, "We got it, missy. We got it."

The medics pulled Wally out of the door opening and lay him across a stretcher as Becky stepped aside and let them work. Karen was at her side almost instantly and she put a bloody arm around Becky's shoulder. She and Becky began shedding tears and then their shoulders started shaking as the tears fell from their dirt streaked faces.

Karen pulled Becky closer and put a hand on her cheek as she whispered, "We can be little girls now, Becky."

It was seven-thirty at night and the hospital emergency waiting room had Jo Ann, Bob, and Allie all sitting in hard cushioned chairs and talking among themselves. Wally was still in emergency surgery.

Bob was telling Jo Ann as much as he could in regard to the incident, but his information was second hand facts provided by Sam Linden. He and Allie sat directly across from Jo Ann and they held each other's hands. He spoke very softly as he explained, "Sam said Jesse's rifle discharged and the bullet hit Wally. He saw the animal kill Jesse, and then he saw it get ready to attack Wally."

Jo Ann sniffled, but otherwise remained quiet. Bob continued, "Sam said the wolf seemed to sniff Wally, then it backed away from him like it was scared or something."

Jo Ann stiffened, "Scared?"

"Uh-huh. He said it sniffed Wally and then started backing away. He said that's when he shot at the wolf, but he only wounded it again."

Jo Ann replied, "Then?"

"Then the wolf ran away and tried to escape. Becky and Karen killed it when it tried to leave the gulch."

Jo Ann choked back a cry and wiped a tear from her face with the backside of her right hand. She turned to Allie and asked, "The two girls...they saved my husband's life, didn't they?"

Allie only shook her head in the affirmative as Bob continued, "Becky and Karen bandaged him up and drove like hell to get to Meacon. Allie had an ambulance meet the girls on the road, so they brought Wally in."

Jo Ann sniffled again and said, "He's been in surgery for a long time."

Bob continued, "I came in with the body of Jesse Blount. I had to ride in the ambulance with him because the deputies took my Jeep away for evidence."

An announcement over the loud speaker interrupted the conversation, so they all took a breath and then Jo Ann spoke again, "Bob...the wolf...he...was scared off by Wally? How can that be?"

Wally was hesitant to say anything, but he felt that he

had to be honest with Jo Ann, so he offered an explanation. "Jo Ann…a wolf…especially a wolf, won't attack an animal that has a disease. They smell it and they won't kill it for fear of getting sick themselves."

Jo Ann's hands shot to her mouth! Her words were muffled, but both Bob and Allie understood her to say, "Oh my God!"

Bob started to put a hand on Jo Ann's shoulder, but he stopped when he saw Jo Ann drop her hands and there was a huge grin on her face. Tears flowed down Jo Ann's cheeks and she muttered again, "Oh my God!"

Bob was very confused. He tried to ask her if she was alright, but it only came out as a form of a question, "Jo Ann?"

Jo Ann continued to cry and laugh and the scene made Bob and Allie both very uncomfortable. They fidgeted and each tried to understand Jo Ann's reaction.

Suddenly Doctor Wilson appeared at Jo Ann's side. He interrupted her crying and laughing and simply said, "Jo Ann… he's out of surgery. Everything looks fine. You want to go to his room and wait for him to get out of recovery? He won't be in there very long."

Jo Ann jumped to her feet and wiped away the tears from her eyes, "Oh, yes!" She then spoke to Bob and Allie, "I'll be here all night! Will you two come see me in the morning?"

She didn't wait for an answer. She let doctor Wilson lead her away and they disappeared behind two heavy wooden doors that swung open automatically.

Allie and Bob stood up and Allie whispered to him, "You understand any of that?"

He put her hand on his elbow and led her out of the waiting room and replied as they walked away, "Nope."

Jo Ann was sitting on a cushioned chair in Wally's room as two male nurses pushed his gurney through the open door. They parked him next to his regular bed and moved him from the gurney to the sheets.

Jo Ann was instantly at his side, but she kept out of the way while the two nurses connected his drip bottle and electrodes to the wall monitor. He was semi-conscious as they worked and he tried to speak to Jo Ann. She hushed him immediately and brushed her hand across his cheek.

The nurses completed their work and then silently left the room. Wally fell asleep and Jo Ann remained at his side while she continued touching his face. She was smiling as she whispered, "Oh...my husband! You might be the only man alive that has had his life saved by Agent Orange.

THE END